I0573340

Mcguffin

Gene Murray

A Wings ePress, Inc.
General Fiction

Wings ePress, Inc.

Edited by: Jeanne Smith
Copy Edited by: Rebecca Smith
Executive Editor: Jeanne Smith
Cover Artist: Trisha FitzGerald-Jung
Images from Pixabay
Couple image: von Yuting Gao von Pexels

All rights reserved

Wings ePress Books
www.wingsepress.com

Copyright © 2021 by: Gene Murray
ISBN-13: 978-1-61309-532-4

Published In the United States Of America

Wings ePress Inc.
3000 N. Rock Road
Newton, KS 67114

Dedication

To Dolores, of course

* * *

Part I

The old man woke early that morning and remembered that this would be the last day of his life. He was a homely man, pig-faced and baldheaded, with the broad shoulders and strong hands of a stonemason. Once the sun was up, he walked unhurriedly around the small room thinking about his seventy years and avoiding the doleful eyes of the friends waiting for his execution.

"There still may be time to escape to exile," Crito said. "There are still many places where you are admired. I have enough money to bribe the guards; it only needs for you to agree."

"Is that the right thing, my friend?" the old man asked. "Wouldn't that prove their accusations? My whole life has been a struggle to live according to my principles. Is preserving my life more important than honoring it?" he asked.

Questions. Decades of hard questions without simple answers. That was what he had really been convicted of; asking difficult questions of men who were too satisfied with easy answers. The citizens of his hometown had found him guilty of impiety and sentenced him to death. He had been an artisan in this city and a soldier in its defense, and was at one time considered its wisest citizen. Perhaps this was the price of wisdom.

A small crowd had formed around the house where he was kept prisoner, and the old man could hear them outside murmuring and shuffling. There were no windows here as at his pupil Alcibiades' estate, but he knew what the crowd's restlessness meant. The guards would be coming soon, one to unlock the door and the other to present the cup containing the poison.

His friends looked at him with horror and doubt on their faces, but he simply smiled and walked toward the door. It swung open and the crowd parted slowly. A young citizen moved carefully through the crowd, holding the deadly cup in his two hands.

The silver cup, more of a bowl, was scratched and dented and dulled by time and use. The old man thought, but not sadly, "No luxury in life, and none in death."

The eyes of his friends and of the crowd and of the cupbearer were all on this crude vessel half full of poison made from the juice of the hemlock plant. The cupbearer stopped in the doorway. The old man looked beyond the crowd to the hills and beyond the hills to the sea. He said a small prayer of offering to the gods.

At the moment he took it from the cupbearer, it began to tremble slightly and then glow. The cup and the hands holding it were glowing with a light that had no origin. The crowd fell silent as the color changed from a pale silver color to a bright golden light and then back to silver.

The old man stood, unmoving, with the cup held to his lips until the light faded. Then he drank deeply.

One

"Over there," the younger, thinner one was saying, "just behind those hills was a prehistoric sea, miles across and maybe a couple of hundred feet deep."

The heavier man, lying on the grass, squinted at the thinner one. "Oh yeah, like with plesiosaurs and ichthyosaurs and like that."

"No, I'm talking about a billion years or so before life developed. The water was just chemicals. Pre-organic chemicals."

"Pre-organic, like primeval soup."

"Primordial. You mean primordial soup."

"Same difference, man. Like 'potato,' 'potahto.'

"No. Different. A shade of difference. Primordial refers to the first, as opposed to primeval which is *among* the first. Small difference, but an important one."

"Oh sure, that makes all the difference. I stand corrected. I must have been thinking of the band."

"What band?"

"Primeval Soup. Eighties big hair band. Lead singer's voice was too thin, but they had a kick-ass keyboard player."

The younger man squatted, snorted, and picked at some grass. "This is part of the reason the United States no longer competes with the Chinese," he said. "I'm discussing the geological and topological development of this area in pre-history, and you change the subject to piano players."

The heavy man pulled himself up on one elbow and stared for a long moment. "Jason. Your name is Jason, right?" He pointed a pudgy finger up at Jason's nose. "First, we weren't discussing jack squat. You are lecturing me, like you've been lecturing me since I handcuffed your sorry ass into the back seat about a hundred miles ago. Second, I said 'keyboard,' not 'piano.' There is a world of difference, or should I say a shade of difference but an important one. Keyboards are electronic instruments that can be programmed and adapted to create a staggering variety of sounds. They are light, portable and adaptable. Pianos are acoustic instruments, unchanged in their basic design since the time of Johann Sebastian Bach. Their sound is rich and resonant, and they are heavy as a son of a bitch. And I ought to know. And third, I'm not the one being transported for psychiatric evaluation. That, my erudite companion, would be you. And if you are gonna ask me about Erudite, they were a five-man jazz combo, and they sucked. Rhythm section really dragged it. Their keyboard player had fingers that didn't seem attached to his hands. Kinda tinkly, you know? Their sound did not come across well in a crowded venue."

The two men were relaxing on a hillside looking down at the New York State Thruway. A line of parked cars along the highway led north to a tangle of police cruisers and ambulances about a half mile north of them. Andrew, the heavier man, shading his eyes from the afternoon sun, could make out cars toppled and tossed across the road at odd angles, small enough in the distance to remind him of the models he used to crash together in the living room when he was a kid. He thought of the people in those cars, frail bone and flesh colliding with steel at high speeds. Immediately, reflexively, he whispered "good luck." That was the closest thing to a prayer he had uttered in years.

Most of the parked cars stuck in traffic behind the crash were abandoned and left open to keep the insides cool, and the passengers were wondering "what the hell" and looking for ways to kill time. A few gathered together on the hill, talking and pointing toward the accident. A few sat on rooftops of the cars, getting a September suntan, and most of the others had spread themselves around on the hillside with frisbees and headphones.

A few feet from Andrew and Jason, three girls, about college age, ate sandwiches and drank bottled water and occasionally laughed at something or other.

One of the girls, thin but with a jowly face and eyes that weren't quite symmetrical, had a guitar and was clubbing her way through "Let It Be." She had the first couple of chords right, but skipped right over the minor she needed to set up the fourth.

Andrew kept time with his head and hummed, "da da da da da, A minor, A minor, A minor, F."

The girl tried again, and again skipped over the A minor.

Andrew called over, "You need an A minor in there, after the G and before the F." The girl didn't hear, or at least didn't respond, so he shouted louder. "An A minor! You need an A minor in there."

She looked over at him, not angrily, and said, "I don't know how to play an A minor. I don't know what that is."

Andrew said, "Oh," and looked away. "Sorry."

Jason, the thinner and younger man, giggled. "In a former life you were a music teacher, right?"

"No," said Andrew. "In a former life I was a music accessory."

"Well that certainly clarifies the situation," Jason said. He was trim, broad shouldered and athletic looking without being athletic. He had a narrow face and long aquiline nose. His hair was neatly trimmed and parted in a very straight line down the left side of his scalp. His glasses seemed perfectly adapted for reading either the *Wall Street Journal* or the *Selected Works of Cicero.*

They sat quietly again for a few minutes, and he said, "You think we'll be here for long, maestro?"

"Yes. I do," Andrew said, trying to ignore Jason. He was overweight, with thick arms and hands, a broad face with an easy smile. His thick, unkempt hair spilled over his ears. *There is something about this scene,* he thought. *Something.*

"Well," Jason continued, "since we have time, let me tell you what the Ice Age was like around here."

Andrew groaned, flopped back on the grass and stared at the high blue sky for a moment. There were a few wisps of clouds off to the far west, and a slight breeze rustled the trees in the woods behind him. He was afraid he might fall asleep, but then he heard the familiar crackle in his ears, and a slow shifting of his visual spectrum, a sound and a sight he was sure no one around him noticed.

Oh, he thought, *here comes another one.* He opened his eyes slowly, not frightened, but curious about which one he would see this time. Of late, there were only a few different scenes that rotated through at no sequence or logic that he could see. He had gotten familiar with them all over the years and had even learned to enjoy them. Well, most of them. He called them his "dry dreams," and his main objection was that the good ones ended too soon.

~ * ~

The sky is a streaky, sodden orange, and meets the purple grass at a horizon that tilted downward at about forty-five degrees. Trees curve and grow into one another, and leaves hum with a tinny, shimmering melody. He is surrounded by people, all young, all smiling, staggering and caked with mud, and singing as loud as they can. He can't quite make out the song they are singing, it's so garbled. And it seems to be important to them. What is it? And why is everyone singing?

He turns toward a wide wooden platform off in the distance, in a small valley. There is a woman up there, floating all alone, playing an acoustic guitar and singing. She is round-faced and starry-eyed and has long, long golden-brown hair. She stands singing in the rain and the wind (what is that song she's singing?), her long flowered dress blows against her legs, she plays her guitar and sings.

He struggles to understand the words but the crowd, singing along, is drowning her out. He turns to the guy next to him who is pointing at himself. Letters began to flow out of his mouth. T....H...E... The boy points at the stage at the singer, and now the full words flow easily out of her mouth. They are new to him, but he knows them. She is new, and yet he remembers seeing her before. He listens and tries to connect then with now, but all he can understand is that this angel believes in peace.

It suddenly falls into place for him, and he understands. "I know that song!" he shouts. He looks around him at the crowd, at the stage, at the purple sky, at the smiling woman singing in the rain. I'm home, he thinks. I'm at Woodstock, I'm nineteen years old, and there's a chance peace will come in my life.

~ * ~

He heard a siren then and a murmur of voices and felt the breeze on his face. He opened his eyes to a blue sky, green grass, and those same wispy clouds. He blinked. His vision cleared just in time to see an ambulance heading southbound at top speed.

"They're starting to clear it out," Jason said.

"Thanks for the update, now shut up. Some of the adults are trying to relax."

There were still two wrecked cars to be cleared and a couple of miles of bumper-to-bumper traffic to sort out, but people on the hill were becoming restless. The guitar player had given it up and was braiding her hair. *Probably won't get that right either*, Andrew thought. A few frisbees sliced through the air. A boom box in the distance was playing "Purple Rain."

"Oh, man. This feels so familiar," he said mostly to himself.

"Uh-huh," Jason said, unused to and unhappy about being told to shut up.

"Yep. I was in a backup like this before, years ago, decades ago now, on the way to the Woodstock Festival. There was such a jam-up that thousands of us just abandoned our cars and walked a couple hours to get to the concert."

"Oh, right, Woodstock. Are you one of the thousands that actually went, or one of the hundreds of thousands who claimed they actually went?"

Andrew looked over at him. "Oh, I was there, man. I did the whole scene. The music, the mud, the drugs, the chicks. Man, I even got Pete's ax." He was a little surprised to hear himself say this out loud. He hadn't mentioned it to anyone in years.

"I know I'm supposed to ask you about the Pete's ax thing," Jason said, "but I really don't care. And if anybody should shut up, it's you. Woodstock is a myth, you moron. A stupid, hippie hash pipe dream."

Andrew laughed. "Except that it wasn't. And you're missing my point, man. I got Pete's ax. Me. Andrew, the Druid, the Drusome one, caught the guitar that Pete Townshend threw into the crowd at Woodstock."

This was his latest "dry dream," but one of the most satisfying. He was up near the stage as The Who were finishing their set. Andrew was wasted, as he had been much of the weekend. It was dark, the kind of deep darkness that happens on a cloudy, drizzling night far from the lights of a city. A single spotlight on the stage lit up Townshend in his white jump suit as he danced and hopped around on stage and assaulted his guitar. He smashed it a few times, and then carried it, almost tenderly, to the end of the stage and tossed it into the crowd.

"I don't know what the hell you're talking about," Jason said, "and I don't imagine you do either." But he turned and looked over at Andrew, interested.

"It was their thing, or one of them. They would trash their equipment at the end of a show. I don't know why, maybe a political, social, 'fuck you' kind of thing that says 'Hedonism, man! We don't need all this capitalist, consumerism crap.' I always thought it was kind of stupid, but fun to watch. So when he threw it, there was this big pile-on of maybe a dozen guys, and I guess I was the least stoned. I came away with it. Hugged it like a football and ran like a halfback. Goddamn. Pete's ax."

"And you keep it in your mom's basement near your inflatable furniture."

"Sorry to say it is not. I buried it. Well, I'm pretty sure I buried it, but when I went back for it, it was gone. Not a trace. Just one little piece, a little silver thing, a tuning key. Man, that was a kick in the ass."

"Pete Townsley threw an ax off stage, and you were stupid enough to catch it? And then even more stupid when you lost it?"

Andrew stared at him for a long moment. "No. No, you dipweed. It wasn't an ax, it was a guitar. Pete Townshend. Pete Townshend of The Who."

"Who? Pete Townshend of what?" He turned away from Andrew with a sly smile.

"Not what. The Who, goddammit! What is this...Abbott and Costello? The Who!"

Jason scratched his head for a moment, pretending to think. "The Who. Like in *Horton Hears A Who*."

"Jesus, you are dense. The British rock band of the sixties, The Who. Pete Townshend, Roger Daltrey, Keith Moon, John Entwistle."

"Oh. Oh, yeah. Didn't they do some kind of opera or something?"

"Yes! Jesus, finally a glimmer of hope. They did *Tommy*, the first and best rock opera."

"Something about playing pinball, right? 'Pinball Genius' or something? I remember hearing it as background music to a video game I used to play."

"'Pinball Wizard.' And that was not background music, man. That was genius."

"Genius? Genius? Mozart was a genius. Beethoven, Wagner, Mahler, maybe Leonard Bernstein. But Pete Townley? You gotta be kidding me."

"Townshend, butthead, Pete Townshend."

"Potato, potahto, maestro. He was not a genius. And I'm not a butthead, and I don't like being called names or being told to shut up by an underachieving music accessory with delusions of grandeur."

A frisbee landed close to Jason, and he took a moment to toss it back. The frisbee wobbled and landed about ten feet ahead of the guy he was throwing it to.

"You throw like a girl, too." Andrew called.

"I happen to have a master's degree in History, and am a few short steps away from my Ph.D.," Jason sneered. "Did you get your GED yet?"

"That's not the way I heard it," Andrew said. "The way I heard it, after your little camping trip, you're several light years from your Ph.D."

"What?" Jason yelled. "What did you hear? What do you know? How could someone like you know anything?"

"Got a buddy with access to the court records, and he gave me a heads up about yours. We're working up a list of top ten wingnuts, and you're looking good for the list. Camping on some little old grandma's lawn? Stalking her? You might make the top five."

"That's not what happened! That is not what happened! I didn't do anything wrong! I had a legitimate reason to be there!"

"You had a legitimate reason to pitch a tent on the front lawn of a sixty-five-year-old secretary and grill some burgers. Is that what you're trying to sell me, Professor?"

"You just don't understand what they did to me. They ignored years of work and research and planning. They denied me the chance to prove something I know is true and that will have a major impact on how we view world history. And they had me arrested. Arrested! Jesus, what a mess."

"The major impact on world history would come from your research, I gather."

Jason sat up straighter and pushed his glasses up on his nose. "Yes," he said firmly. "I believe my thesis has the potential to shake the academic world to its roots."

"You discover that we're descended from apes? No, Darwin did that already. You found the Titanic and hauled up some of its treasures? Nope. Nope, I'm pretty sure that big-ass boat is still bumping along on the floor of the Atlantic. I got it! You found Al Capone's safe! No, nope. Geraldo Rivera already did that."

"Ha, ha, ha," Jason said. "You must have to work at being this obnoxious. Or maybe it just comes naturally to you, like your odor?"

"I'm sorry, man, but you have to admit that's kind of a heavy lift, shaking the academic world to its roots."

"What the hell do you know about the academic world? And what do you know about my theory?"

"Okay, okay, you're right. I'm just a gorilla who learned how to use the keys to open your handcuffs, which, you may have noticed, are not on you right now. And you're welcome."

"Yeah, I was surprised you didn't put them back on me. I appreciate that."

"Just appreciate it enough to stay put. I'm not really in the mood to kick your ass. And don't start your monologue about the ice age again. I'm really not interested. I'm a summertime kind of guy."

Jason stood and walked in a circle. Andrew kept an eye on him, hoping he wouldn't run.

"I wasn't trying to hurt that lady, I just needed her to do her job. I needed her help to get my thesis approved, and she was just ignoring me."

"Your thesis. Tell you what, as long as we're stuck here, why don't you tell me your story. You tell me about your earth-shattering thesis. Gotta be better than the ice age."

"I'm not saying anything to you."

"C'mon man," Andrew said. "Tell you what, we can trade. I'll tell you something crazy about me first. Then your turn."

"I think you already told me something crazy."

"No, I mean really crazy. Come on, we're both bored, we're stuck here. Is it a deal? I tell you my crazy thing and you tell me your theory."

Jason hesitated, but not for long.

"Okay," he said. "I'm tired of telling my story to someone who charges by the hour. But here's the deal. I take you seriously, you take me seriously. Deal?"

"Deal." Andrew said. "Seriously." He took a deep breath and let it out slowly like a guru preparing for a trip to his inner world. "I think, actually I'm pretty sure, that I may have seen God one night," he said. Jason didn't move. He sat stone faced and waiting, so Andrew continued. "It was only for the briefest moment and I only saw him from the back, but wow, this is really the weird part. He was climbing a tree and holding onto a star. It's so clear to me, I can still see it. He's halfway up, hugging a tree, and his left-hand is extended straight up, holding something kinda pointy, and it's glowing like a star. The way his arms were out it was sorta like Christ on the cross."

Jason counted to five, silently. "Are you sure you weren't just stoned?"

"I've been stoned often enough to know the difference between real and delusion. This was real. I'm sure of it."

"Well, look, I'm really trying to take you seriously, but seeing God? A lot of, um, unbalanced people see god. But climbing a tree and holding a star? That's new."

"Yeah, I know. Pretty far out there, but I saw it."

He shredded some more grass and watched the third ambulance pull away from the accident scene and scream away.

"All right," Jason said. "I'll tell you about my thesis."

"You know, on second thought, man, it's okay, you don't..."

Jason interrupted. "I have discovered that there is a basic force, something elemental, primordial if you will, that holds the world together."

"Huh," Andrew said, and turned away, bored already.

"Philosophers have been searching for centuries, even millennia, to figure it out. Heraclitus thought it was change, Plato thought it was goodness, Christians thought it was love, Nietzsche posited in great detail that it was strength, now they talk about a grand unified theory. But suppose..."

Andrew was still shredding grass. He stared at the girl braiding her hair and mumbled, "It seemed so real, and I remember it so vividly." He was hoping for a dry dream right about now, but they never came when you wanted them to.

Jason continued without pause. "...suppose the force is something physical. Something tangible. Wouldn't someone have seen evidence of it, you ask? Of course, of course, but would they recognize it for what it was? Of course not. I have found records..."

Andrew kept talking to himself, "...and that star he was holding. Bright as the sun but didn't hurt my eyes a bit. Actually, I think it coulda been my guitar."

"...records from four different historical eras of a phenomenon occurring at an important time in history. The death of Socrates, Constantine's conversion to Christianity, the crowning of Charlemagne, the bubonic plague. There is a whole chronological pattern..."

"I remember the glow had a kind of a pattern to it," Andrew said to himself. "It was silver first, then gold and silver again before it faded away..."

"The stories are all amazingly similar," Jason went on. "In each, an ordinary object begins to glow. It pulses from silver to gold and back to silver over about thirty seconds. And then it's gone without a trace and has no after effect on the observer. Socrates went ahead and drank the hemlock, obviously. And Charlemagne permitted the crown to be placed on his head. I haven't found enough data on the bubonic plague incident, or on Constantine. But if I can swing a grant and afford some serious research, I can get this done right."

Andrew shook his head sadly. "That damned guitar is in my head, man. Has been for decades."

Jason didn't hear him. "A pattern of emergence, emergence becoming an esoteric term in my thesis, in alternating four hundred or sometimes eight hundred year intervals. Well, approximately. When we're talking about cosmic phenomenon of this magnitude, the concept of a year or even a century is virtually meaningless."

"I just wish to hell I knew what it meant."

"I suppose you're wondering what all this means," Jason said.

"Yes," Andrew said, still only half listening. "What does all that mean?"

"It means, as my thesis concluded, that there is a natural force in the world, perhaps a universal force, which is systematically observing human activity, and perhaps even influencing it. It's moving southeast to northwest in a somewhat predictable schedule like a seam running across the earth."

"A seam?"

"As I envision it—and I grant you the image is somewhat fanciful—the actual force is like a needle, hopping up and down in the fabric of time."

Andrew sat up, focused now, and looked at him. "Well, man, I'm trying to take you seriously, but your explosive idea is some kind of a cosmic sewing needle? That's a tough sell."

"Yeah," Jason admitted. They both sat quietly for a few minutes, looking at the traffic jam.

Andrew said, thoughtfully, "I think I saw the back of God at Woodstock."

Jason thought, but didn't say, *That's the craziest thing I've ever heard.*

Jason said, thoughtfully, "I think there is a cosmic force in the universe moving through the fabric of time like a needle."

Andrew thought, but didn't say, *That's the craziest thing I've ever heard.*

Two

In the year 1629, there was a shaky peace between the Delaware and Mohican tribes who had been enemies for generations. Delaware scouts, who had ridden cautiously along the ridge that separated the two territories, now told of something strange and deeply troubling among the Mohican. A new race of men, fair skinned, oddly dressed, and with powerful weapons that could spit fire and smoke were camping with the Mohican. Most didn't believe this, but Anshu, the chief's oldest son, was not so sure. He believed the world to be large, full of mystery and powerful medicine. And he believed the Mohican to be a ruthless and dishonorable enemy capable of dark magic.

This morning, two of the Mohicans that Anshu had traded with before came up over the rise with one of the strange, pale creatures. They approached close enough for him to be repelled by the pale man's smell and his foul appearance.

Through his two companions, the stranger explained that the pale strangers were peaceful, and very much desired to trade with the Delaware.

Anshu asked, "We have skins and we have meat and we have horses, but what does the pale, dirty one have to trade?"

The stranger reached into his bag and pulled out an earthen container, pulled the stopper, and handed it to Anshu.

Suspicious, he held it carefully, looked inside, sniffed it, and took a small sip. The two Mohicans watched him with broad smiles. The stranger only stared, and Anshu took a bigger drink. He nodded and smiled and asked the pale, smelly stranger if he had any more of this drink. At that exact moment, the fire burning in his tent flared up to double its height, and quickly faded to its former size. No one noticed.

~ * ~

Three hundred and forty years later, on the spot of Anshu's lodge tent, a woman looked out the window of a shop that had once been the Liberty Wine and Spirits Emporium. It was now called the Penultimate Pickle and sold everything from paperback books to penny whistles to hand crafted pottery.

The owner, an energetic, buxom blonde in her forties with some gray trails in her hair, turned away from the window quickly as two customers entered her store and began to browse.

"Is this a bit tight on me?" the customer asked. She was trying on a tie-dyed T-shirt that was about two sizes too small.

"Yes, a little," the store owner said, thinking the shirt would be stretched out of shape now and would need to be washed before being sellable. "I think you would fit nicely in the next size."

The older woman turned and posed sideways in front of the mirror. "I like it a little small, you know, to make my bosom look bigger."

"Bigger tits," the store owner said, and slapped herself on the thigh.

"I beg your pardon," the customer said.

"I'm sorry," the store owner said, clearly embarrassed. "Please forgive me. I just get carried away sometimes. It won't happen again. Would you like to take the shirt?"

"Well, it does look nice on me," she said, turning back to the mirror. "Yes, I think it's nice."

"Bitchin', sister."

"I'm sorry, what did you just say? Did you call me a bitch?"

"No, no. I said 'bitchin'. Like something really attractive, appealing. Please, I have this terrible nervous habit. I...I translate things people say."

"Translate? It didn't sound like a foreign language to me, it just sounded vulgar."

"Again, my apology. I didn't mean to offend you. There are several others tees on this rack you might like as well. I dye them myself. Please look around, take your time. I'll go check on my other customer."

"That's my husband," the older woman said, nodding toward the man scowling near the counter.

"Your old man, that's righteous." the owner said. "Well, excuse me. I'll be right back. He looks like he could use some attention."

He was a big, barrel-chested man wearing a turquoise string tie. "This is incense, isn't it?" He was holding a grayish stick.

"Yes. That one is sandalwood. We also have...."

He looked around at the rock concert posters on the wall and the life-size cardboard cutout of Paul McCartney. There was a shelf with lava lamps and peace signs, heart shaped sunglasses, and "make love not war" ceramic cups. There was a huge mural of the Woodstock poster, the one with a dove perched on a guitar neck, and another of a Volkswagen bus painted in psychedelic colors. The far wall was a stained glass representation of a garden.

"What is that music?" he asked. "Is that like, psychedelic?"

"No, that's the Percy Faith Orchestra playing Beatle melodies."

He just grunted. "Jesus, the joints Sharon drags me into. Look at all of this long haired, freaky crap. When I was on the force, we used to arrest kids for burning this stuff."

She nodded and smiled. "You were a pig, and you busted hippies."

A moment passed quietly while each of them stepped back 30 years, looked up "pig" in their respective Funk and Wagnalls encyclopedia and then hustled back to the Penultimate Pickle. He stared at her, and she at him, for that long moment.

"I'm so sorry, I didn't mean," she began to explain. "You see, I have this condition..."

"Sharon!" he bellowed. "We're getting out of here. We're not buying anything in this freak shop!"

She tried again to explain. "It wasn't meant to be disrespectful, it's just that I have this habit, this condition of..."

But he had already stormed away from her and was pulling his wife toward the door.

"It's just...well, it's very hard to explain."

"I'm not going to stay here and be insulted," he yelled back at her.

"The words aren't really mine," she cried. "I think I'm channeling someone." The door closed with a crash behind them.

She walked slowly back to the counter, pausing to refold the abandoned T-shirt. She found a brush and began to stroke her waist length, greying hair. "This is such a bad trip," she said. "I wish they would just get here."

She put the discarded blouse in the back to be washed and went back to the roped off ceramics corner of the store. She sat next to the kiln and carefully painted a small lawn ornament, a gnome, to be added to her village display. She looked worriedly at one of the paintings in the window and said again, "This is such a bad trip."

The bells over the door jangled and an older woman came in with a younger woman pushing a stroller.

"We have passed your store before and always wanted to stop in. I'm glad I finally did. It's very unusual. It's homey and inviting."

"Yes," the owner said. "It's real funky. Please feel free to look around. I'll be hanging out, but I won't hassle you."

"You are the owner?"

"I'm the man, yes. I painted most of those pictures in the window, I fire and paint my own ceramics, and I tie-dye all the shirts and scarves."

"Wow, keeps you busy, I'm sure."

"It can get pretty heavy, but I'm cool with it."

"And I love the ambience in here. That's sandalwood, isn't it?" the younger woman said.

"Yes, it's a gas. Makes for a really mellow vibe."

The little girl in the stroller, about three years old, began twisting and calling out. "Would you mind if I took her out and let her walk around a little? She's getting cranky."

"Sure, that's cool, just please stay with her. It's been a number of years since this place was child proof. And of course, the kiln area over there is very hot, so off limits."

"Of course, we'll be careful. Thank you."

"Far out."

She moved a couple of display racks over to block off the kiln area and busied herself straightening shirts and re-arranging knick-knacks. The two women bought a couple of T-shirts and a bracelet. As they were leaving, the owner said, "Oh, I almost forgot...we're having an end of summer sale on stuffed animals." She picked out a unicorn for the little girl.

"Oh, that's cute. How much is that?"

"My end of summer sale means that it's free if you will try to come back again next summer."

A big smile from Mom. "Wow, that's wonderful. We certainly will try to come back next summer. And thank you." The little girl took it and hugged it.

"Groovy. Far out."

The older woman came over and said, "I love the way you set the atmosphere in here by talking like a hippie from the sixties. It's theatrical, but it's fun." As she left the store, she turned back and waved.

"Peace and love," the store owner said.

Three

Andrew had gotten off the highway a few exits early and was driving up Route 50 toward Saratoga. After spending so much of his life on highways, he preferred the stop and go driving through small towns.

"Milton Hill," Jason read, pointing out the car window at a sign. AREA OF TOWN FIRST SETTLED c. 1772 BY DAVID WOOD FAMILY. POWELL'S STORE, EPISCOPAL & PRESBYTERIAN CHURCHES UNTIL c. 1850; SCHOOL #3 TO 1950'S

Andrew, who had briefly been in love with his high school history teacher, always stopped to read these historical notices. He had seen this one before and listened to Jason with only half an ear. He was thinking about his guitar and replaying the conversation he had with Jason on the hill. "Hang on a second," he said. "What did you say back there? Something about a pulse? Pulsing?"

"Pulse? Um, no. I said Powell. Powell's store until circa 1850."

"No, no. Before. On the hill. You said some of those dead guys wrote about something pulsing, right? Something pulsing, and changing colors? I thought I heard you say something like that. What I saw, the star, that whatever I saw was holding, went silver, gold, silver and then faded away. Seems kinda like pulsing, no?"

"Come on, pal, I thought we had some kind of a truce. I take you seriously, you take me seriously, no raggin' on each other. I'm trying to hold up my end."

"I'm not raggin' on you, man. This is what it was. Some dude or angel or devil or superhero holding on to something bright, glowing and changing from silver to bright gold and then back down to silver. The straight dope, man. Pulsing. Silver to gold and then back to silver."

Jason was still for a long moment. "Just wait a minute," he said in a strained, slightly high pitched voice.

In the rear-view mirror, Andrew watched Jason squirm in his seat, blink a few times and then decelerate, until nothing moved but his eyes. They slid from side to side at a steady pace, like someone in a neck brace watching a ping pong game.

Jason said very softly. "Is it possible? The time is just about right, late twentieth century. The place is approximately right, especially considering the ocean, it is a common enough object, a guitar. Just maybe a little bit too big. The only question is the meaning. Woodstock, music, flower power, rebellious youth, the counterculture, no, no, none of those. Well, maybe, who knows. Maybe some correlation, but how crazy would that..." His voice trailed off, but his eyes continued to sweep back and forth.

"Tell me again what you saw," he yelled. "Andrew! Sir! Tell me. Tell me. Tell me!"

This was the first time Andrew had seen him agitated. He had been calm and cooperative in the jail, in the car and sitting on that hill. "You sure you're okay back there? You're cuffed into the seat, man, and I got pepper spray. Please don't make me use it."

Jason sucked in a couple of deep breaths, and forced his eyes to focus ahead. "No, no, I'm fine. Just excited. I think you may have seen something enormously important. I'll stay calm, I promise, just please, tell me again what you saw. With details."

"Just chill for a minute. That's right, more deep breaths." He pulled into a parking lot, and turned around to look at Jason. "It was at night, no, actually early morning. The sun was just coming up."

"Early morning, that's another constant," Jason said. "Continue, please."

"I was walking. Coming from somewhere, I think maybe I was swimming. I'm not sure where, but I was feeling okay, you know. But I was straight, the swim cleared my head, I'm almost sure of it."

"You hadn't buried the guitar as of yet, right?"

Andrew thought for a moment, then scratched the stubble on his chin. "I did bury it. I'm almost sure. I'm sure I had buried it. I was feeling good because I thought it was safe and I could come back for it."

"But you said you lost it. When did you lose it? How?"

Andrew turned and tapped his palm against the steering wheel. "I don't even know, man. I have kicked myself and thought about it and it's just a blank. I had it, I went for a swim and then I couldn't find it. I was probably still high, but not that high. I wouldn't just lose it. I looked all over for it, and then I saw the thing in the tree."

"So, after you hid it, you're walking, after you swam somewhere, and you're looking for the thing, and you see something or hear something and then you turned around and saw what?"

"Nope. Didn't have to turn around. It was like right there in front of me. The sky was getting light in front of me, so I must have been looking east, into the sunrise. There was just an outline of the body, maybe ten or twelve feet up, hugging a tree. In his left hand—I'm pretty sure it was a guy—was a shape, kind of like a guitar with a weird glow."

"What kind of glow? The whole body, the whole tree, what?"

"I don't know, but it wasn't like a light bulb. I guess it was the shape of the guy and the star, guitar, whatever, and it kept changing, like a throb. It was silver, and got brighter and brighter, then it turned to gold, and kept getting brighter. Then it turns silver again, and then it was like, gone. All of it was gone. The light, the guy, all of it. Only the dim sunrise light in the woods."

"What did you do? What happened to the guy in the tree?"

"Well, I don't know. I freaked. I was afraid I was really losing it, you know? I just bolted, man. I turned and ran. I think I ended up back at my tent. You see Jesus in a tree, man, what would you do?"

Jason began rocking back and forth. "It's okay," he said, his eyes wide. And as he talked, his voice got steadily louder until he was yelling. "It's okay. You witness one of the most important events, probably the most important event of at least the last twenty-five hundred years, and you run away! What the hell is wrong with you?"

Andrew was watching him closely in the rear-view mirror. His hand reached for the pepper spray. "Let's both just chill for a few minutes. This is getting away from us." He got out and sat on the fender for a few minutes, keeping Jason in his peripheral vision, and watching the wind turn a small cloud into a biplane, and then into a flag, but bars without stars, shredding and stretching into dissipation. After a few minutes of calm, he leaned in the driver's window and said, "You okay now? Got that out of your system?"

"Yeah, yeah. I'm fine."

"So, we're both thinking the same thing. There's a connection, right, between what I saw and what your dead guys wrote about?"

"They're not my dead guys. They are historians. Although they're not held in high regard by current mainstream academics. But yes. If what you're telling me is accurate, I think there is a connection."

"Whatever lit up my guitar and your needle thing are maybe the same thing."

"Maybe. Maybe the same thing."

Jason squeezed into the corner and stared out the window to avoid Andrew's gaze.

The CD player, which was off, suddenly popped out the CD, and then the tray pulled back in. No one noticed.

"I gotta deliver you up to Halcyon Harbor, but you know we just can't leave it like this."

Jason pulled away from the corner a little bit. "I know, but I'm not gonna say it."

"Say what?"

"You know what. What we need to do about it."

"Right, so okay. I'll say it. Why don't we team up? You want to find your needle thing, and I want to find my guitar."

"You had that experience, and I know the science. So, you think we need each other? Is that what you're saying?"

"Hard to believe, but yeah," Andrew said. "That's what I'm saying. A team. We'll be like peanut butter and anchovies, Roger Maris and Mickey Mouse.

"Glorious," Jason said. "Bud Abbott and Al Capone. It'll be great."

"We find the guitar, right?"

"We find the guitar, and we find the tree," Jason said. "Yeah, a team. We'll be just like two fish out of water."

A quiet half hour later, they pulled into the parking lot at Halcyon and Andrew unlocked the handcuffs to let Jason out. "I'm sorry, man, I gotta put them back on you to go inside. Rules and regs, man."

Jason just sighed and held out his hands.

Andrew hung his ID badge around his neck and signed them in. They were buzzed through a thick security door. Inside, it seemed less like a prison than a hospital with long, white corridors and too bright fluorescent lights. As they walked toward a reception desk, Andrew whispered, "You want to get out of here as soon as possible, right?"

"Of course. You and I have plans. Peanut butter and anchovies."

"It won't be so bad. Just keep your head."

"I don't think I'll have to be here that long. A week, two at the most. I can fake out these community college morons in no time."

Andrew stopped and looked at him. "Wrong attitude, man. I've been doing this gig for almost a year, and I think I got it figured. Half of the game is that you can't be smarter than them, especially if you are smarter than them. That's gonna be tough for you, because of that short you got between your brain and your mouth. Just keep in mind, they got the fancy uniforms, they got the paperwork, and most of all, they got the keys. Therefore, and ergo, you are a lesser life form, and you had better act like it. If not, they will prove to you that they still got the paperwork and they still got the keys."

At the desk, the beefy guard with the blue trousers and starched white shirt said, "Welcome to Halcyon Harbor."

Jason said, "You may not know the meaning of the unusual word, halcyon. It is a reference to a Greek myth about a divinely inspired bird that can calm stormy seas just by flying over them. So, the phrase 'halcyon days' suggests tranquility and..."

The guard stood and poked Jason's chest with a stubby index finger. "You should probably shut up now," he said in a low voice that was nearly a growl. He took the manila envelope with the court order from Andrew and read carefully through it.

Andrew whispered, "Nearly a Ph.D., and dumb as a bag of hammers." He watched as the security guard, whose pants didn't quite reach his shoes, took Jason by the elbow and escorted him down the hallway.

~ * ~

Later, driving south on the Northway, an often-unrecognized local oxymoron, Andrew was enjoying the solitude and the easy performance of the New York State official Impala that was used to transport the less dangerous detainees to the upstate evaluation facility. They were 'detainees' because, like Jason, they weren't quite criminals, and they weren't quite trusted citizens.

On long trips, he usually brought along his 'driving music' from his salad days, rock classics like Bachman Turner Overdrive or Steve Miller. Lately though, mellow nostalgia had overruled. Crosby, Stills and Nash, or maybe the Eagles, would turn on his lights. The music he heard on commercial radio made him want to open the window and spit. Sometimes he did.

He lived now, temporarily, in his nephew's apartment while the nephew was doing his Army Reserve duty. This nephew was the son of Andrew's younger sister, the only one who would still have anything to do with him, and even that was sporadic. The apartment, though, was great. The nephew, Drake, was some kind of corporate drone... insurance maybe or accounting, whatever, but the apartment was an amusement park. A balcony, walk-in closet, a serious sound system (although his choice of music sucked), track lighting, a big, flat screen TV with every station imaginable. Andrew's responsibility there was to water the plants, close the windows when it rained, and not to track mud onto the carpet. He had been there for almost three weeks, and so far, mission accomplished. No mud, no water on the floor, and no dead spider plants.

Most of his worldly possessions were in a storage locker on the outskirts of Cleveland. Here in Brooklyn, he only had two suitcases and a backpack, but they were enough. Having lived on the road for so many years, he was an avowed minimalist. His two suitcases were open on the floor in the bedroom, and he lived out of them. It never occurred to him to pack anything away in a dresser drawer. Stuffed in there were jeans, sneakers, underwear, socks for the winter, moccasins for the summer. He hated hats but, out of deference to his thinning hair, had a couple of baseball caps.

On top of the smaller suitcase was what he called his photo album, actually a plastic bag with a jumble of pictures, CDs and cassettes. An empty album with a few pictures, an abortive attempt one hungover pre-dawn, was tucked in there, too.

He watched television for a while, struggling with the remote, and finally gave it up with a curse. "The guy that said TV is a half-assed wasteland was dead right."

He spread the contents of the plastic bag out on the floor and began to go through the pictures, tossing the duplicates and unrecognizables, labeling the ones he could identify, and arranging them as chronologically as he could remember. When he had about twenty pictures, he started placing them in the album.

Time lurched forward from a seventeen-year-old Andy, hanging with some high school friends, to a twenty-year-old Andrew with a beer and a broad smile on someone's couch, to a heavier twenty-eight-year-old Druid looking serious and stressed, to a photograph taken for his current ID badge, jowly, red-eyed, and vague. That person he referred to as 'Drusome.'

His hair went from just over the ears to shoulder length to an untidy mullet and then slowly receded to his current scruffy gray shag with pink islands of skull beginning to break through.

He went to the full-length mirror in the bedroom closet and stripped down to his shorts, intending to take a long survey of who he was now.

He slammed the door shut after less than a minute. The smiling boy in the family room in Utica had grown into an overweight, sagging, yellow toothed, frowning old man; a man with no future, and not much of a present. *But with a hellacious past*, he thought, scratching the broad area between his navel and the band of his jockey shorts. *I had booze, I had drugs, I had chicks. Most of all, I had music.*

At the bottom of the plastic bag, stuck in the corner, was a small silver object, square at the base and extending to a key shape. It was the tuning peg for Pete's ax that he had dug up among the roots and mud where he had hidden the guitar. It was the only thing he had left of it. He thought sadly of the red Gibson SG Special that Townshend had bashed around on stage, and then, as usual, he thought of his father.

That would do it, he thought. *I could survive this half-ass life if I had something from back in my real life. If I could hang Pete's ax on my wall, I wouldn't feel like hanging myself.* He clipped the tuning key to his keychain.

~ * ~

Three weeks later, Jason was feeling resentful, abused, and seriously patronized, but far from defeated. This was not the most complicated game Jason had ever played. Graduate school in its entirety probably held that honor. But this was a subtle one. How to prove something he was sure was true without appearing to be trying to prove anything. He had to prove that his behavior had been desperate, but not irrational.

Halcyon Harbor was a hothouse of exotic therapists and professionals. The halls hummed with psychologists, psychiatrists, social workers, someone calling himself a psychopharmacologist (which sounded like an insane druggist but was probably not), and each discipline had a cadre of interns. It was easy to tell the interns because they were younger and tended to carry clipboards. All had name tags, and a few of the name tags had the professional title underneath. These people would come into his room or approach him in the hall and begin talking to him without preamble. Apparently, the courtesy of introductions was not considered therapeutic. It was only one of the oddities that Jason mused over.

This was his third week and his fourth psychologist. Actually, one psychiatrist, two psychologists and one clinical social worker. Jason also wondered, but not out loud, what a non-clinical social worker would be. A whimsical social worker? Perhaps a libidinous social worker? He never saw a sign of either joy or passion in any of them. But after that first incident with the guard, he had stifled his intellect and his sarcasm and had so far stumbled through the maze without serious incident. He tried to keep his eye on the prize, but arrogance is a disease that lingers, and he schemed to prove his superiority. Lying in his room, struggling to ignore his roommate, he constructed a complete misdirection for his latest adversary.

They met this morning in the cafeteria at the psychologist's request, if a psychologist was what he was. It had been a very frustrating period for Jason. He had carefully cultivated the other therapists, laid down an intimate pattern of remorse and gradual enlightenment, but each had disappeared before he was able to manage a miraculous breakthrough.

The first three had each been well spoken, well dressed, and had a degree from a reputable, brand name university. This fourth one was different. He said very little, needed to be introduced to a dry cleaner, and was a graduate of a state university program. He had thin hair, thick glasses and a nose shaped like a ten-watt lightbulb. He looked so dumb that Jason was sure he was the smartest of the bunch.

They sat facing each other, Jason slurping cream of broccoli soup from a plastic bowl and his adversary assiduously probing each space between his teeth with a toothpick.

"Lettuce," he said, "always gives me a problem. I had periodontal work once, I would not want to go through that again."

R. Hotchkiss was the name on his identification badge, but Jason did not know what the R. was for. He was thinking it was either Richard or Robert.

R. Hotchkiss put his toothpick down on his salad plate and said, "What do you think the difference is? I mean the difference in your attitude now and that of a month ago?"

There it was, the opening he needed, a wide door with a paved road to stroll through. The real crime, he knew, was not pestering a secretary, but pestering a tenured professor and vice-chair of a prestigious history department. If he could shift focus back to his immoderate behavior, and convincingly beg forgiveness for it, the game was over.

"Look, Doctor, I won't insult your intelligence by saying I'm sorry for what I did, but I'm beginning to see my actions from..." he paused for a moment, for dramatic effect, and tore off a piece of his grilled cheese sandwich. R. Hotchkiss leaned back and smiled, just a bit.

Still staring at his sandwich, Jason said, "I can analyze my actions from the perspective of other people."

"Specifically, which people?" Hotchkiss asked. That was the other difference between R. Hotchkiss (Ryan maybe? Roger?) and the first three. They had the answers and appeared to enjoy the sound of their voices. This guy had questions and listened to the answers. This guy was going to be tough.

"You want to know if I feel bad about scaring Mrs. Koch, right?"

"Mrs. Koch?" Another question.

"She's a department secretary that I..."

"Stalked." A statement that time.

"Well, 'stalk' is the word the police used, but I think of it as lobbying."

"Well, I don't really know the whole story. Would you tell it to me?"

"I have told this story to your predecessors, all three of them. It must be somewhere in your file, Doctor. Are you a doctor by the way?"

R. Hotchkiss just smiled. "Of course, there is a description of the incident on the front lawn, the camping, I mean, but I want to know what preceded that event. I want to know if you can understand the behavior that led to your 'lobbying' in such an unusual manner."

Ah, Jason thought. *I got it. The R must stand for rat bastard.*

Jason hesitated for what he thought was the appropriate time. "I really will have a hard time telling you about that," he said. "It's deeply, deeply…" He shook his head.

R. Hotchkiss smiled again, a genuine, wide "gotcha" kind of smile, and Jason did see a small piece of lettuce clinging near his eyetooth. *Good*, Jason thought. *I hope it rots your gums right down to the nerve.*

R. Hotchkiss said, "It's my responsibility to advise the court whether or not you truly understand your actions and whether you truly feel remorse for them. You're an intelligent man, Jason, and the other professionals you have interviewed with have some suspicion that you are a very good chess player as well. Do you think…"

Another goddamn question, thought Jason.

"…do you really think a person who can't describe his actions can be said to understand them? Or to regret them?"

The others had not gotten to this crux with him, always nibbling around the edges of it, talking when they should have been listening. Jason flushed, ready to angrily refuse to discuss it, but then re-focused on his opportunity. *Checkmate*, he thought. *Endgame. You have me right where I want you. I need to explain what I did and why it was wrong, and that wraps the whole bizarre incident into a big package of immaturity, remorse and a return to rational thought. Right. Okay, I can do this. They are ready for me, and I am ready for this. I can do this.*

"I don't know what your first name is," Jason said, sincerely.

"Raymond," the psychologist said without expression.

Jason scraped at his empty bowl for a minute, and then began. "It's a reasonable surmise, well after the fact, that Mrs. Koch was an innocent in this whole debacle. But at the time," deep breath, "I did not see her as such."

"Secretary, I believe you said."

"Yes, senior clerk, I think was her formal title. She and I used to be friendly. I used to bring her packets of Sweet and Low."

"She kept you from seeing your thesis advisor."

"Yes."

"Difficult as it may be for you, Mr. Nelson, you are going to have to narrate this part of our interview. A long skein of questions and answers are not going to bring us to the center of what you called the debacle."

"Yes, I don't think I ever gave a full description of the prelude to our um, episode."

"My colleagues felt that you weren't ready."

"Um, I suppose not," Jason said to his empty soup bowl. He thought *I'm goddamn good and ready now*!

"So." The half-smile, the lettuce in the teeth.

"My thesis," he began, "had become an object of ridicule among the faculty at NYU and especially to my advisor, Dr. Braithwaite. To be clear, Braithwaite should never have been my advisor. His bailiwick, his parochial area of interest, was the Carolingian Renaissance. A portion of my thesis, and a peripheral portion I might add, involved the Middle Ages, and thus he was chosen as my advisor. Completely inadequate for a theory that encompassed millennia."

Raymond Hotchkiss scribbled a quick note of the word 'millennia.'

"Doctor Braithwaite rejected my theory and my thesis out of hand in a brief letter to me that was insulting, and demonstrated that he had not bothered to read my work all the way through. I followed appropriate university protocol, asking that another advisor be assigned, and was refused. I asked again and was refused more firmly. I asked for a consultation with Dr. Braithwaite, either by telephone or face to face, and that was also refused. I asked again for some form of communication with Braithwaite or another of the History Department faculty—actually, two requests, I believe—and was refused rather rudely both times."

"And all of this 'protocol' went through Mrs. Koch, I suppose."

"Yes, I suppose it would have, but I developed no particular enmity toward Mrs. Koch at that stage. I understood her role as simply a gatekeeper. And I made sure to follow, to the letter, the formal agreement between student and advisor. For all the good it did me."

Raymond Hotchkiss, who had several years' experience with anger management disorders, could see the signs developing in Jason. His speech sped up, his color deepened, his gestures became more pronounced, his volume raised. None of this was at a critical level, but Hotchkiss did stop picking at his teeth and paid closer attention.

"But the effect on you was to perceive Mrs. Koch as a barrier to your objectives."

Jason, from some corner of his mind that remained analytical, thought, *Huh. I'm now getting statements and not questions. Must be some kind of technique.* And from this sanctuary, he surveyed the strategic chessboard. Mrs. Koch, whom he barely knew and rarely acknowledged, had become the pivot point, or at least one of them, in his apparent capitulation and restoration to reason. But the pivot could not be rushed.

"I don't know about that. As I said, we were on friendly terms. I used to bring her stirrers and sugar packets for her coffee."

"A nice gesture. Mentioned several times by your attorney." Again, a statement. "But that seems a huge leap, a quantum leap if you will, from that amiability to camping on her front lawn."

Jason suppressed a smile. He imagined talking to Hotchkiss in a lecture hall. *I don't think you are smarter than the others. A quantum leap is the distance an electron makes between one energy state and another inside an atom. Essentially, the smallest distance known to science.*

Jason said quietly, "She was not the problem. Braithwaite was the problem. I am not stupid, sir. At some level I understood that."

"And yet you acted, you set a plan in motion, against Mrs. Koch. Not Dr. Braithwaite."

"Yes. For a very good reason. The student-advisor agreement stated that once an appointment had been made between the student and the advisor, it could not be cancelled, could not be ignored. Had Mrs. Koch made that appointment, it would have required, literally required, Braithwaite, to meet with me. I was, again, following protocol."

Hotchkiss excused himself, saying he needed something to drink, and it might be a good idea if Mr. Nelson thought a bit about his last statement. He came back in a few minutes with a soda, sat down and avoided eye contact. Jason returned the gesture, staring over R. Hotchkiss, now 'Rat Bastard Hotchkiss', shoulder. They were seated together, but like two electrons, an unfathomable distance apart.

After a few minutes, the psychologist, if that's what he was, said. "Straight talk now, Mr. Nelson. There is no such clause in the student-advisor agreement."

"I believe there is."

"Mrs. Koch does not drink coffee. It gives her heartburn and you never brought her stirrers or Sweet and Low or anything else. Her statement during court proceedings was that you had hardly ever exchanged a word in two years of being acquainted. She thought of you as a snob."

He looked hard at Rat Bastard now and breathed deeply. "I only wanted a chance to defend my thesis. Two years of work, and I couldn't even get an appointment. How does that make sense? How is that academic freedom?"

"And so you made plans to hound, or as the complaint said, stalk, the gatekeeper until she let you communicate with the person who really should have been your target. Doctor Braithwaite."

"But Mrs. Koch, she was the one that had to..." he stopped and turned away from Hotchkiss. "She wouldn't even..."

He wanted to wrap his arms around himself and begin to rock but thought that might be overdoing it. He just stared at a tastefully rendered wall of flowers. Hibiscus maybe? Daffodils?

There it is, Jason thought. *Pivot complete. Check. Checkmate. Game, set and match. Let me out.*

He took a deep shaky breath and looked for a long time at R. Hotchkiss. He said softly, "Okay, okay. What you want is an acknowledgement that targeting Koch was not logical. Not strategic."

"Nor rational," Hotchkiss said.

"Yes," Jason said to the table. "And I have understood at some level since I was arrested that Mrs. Koch was not my adversary. It was Braithwaite. My god, I treated that sweet old lady so poorly and she was not the problem. You need me to say it out loud, I suppose, well okay. She was only in the way. Braithwaite was the problem."

Jason expected a small degree of sympathy from Hotchkiss. Perhaps an "understandable under the circumstances," or perhaps even a hand on the shoulder. But Hotchkiss was silent. He gathered up his papers and stood, looking at Jason with that half smile. "But was he really, Mr. Nelson?"

"But you just said…"

"We need to go a little deeper, Mr. Nelson. You know full well that the real obstacle was not Dr. Braithwaite."

"Well then, who?"

Hotchkiss smiled, the lettuce gone now, and said, "This has been a very productive session, Mr. Nelson. We can proceed further tomorrow."

His wobbly fiction collapsed, and Jason went back to his room.

~ * ~

"Tomorrow" turned out to be three days later, in Rat Bastard's office, which, thought Jason, had to be a converted janitor's closet. A narrow, cinderblock room just wide enough for a desk, and just long enough for two people to sit without becoming intimate. This was the first interview that Jason was not prepared for. The collapse of his narrative had caused him a couple of restless nights.

"My last statement to you, Mr. Nelson, was to the effect that you know the obstacle to your research was not Dr. Braithwaite. Nor, as you realized, was it Mrs. Koch. Have you thought more about what the actual impediment might be?"

It was still too early, and his morning coffee was too bitter for Jason to be polite and pleasant. He was worried, and he was galled by Rat Bastard's superior gamesmanship.

"Braithwaite scoffed at two years of my work. Mrs. Koch kept me from either resolving it with him or speaking to another advisor.

Perhaps we have different definitions of the word, but that sounds like an impediment to me."

"Your research extends all the way to the Classical Greek period, correct? And proceeds to the Early Middle Ages, I believe, and you make reference to the fourteenth century plague."

"Please don't pretend that you read it."

"No, excerpts only. A digest of sorts. But reading that much has given me an insight into your problem, and perhaps a solution."

"Which problem would that be? They seem to be multiplying like rabbits on a moonlit night."

R. Hotchkiss turned back to his desk and straightened some papers. The desk was loaded but organized in neat piles.

"We are approaching endgame here, Mister Nelson, where I need to make a recommendation to the court. If I may continue the chess analogy, I am only a few moves away from checkmate. I would not like to see you in jail, nor, I think, would that soften your perspective. So, can we compromise? Will you stop fencing with me? Work toward a solution?"

It took a minute, but Jason said, "I don't want to go to jail. What do you have in mind?"

"Braithwaite has written that your research is unsupportable. I think that it is, perhaps, not unsupportable but only unsupported. Data, Mr. Nelson. Your contention, your dogged research, has a scarcity of data. You know, I am sure, that theories are as common as air and are incoherent without supporting facts."

"Yes."

"I am suggesting that you either find some supporting facts or come to the conclusion, the stated and clearly acknowledged conclusion, that those facts are not obtainable. That gives you an out, Mister Nelson, and permits me to report that you are evaluating your past behavior in a more rational manner. Believe whatever you want, but in this situation, you need to prove it."

"Ah. Senator Moynihan."

Hotchkiss took a few seconds to reach into his memory. "Yes, the quote from Senator Moynihan. 'You are entitled to you own opinion, but not your own facts.'"

"Data," Jason said. "Facts."

"Yes." They looked at each other for a long moment, each uncertain who had won the game. "What I will do is release you but keep you on a short tether. You will need to come back here on a scheduled basis, and we can dissect the barrier between fact and opinion. But the endgame is approaching, Mr. Nelson, after which there will be no more chess."

Four

Hydrogen was the first element to coalesce after the big bang, with one proton and one electron. Helium came next, with two protons and two electrons. Lithium came next, then beryllium. Boron was fifth, carbon sixth, nitrogen was seventh, and oxygen was number...

"Eight!" Jason complained. "Eight more boring, embarrassing, insulting, stifling days in that cage, even after Hotchkiss promised to let me out! That guy! God, what a rat bastard bonehead!"

After his release, Jason had spent a couple days at home, lying to his family, and shedding his Halcyon experience. On his second day, his mother asked the question he had expected. They were sitting poolside, sipping lemonade and shading their eyes from the afternoon sun. "Are you now considered a criminal?" she asked. "I mean technically."

"No, Mother. The arrest and my time in that facility were based on a monstrous misunderstanding on the part of one of the clerical staff at school. I managed to untangle it all, and I am free and clear, without a blemish on my reputation."

"That's fine, dear. You know how proud we all are of you."

Soon after that conversation, Jason packed a bag and drove to meet Andrew at the apartment in Brooklyn.

"This is where you live?" he asked.

"Yeah, why? What's not to like?"

"It just doesn't seem to match up with your overall, um, gestalt."

"Well, before I left home, my mom made me promise to always wear a clean pair of gestalts. I always listen to my mom's advice. I have the best gestalts anybody's ever seen."

In Jason's Volvo, they stopped at a 7-Eleven for coffee and gyros. They drove through Brooklyn into Queens, over the Whitestone Bridge and through the Bronx until Route 87, the Northway, correctly heading north this time, opened up into a smooth pleasant highway.

"How was court last week, J?"

"J? Really? Now I'm J?"

"Didn't know it would piss you off, or I would have called you that an hour ago. So, Jason, how did it go in court the other day?"

"It was just a legal formality and a chance for my lawyer to put his hand in my pocket again. Once Rat Bastard green-lighted me, I was good to go. A suspended sentence, but I have to check in with a court-appointed Rat Bastard every month. You were right about that place. Once they get you, they do not want to let you go."

Andrew was doing his best to resist putting his feet up on the dashboard. "So, good to go, right? The adventure begins."

"The adventure begins. I got maps and Triple A directions to Woodstock, but I'm thinking maybe you know how to get there."

"Sometimes it's as easy as closing my eyes and watching the colors change. Other times, not so much."

They cruised down the highway at a speed undreamed of during 99.7% of the existence of human beings, using a fuel made of compressed remnants of plant and animal life which had been dead for 50 million years. Of course, they were completely oblivious to this.

Andrew soon slipped into the semi-stupor he had learned to adopt during long trips. The road hummed the same tune and was set in the same key, no matter what highway he was on. The DJs had the same pitch, "more music, no repeats, the hottest sounds of today, yesterday and tomorrow...when a pair of tickets to...set your dial." Each rest stop looked like a hundred others where he had wrapped both hands around the largest coffee he could afford and tried to remember what city they were driving to. It was hard to believe how much he had once loved life on the road, and hard to believe how much he had come to hate it.

Jason drove the way he did everything else: with narrow minded aggression occasionally tempered by moments of mental clarity. There were only about half a dozen cars that he could see, but each one was considered a challenge. He didn't really care about driving fast, just a little faster than the car ahead of him. Once he was past it, Jason was content to match the other's speed.

He nudged Andrew. "So, on my map, Woodstock is exit nineteen. Unless you know a shortcut."

"Nope, not nineteen. A couple exits before that," said Andrew.

"But nineteen is the exit for Woodstock."

"Yep. But the Woodstock Festival and Art Fair wasn't at Woodstock. It was at White Lake, sort of, about fifty miles southwest of Woodstock."

"Well, sure. That makes perfect sense. Why would Woodstock be at Woodstock? I keep forgetting that this was the sixties. Nothing was normal."

Andrew shook himself awake and thought immediately about a cup of coffee. "Tell you what, mister historian, PhD candidate, camping aficionado. You pull into the next pitstop and I'll educate you a little about Woodstock. It's stuff you may need to know if we're gonna find the holy grail."

Jason parked at the far corner of the parking lot, safely away from all other cars and trucks. "A little exercise won't kill you," he said.

They sat on red plastic chairs at a shiny table, some unrecognizable music bouncing off the walls, but at least at a reasonable volume.

Andrew sat with his large coffee, Jason with a bagel and fruit juice. Jason watched as Andrew ripped a small opening in the lid.

"What's that for?" Jason asked. "You're sitting at a table. It won't spill."

"Force of habit," Andrew said. "The lids all have spouts now, but I come from that ancient civilization where we were forced to make holes in the lids of our coffee cups. It was an era of dreadful vexation."

Everything in the restaurant was made of plastic, or covered with plastic. Every square inch from floor to ceiling could be wiped clean with a damp cloth.

"Okay," Andrew said, "here comes the history lesson, Professor. Dylan lived in Woodstock for a while after his motorcycle accident. That's where the idea came from. The organizers thought that just his name would create interest. They were probably right; he was that popular."

"Bob Dylan, you mean? The guy with the adenoids or nasal blockage or whatever the hell is wrong with him? That guy? I never did understand his appeal."

"Timing. I guess you could think of it kinda like Elvis, coming along at the right time. When the king hit the airwaves, R and B was just becoming popular and he was a white guy that could sing it. The Beatles, same thing. Just making the right sound at the right time. Dylan had that social consciousness vibe at just the right moment."

"Dylan."

"Yep, that's the guy. And these four promoters, two money guys and two music guys, thought they could have a big music and arts festival and Dylan would pull in fans, and he would be the headliner. Of course, he didn't live in Woodstock anymore and wasn't interested anyway, but by the time they figured that out, they had momentum, and the name stuck.

They originally thought maybe fifty or sixty or seventy-five thousand people. When they were looking for a place where that many people could camp out, the nearest site was some half-assed industrial park in Wallkill."

"But you told me white something or other."

"Yeah, White Lake. The town government in Wallkill learned it was about to be invaded by, like, fifty thousand hippies, and they just freaked. Refused the permits and paperwork necessary and just pulled the plug on the whole thing. Boom!"

"Can't really blame them when you think how it all turned out. All the problems it caused. The traffic jam, the food shortages."

"Yeah, because nobody ever remembers the Woodstock Music and Arts Festival, but all the towns around here are famous. No tourists are curious about the Woodstock festival. No one has reunion concerts, no one ever made a movie of it or wrote a book about it. None of the original performers ever made it big, right?"

"Okay, okay. A group of moony bozos hit the jackpot. Epic. Legendary, blah, blah, blah."

"So, anyway, moony bozo incorporated moves the Woodstock concert out of Wallkill to White Lake, right? At least it was all Ws. Makes it easier to remember, almost like a...what do you call it, a metonic."

Jason thought for a moment. "Oh, you mean a mnemonic, Professor. A memory aid."

"Yeah, one of them. Well, a guy in White Lake had a permit for some kind of a festival, but his place wasn't near big enough. So, last minute, these four guys found Yasgur's farm in Bethel, and that's where they finally had it. Max Yasgur had a dairy farm about the size of New England."

"So the Woodstock festival, which was never in Woodstock, was kicked out of Wallkill and ended up in Bethel on a permit issued for White Lake. I think I got it. I don't care, but I got it."

"Like you said, man. This was the sixties. Wasn't much that was normal."

"So, if they were still figuring maybe fifty to seventy-five thousand stoners, where did the rest of the horde come from?"

Andrew laughed and took a long swig of coffee. "You're still not getting it, man. This was the sixties, and people were different. There was a war, there was Nixon, there was pot, there was civil rights, there was free love, and there were college kids, I mean college kids everywhere. Word spread that there was a major concert happening in Dylan's home town. It was like a party at a friend's house when his parents were away. Everybody just showed up. I mean everybody. Man, we just showed up."

Jason knew he shouldn't ask this question but couldn't resist. "But what do you think it all meant?"

"What do you mean, what it meant?"

"I'm a historian, you know, and trying to look at this thing like it was history. History sets the course of the future. Life isn't random, things build on other things. So, it had to have a reason. If my needle was the same phenomenon that found Socrates and Charlemagne, then it had to be something significant. World shaking. Not just college students sliding around in the mud. It had to have some meaning."

"I don't know what to tell you, man. To me, not everything has a reason. In fact, most things don't. Not everything has to be about something big, cosmic, world shaking. Some things just are, man, and you just have to dig it. There's nothing else you can do with it except get out of the way and just dig it."

"Oh, please, don't give me that hippie 'dig it' shit. I'm trying hard to hear you, but I can't buy that. Things have a reason. Things are about something. Greece and Rome were about culture and civilization. The Crusades were about religion. The Holy Roman Empire was about trying to build order out of chaos. Life is not random. Things are about something."

"I don't know what to tell you, mister history professor. I was there. I got stoned, I heard the music, I got covered with mud and I got totally lost, and it was the best, I mean the best, time of my life. It was never about anything but itself. Woodstock was always just about Woodstock."

"Crap," Jason said. Andrew just shrugged. Jason finished his bagel in silence, and Andrew pulled the lid off his coffee and stared at a blonde in a Ramones T-shirt.

They left the interstate at exit eighteen, and took local roads west and south and then west again, and then south again. It was September, so the trees were still full of leaves, with only a few curling, turning brown and twirling to the rolling hills below. Jason drove through Catskill Park, past lakes and dairy farms and through communities too small to be considered towns. What looked like an hour's drive on the map stretched into two hours, and then to two and a half. At a stoplight in Liberty, the first real town they had gone through since the highway, Jason said, "Are we lost?"

Andrew glanced down at the map balanced on his knee. "Nope. We're just where we should be. Keep heading south on this for a while, we'll come to White Lake and 17B takes us just past it."

"Amazing," Jason said. "Amazing that a hundred thousand stoned out freaks could find this place at all, much less on the same weekend."

Along 17B, there were signs that led them to "The Original Site Of The Woodstock Festival." A few miles up the road, the woods thinned to a wide pasture behind a fence.

~ * ~

"Stop here, man. Pull over," Andrew said. He crossed the road and leaned on the high white fence. Inside the fence was a stone block with a plaque set on it. It was too far away to read the inscription.

"This is the place," Andrew said softly, a wide smile on his face. "Just over that hill, the land slopes down into kind of a bowl shape. At the back edge of the bowl there was a little rise where the stage was built. Jesus, man. Jesus, I can see it."

"Don't have an orgasm just yet," Jason said. "Where is the tree? Where did you bury that guitar?"

Andrew leaned on the top rail and pointed to his right. "Down beyond the hollow, you can see a roof. I think that may have been for the stage. Behind the stage there's a dirt road that heads off to the left, uh, northwest, I think, and leads to a pond and a little stand of trees. It was somewhere in those woods."

Jason put his foot up to climb the fence. "What are you going, man?" Andrew called. "This is somebody's property. If you're looking to get arrested again, at least give me your car keys so I'm not stuck here."

Jason climbed down slowly. "Great. I got a burned-out former freak giving me lessons about trespassing. You were trespassing the whole three days you were here."

"Not burned out, probably still a freak, but not currently limited by any court orders, thank you very much." They glared at each other for a moment, then Andrew walked about 20 feet away. He leaned against the fence again and stared at the pastureland until he heard that familiar crackle and waited for the color shift. This time was a little different. The green of the grass and the white of the fence faded into the pale black and gray of an old photograph.

~ * ~

The three of them are walking, west along 17B. Rich first, gangly, pimpled, always smiling Rich. Carl next, with his big head and his cow eyes, and then him. He is having trouble keeping up because the top strap on his sandal is digging into his instep and he is beginning to limp, so he takes off his sandals and stuffs them into his duffel bag. His bell bottom jeans are a little too long for him and he can hear the flap of the cuff against the road with every step he takes. They have been walking for about two hours since they parked his car on the shoulder of 17B, among the hundreds of other cars stuck and abandoned. Rich is about ten yards ahead of them and he can spot the orange peace symbol on the back of his backpack. He has watched that peace sign bounce up and down the last three miles, but it has stopped moving now. Rich has left the road, climbed the hill and stopped in his tracks.

Carl calls to him, "Rich?" Rich doesn't even turn around, he just waves them forward with a weak motion of his arm. Carl runs up the hill and stops, too. Andrew climbs up the hill and says, "What the hell is wrong with..."

He hears it before he actually sees it, the distant murmur of thousands and thousands of voices. He stares down, like Carl and Rich, and tries to interpret what he sees. There is a layer of people, heads and shoulders mostly, that fills the little valley. From his place on the hill, he can't distinguish male from female, black from white or young from old. It is just a wide and deep concentration of murmuring, mobile flesh. More figures are streaming in from all sides and the humongous mass in the middle seem to be bulging, rippling outward and forward toward the enormous stage at the far edge.

Carl is the first to move. He points, "Look," he says. "Look at all these people. Look."

~ * ~

"Look," Jason called to him. Andrew jolted out of his flashback and staggered back a couple of steps.

"I didn't mean to startle you, but look, we need to work out some boundaries here or this partnership is not gonna work."

Andrew rubbed his eyes and banged the palm of his hand against the fence. *Man, I wish I could stay there*, he thought. *Why can I never stay there?*

Jason continued. "You're right. That burned-out freak crack was out of line, but you've hit me with some good shots, too. You and I need to come to some kind of understanding if we're gonna get this done."

Andrew reached out and patted him on the shoulder, making sure he was real. "What do you have in mind?"

"A reset. Complete reset. We go back to square one and start from scratch. Both of us. No more attitude, no more cracks, no more pissing each other off. Okay? We already established that we don't like each other, but it doesn't matter if we don't like each other. Let's just zip it until we can get this done. Agreed?"

Andrew nodded. "Yeah. Just until we can get it done, right?" he said.

"Yep. We find the Mcguffin and we go our separate ways. You get your guitar, I get my data. But we stay civil until we get it done."

Andrew laughed. "Mcguffin, ha! I haven't heard that word in a long time. My father used to...never mind."

Jason just nodded. "Okay. But past the truce, nothing has changed. You're still a smelly lard ass with no life, okay? Truce?"

"Yeah, and past the truce, you're still an ignorant digit head who couldn't find his ass if his hands were in his back pockets. Right, truce."

~ * ~

They stared and pointed over the fence for a few minutes, trying to think of something else they could do. Andrew did his best to remember and point out where things were in '69, and Jason nodded and grunted some, but didn't really care. Finally, Jason said, "We'll come back tonight, comb through those woods."

They rented a room at the Liberty Motor Lodge, about half an hour away. Two full sized beds, paneled walls, cable TV, and breakfast at the diner down the block is ten percent off.

"Home sweet home," Andrew said, flopping on the bed and hitting the power button on the remote control.

Jason showered and unpacked his suitcase.

"I don't think I've ever actually put anything in a motel room dresser," Andrew said. "I just pull stuff out of my duffel bag."

Jason looked at Andrew, with his stained jeans curled at the waist, a black U2 T-shirt with a hole in the shoulder, and then across at his stained canvas duffel bag. "Truce, okay? I'm trying not to bust on you, but you're not making it easy."

Andrew skipped through the stations quickly, barely noticing what he was watching. Sports show, news, soap opera, soap, soap, cartoon, 70s rerun, 60s rerun, infomercial. Jason looked over for a second and said, "The guy that said TV is a half-assed wasteland was dead right."

"Wow, that's really weird. Like *déjà vu* or something. I said those exact words a couple of weeks ago."

Jason was busy setting up his laptop computer in the far corner of the room.

"Let me ask you something," Andrew said. "What exactly is the problem between you and me?"

"Oh, no. Don't get started on that. I'm not gonna be the one to break the truce. Yeah. Forget it. We're too close."

"Okay, leave me out of it. You seem to have a beef with my whole generation. The whole Baby Boom generation. I'm not trying to start an argument here, just a dialogue. I really want to know."

"A dialogue? Is that like rapping? Oh, no, no, sorry. Forget I said that, that just slipped out. Okay, you want to know my opinion of the Baby Boom generation, right?"

"I really do. And not your opinion as a historian, your personal opinion."

Jason tapped the button on his laptop, and Andrew heard the soft whine as it started up. "I'm not sure I can separate the two, but I'll give it a shot. Do you know that famous analogy about the pig in a python? I read it somewhere, and it fits the boomers perfectly."

"Pig in a python?"

"Yes. A pig. In a python. A large, ignorant, insatiable grunting mammal that has been swallowed by a large, tube-like predator, and is working its way slowly through it guts. In this case, the inner workings of all of American society. Your generation has pretty much stretched the moral, artistic and economic fiber of this country beyond recognition, and your sheer volume is blocking any kind of constructive change."

"Yeah, there are a lot of us. After the war, parents were horny in massive numbers, and poof! Maybe more like waaaah! Here we are. But you owe us. We set the tone, we loosened the chains. We're like the older brother who challenged all the rules so Mom and Dad went easier on the little brother."

Jason struggled, but could not help chuckling at this. "Not exactly. You're like a hyperactive older brother who never shuts up, never gets out of the way, takes your stuff and only gives it back when it's broken."

Andrew thought about this for a moment and couldn't come up with a good argument. "So, like, everybody your age resents us? That's harsh, man. We're traveling on spaceship earth, just like you, and trying to get along. I can't believe everybody hates us."

"Only the ones paying any attention."

"Come on, man, it's not that bad. We're not that bad." He turned the television back on and flipped through a couple of stations without actually looking at them. "What do we block? What do we take that's yours?"

Jason sighed deeply and closed the lid on the computer. "Okay," he said. "Bear with me here. But this is developing history, and I am one of those who *has* paid attention. I will try hard to stay calm, you know, and tell the truth, but just remember that you brought it up. Let's take something you know about...music. Every broadcast market in the country has at least one oldies station. Even the so-called progressive stations mix in a lot of what they call classic rock."

"Now, for once we agree. Radio stations play mush. I think if it's classic rock it's not rock, and if it's rock, it ain't classic."

"Yeah, that's right. But the boomers, because of their numbers, still dictate what gets airtime, and they still want to hear what they grew up with. How many times can you hear "Layla" before you hurl all over your minivan? And while those stations are busy shoving "Help Me Rhonda" down our throats, the new music, the music that my generation writes, isn't getting played, isn't being heard. A lot of talented musicians are stocking shelves or pinning on an ID badge that says 'management trainee.'

"I hate oldies stations," Andrew said. "I think nostalgia is bullshit. Do you know that Sha Na Na played Woodstock? Doo-wop music. A guy did an Elvis thing in a gold lamè suit. How the hell did that happen?"

Jason shook his head for a moment and continued. "And that's just music. You want to talk about economics? You want to talk about how the glut of boomers are sucking the life out of the Social Security system? Let's talk about jobs instead. Know why the government can claim it's creating so many jobs? Because it takes people my age three crappy jobs to support them. And there are so many boomers still working, that when the hard times hit, guess who gets laid off first?"

"Yeah, but that's the way it always is between older and younger generations. My old man used to have us watch Ed Sullivan with, like, monkey acts and jugglers and crap like that. Oh, and Perry Como. You ever see Perry Como, J.? To this day I break out in hives when I try to wear a sweater."

"Sure. There's always a gulf between generations, but with boomers, it's like a full-scale invasion. Between your generation and mine, it's like, I don't know, ants at a picnic."

"I dig, no...I get what you're telling me, but you have to admit, my generation did some good stuff. Civil rights movement, the antiwar movement..."

Jason laughed. "Yeah, movements. You boomer types have social movements as easy as vegetarians have bowel movements. Civil rights, antiwar, women's rights, gay rights, Indian rights. You and your hero Dylan fired up all this social consciousness into high gear, but you never finished any of your movements. You all—well not you— but most of you grew up and got haircuts and investment accounts and drove their BMWs out to the suburbs. Things have changed, sure. You may have pointed out the issues, opened a few minds, but the problems are still there. Everybody just boogaloos right past their elevated consciousness when things get complicated. There is still race discrimination, gender discrimination, lifestyle discrimination...and by the way, for my money, the worst thing to come out of the boomer generation is that word 'lifestyle.' If you're gay, or bi or whatever, have at it. But it's a life, not a life *style*."

"Maybe some of that's true, but we did stop the war."

Jason shook his head. "Another popular myth. America pulled out of Vietnam, a political and military decision, when it became clear we could not win. I will admit to respect for the people that demonstrated against the war, but you didn't end it."

Andrew surfed around on the television for a few more minutes. "In the spirit of the truce, I'm working hard at seeing your point of view, but I do have an, uh, what do they call an argument in a debate?

"A counterpoint. Or sometimes a rebuttal."

"Rebuttal, I like that word better."

"Because it has the word 'butt' in it."

"See, we're really getting to know each other. This is good."

"Yes, really special. What's your, um, counter argument?"

Andrew shut off the TV and looked over at him. "Well, you said the boomers never finished their movements. But at least they started them, right? Generations before us didn't. And that shot about the investment accounts and the BMWs? That's more you guys than us. Most people my age are trying to drag their kids through high school or maybe saving for college. BMWs are no longer in the plan."

"Okay," Jason said. "In the spirit of the truce, I'm working hard to see your point of view."

"Ha, ha, okay, fair enough, but I got more. I'm remembering this bar conversation with this guy. He was a lot like you, kind of a brainiac. You know, a progeny."

"Progeny? Oh, maybe you mean prodigy."

"Yeah, okay, that. He was halfway hammered and going on about this concept of addition by subtraction, which sounded pretty stupid to me, until he finally, I mean finally, got to the point."

"And you're gonna get there, too?"

"In this adding by subtracting thing, you take something big away from your life, and see how much changes. So, for example, take away the Boomer generation, what do you have?"

"Better jobs, social security, better music and art, a reasonable national debt. I could go on, but I think I made my point."

"Maybe all that, yeah. But also, no Beatles, no Springsteen, so where does that leave current music? No Stephen Hawking, that's the genius in the wheelchair, right? So all of his theories and stuff are gone. No George Lucas, not to mention Luke Skywalker, Princess Leia, Han Solo. They're all boomers. Apple computers, Bill Gates, the moon landing...who did that? And the war in 'Nam. You can argue that we weren't the ones who stopped it, but we definitely got the ball rolling. I could go on, but..."

Jason put his hands up in surrender. "Okay, you make some good points, and all things considered, I don't want to argue. But after we find that guitar, let's make a date to finish this conversation."

Andrew just smiled. "Okay, man, we'll honor the truce, but one last thing. Pig in a python?"

"Yep. Pig in a python."

"That's just a kick ass name for a rock band."

~ * ~

After a quick but meager dinner, Cobb salad and coffee for Jason, barbecue chicken wings and more coffee for Andrew, they drove down 17B and across Route 55 into Liberty to find a hardware store. The town of Liberty stretched for a mile or so down Main Street, and then North Main Street. It was filled with insurance brokers, dry cleaners, real estate offices and bookstores before it narrowed and became houses and apartment buildings and gas stations. They turned off North Main Street onto James Street when Jason spotted a hardware store.

"I made a list of what I think we need," Andrew said. "Shovels, a lantern, flashlights, work gloves, maybe some kind of boots, a compass, and a can of spray paint."

"Spray paint? What do we need that for?"

"To mark the trees where we've already looked."

Jason said. "I'm impressed. You really got yourself organized."

"Yeah, well, we got a cease fire going, but don't push it, man. It doesn't mean we have to say nice things to each other."

The hardware store took up a hundred feet of James Street frontage next to a gift shop with an unusual name. They parked, and Andrew headed to the hardware store while Jason put a quarter in the meter.

"I hate this," he said to the meter. "Government at its worst. I'm only here for ten minutes and I have to pay for a complete half-hour." As he was crossing the street, he noticed Andrew had stopped at the edge of the hardware store. He was looking over at the window of the shop next door, the Penultimate Pickle.

Jason figured he was staring at a cute girl in the store, but he couldn't see anyone, just T-shirts, jewelry and a couple of paintings. Lights were being turned off in the store, too.

He came up behind and tapped Andrew on the shoulder. "Come on. Let's get this done. Hardware store's right over here."

Andrew said nothing. His hand popped up, almost involuntarily pointing ahead, and he walked slowly toward the display window of the little shop.

Jason called, "Yo, Andrew. Dude. Hardware store, remember? Shovels, flashlights, spray-paint?"

Without turning, Andrew said evenly, "That's it. That's exactly what I saw."

Jason walked over to him, thinking *"Oh, great timing. Today is the day this guy's brain finally turns to oatmeal."* He looked where Andrew was pointing. In the corner of the wide display window was a painting, unframed on canvas. It showed the back of a man climbing a tree with something in his outstretched left hand, and he was glowing.

"That's it," Andrew repeated. "That's it exactly. That's what I saw."

They both bent down and waddled closer to the window. Jason said, "I guess that proves we're not crazy."

"I'm not so sure," Andrew said. "It may just mean that there is a third person who's just as crazy as we are."

They stared at the painting for a few minutes; Andrew, like it was a home movie of his childhood, and Jason, like it was a treasure map in a foreign language. They moved slowly toward the door like they were about to step onto an alien world.

Five

In July of 1976, the Bicentennial parade marched down North Main Street with flags, banners and streamers all proud in red, white and blue. Adults wore Uncle Sam top hats, children ate ice cream, and fireworks had been going off all day.

She was sitting on the floor, tears trickling down her cheeks, in the middle of a large rectangular room, recently vacated. They had been married for almost six years; she had worked double shifts at the supermarket, and he had picked up weekend work re-surfacing driveways. With the inheritance she received when her father passed away, they were able to afford this store on James Street in Liberty.

She tugged at the lace band at her wrist. "It's so empty it echoes in here," she said. He put an arm around her and kissed her on the forehead. "We'll fill it," he said, "and there will be lots of happy noises in here. I'll put windows in both the east and west walls. The place will be filled with light, we'll have posters on the walls. I want shelves and cabinets and tables and a model train set with a miniature village.

I heard of a guy selling a kiln we can afford. Secondhand books over there, the kitchen area will be in the back, and my table will go right there. Inch by inch, honey, row by row…"

She wiped the tears off her face. "We'll have to think of a good name. Something that stands out."

~ * ~

Twenty-seven years later, Cecelia, the owner at the Penultimate Pickle, heard the knock from her kitchen in the back of the shop and ignored it. She was just putting the lights out. After the third time, she tiptoed over to the front door. It was dusk, and there was an orange glow coming through the blinds as she peeked between them. Two men stood at the door: one big, beefy and sloppy, the other small and neat but nervous looking. They were Laurel and Hardyish, if Laurel had worn glasses and Hardy had been a U2 fan. They didn't look like thieves and they didn't look like salesmen, but they didn't look like customers either.

"I'm closed." She pulled up the blind on the door and waved her hands. "Come back in the morning."

The big one spoke first. "It's the painting." He pointed toward the window. "I saw that! I saw it, too!"

"Tomorrow," she called. "I open at nine-thirty." She let the blind slap down and walked away. *People come up from the city with a little bit of money*, she thought, *and they think us hicks should be at their beck and call all night and day.*

"Please," the voice called. "The light! The guy in the tree! I saw it. At Woodstock."

She stopped in her tracks. *Oh, damn*, she thought, and then said out loud, "It's finally starting." She jumped to the door in two quick steps and yanked it open. "What?" she said, looking back and forth between the two dumbfounded faces. "You saw what? Tell me what you saw." She grabbed the younger one by the sleeve and pulled him into the room.

"I'm the one who saw it," Andrew said calmly, looking carefully at her. He walked over to the window, picked up the picture and began running his fingers gently along the edge. "Where did you get this?"

"I painted it," she said. "I've painted about a dozen of them over the years. This is the worst of them, so I thought I could sell it. But tell me. Tell me what you saw!"

"I was at Woodstock..." Andrew said.

"So was I..." she said.

"And one morning I was walking back to my tent..."

"Yes!" she said. "I was coming out of the medical tent..."

"And I saw this," he pointed to the picture. "I saw this man..."

"...this cat," she said and then winced.

"Climbing a tree, you know?"

"I dig, yeah, I dig. What else?"

"I was behind him, so I couldn't see his face, but he was halfway up the tree, and he was shining. Not shining, glowing. Just like this. And I thought it was Jesus."

"Jesus," she whispered. "This is really far out."

"You saw it too, right?" Jason asked. "You saw it or you wouldn't have painted it. Couldn't have."

She nodded, twisted her hair and draped it over her shoulder. "I saw it, too," she said. And then she looked down at the painting for a long moment.

"Well, give," Andrew said. "Tell us."

"It's a little hard for me to talk about."

"You don't have to worry about us thinking you're crazy or anything," Andrew said. "Both of us actually believe in this thing, whatever the hell it is."

"It's not that," she said. "I believe in it, too. It's the talking. Sometimes when I talk, things come out a little different."

"Tell us what you know," Jason said. "Please tell us."

She sighed deeply and sat on a cedar chest in the middle of the room. "Okay, I'll tell you. I was just a chick at Woodstock, too, and I was like, stoked. It was so groovy. I had lost my friends and my old man—I found out later he was ballin' one of my friends anyway—and he thought I was, like, his groupie. A really bad scene. But the festival, man. That whole scene was just so free, you dig, so beautiful, man, you know? So real! I was walking around with, like, lilies between my toes, you dig? But I stepped on this huge piece of glass. Bummer, right? A real bad trip. Blood all over the place. So, I went to this, like, medical tent, and they were really beautiful there. They fixed up my foot and told me a place where I could, like, crash for a while. And when I left, that's when I saw it, just like you said, man. I saw this cat halfway up a tree and he was like, glowing, man. It freaked me out. I thought I was having a bad trip. But I was straight. Well, mostly. The whole scene was beyond crazy city."

Jason looked at Andrew. Andrew looked at Jason.

Cecilia took another deep breath. "That's what I mean about talking weird. You know, differently. It's, it's, uh…Well, you're here anyway, so that's cool. Would either of you like a cup of tea?"

There was a kitchen at the back of the store, and a big oak table. They sat at the table sipping oolong, all three feeling awkward about being there and edgy about sharing with the other two. Cecilia brought out slices of sesame bread. She patted Andrew gently on the shoulder. "It's all natural," she said. "Low-fat, low-calorie."

He sighed and broke off a small piece. "Good tea," he said.

"Oh yes," Jason agreed with a vigorous nod. "Very good tea."

Cecilia laughed. Not a polite, drawing room giggle, but a full, throaty, bent at the waist laugh. "This is funky," she said. "This is so bizarre. We all knew something special was going to happen here, that we're on some kind of a quest or an adventure together, but we are so stiff and formal and all we talk about is the tea. Very far out."

"Who are you?" Jason asked. "What are you?" She laughed again and gathered her hair into a long ponytail and pulled it over her shoulder.

"My name is Cecilia," she said. "This is my business, and my home." She separated her hair into three equal parts, each almost long enough to spill into her lap, and then began to braid them.

"But the painting," Andrew said. He was watching as she brought one strand across the middle and then pulled the other strand across the middle. She did this as effortlessly and unconsciously as most people change channels with a remote control.

"The painting is an attempt to deal with what I saw there, years ago." she said. "It didn't help much."

Jason was poking at a crumb that had fallen into his tea. "He believes," he nodded over at Andrew, "that it was God climbing a tree." He waited for laughter, or rolling of the eyes, but Cecilia said, "Jesus coming back? No. Too much to hope for."

Too much to hope for? Jason thought. He looked over at Andrew for laughter, or rolling of the eyes, but he was intent on watching her braid her hair.

"This picture," Jason said. "How...?

"Every once in a while, this vision would just, like, surround me, and I would have to paint it or write about it or sculpt it or something. It's been calm lately, but it was very strong sometimes. Almost controlling."

Andrew said, "Visions? Like flashbacks? Weird colors but everything clear?"

"Mmm, no. The visions I had were pretty much that," she pointed at the picture. "But they would be, like, totally everywhere. I could focus for a few minutes, but then, whoa, man! I'd turn my head and it would be, like, right in my face. Totally blew my mind. Lately, I haven't been seeing that cat in the tree, but I've been seeing a lot of new stuff. Real quick and not as clear, but I think connected to this whole scene. It freaks me out."

Jason looked at Andrew. Andrew said, "Oh, I think what I get is flashbacks. Like movies, that I'm the star of, but sort of on a different planet."

"But you see stuff you've already seen, right? Memories?"

"Mostly, yeah, but memories in glorious technicolor with a really good sound system right between my ears. What do you call it, a holograph?"

"Hologram," Jason said. "Like in *Star Trek*."

"Mine are different," Cecelia said. "Most of them are things I've experienced, but not that vivid and not that clear. Or at least they used to be. But I seem to be getting new ones lately, not stuff I've experienced, but new stuff. I knew something was going to meet me at the door, but I wasn't sure what, or when. And it turned out to be you. And I think something, or maybe someone else, is coming. This all started up again a few weeks ago, and I think I'm pretty well freaked by it now."

"Jesus H. Christ," Jason said, louder than he wanted to.

Cecelia smiled at him. "No, we covered that already. I don't think Jesus is involved in this."

Left over right, pull it tight. Right over left, pull it tight again. Her hair was straight and silky, mostly golden light brown but with pale splashes of gray. Andrew's head shifted slightly to the left and right, following her movements.

"I guess you should tell me who you are, too," she said.

"I'm Jason," he said. "I didn't go to Woodstock and I've never been stoned. Can I still be in the club?"

She smiled, looking right at him. She held her hands up and framed his face without touching him. "You're a loaf of bread, aren't you?" she said, matter-of-factly.

He stared at her for a long moment. "Okay, if you want me to be. I'm a loaf of bread. Next week, can I be a jar of pickles? The sweet pickles, not the dill. They make my face all scrunched up."

She smiled and laughed that full throated laugh again. "Yes, definitely a loaf of bread. Not the squishy grocery store kind, but the home baked kind. On the inside you're firm and consistent and sustaining, but you're afraid that it's too soft. So your outside is hard and dark and you think you're protected by it. Yep, loaf of bread."

There was silence in the large, darkening room. She stared at Jason and both Jason and Andrew stared at her. In the snow globe over on the sale table, the last piece of snow settled on the bottom and was still. At the same moment, on the parking meter next to Jason's Volvo, the red "expired" flag popped up and remained motionless. A cuckoo clock in the corner wound down and stopped as they all just stared at each other. A strong breeze blew down the center of Main Street and gusted under the shop door. It rang the bronze wind chimes hanging by the doorway.

"I'm Andrew," Andrew said. He put out his big hand and said, "and I'm very pleased to meet you, Cecilia. And believe me, he is more of a dill pickle than a loaf of bread."

She looked from one to the other, slowly. "You two don't know each other, do you? I mean not really."

"No," Andrew said, "not really. We met about a month ago."

"That's interesting," she said. "It occurred to me there might be two, but I thought you'd be together. A team."

"What the hell are you talking about?" Jason asked. "Who the hell are you"?

"Hey man, lighten up," Andrew said. "Just lighten up."

"Be cool, man." Cecelia said and held her hand up to her mouth.

"Sorry," she said. "This shit just happens, man. And I get so hacked."

"What is that?" Jason said, more evenly. "What is it with that speech pattern?"

"I know," she said. "It's awful. I hate it, but I can't control it. Sometimes I translate what other people say. It's like a reflex."

"Translate? Translate into what? What is that?"

She sighed deeply. "Can we not talk about that now? Please? This is all too exciting, too important. I want to know all about you two."

Andrew began. "We met a few week ago when I was escorting..."

Jason jumped in. "What we are mostly is two tired and hungry guys that want to get out to that farm and look for the Mcguffin."

Cecelia said, "Mcguffin, ha! I haven't heard that word in a long time. My old man used to...never mind."

The two men exchanged a glance. Andrew said, "I think I said those exact words this afternoon. Exact."

Cecelia said, "I can help with the hungry and the tired. How about we mellow out for a while, I'll put something on for dinner, and you can boogie on out to Yasgur's once it's dark?"

"If that hardware store is open, I'll get some flashlights and stuff," Andrew said.

"Cool. Now we're truckin'."

"Are you with us?" Andrew asked.

"Um, can we..." said Jason.

"Don't worry, man," she said to Jason. "Stay mellow. I am with you on the quest, for sure, but I can't make it tonight. I need to stay here."

"Okay,"

"I did mention that there is someone else coming into all this. I'm not sure who or when, but I want to be here when they arrive."

"They? You've got whoever conjured up as more than one?"

"It isn't a certainty, these things never are, but I think there is more than one, and I think they share something. And just so you know, I don't conjure. My eye of newt went bad months ago, and my toe of frog got freezer burn."

Andrew laughed. "Speaking of burn..."

~ * ~

She made them fish tacos and raspberry tea, which Jason ate quietly and quickly, but Andrew mostly pushed around on his plate and longed for a beer and a burger.

Andrew said, "You haven't told me what you think I am? I hope not another loaf of bread."

She pushed her chair back and looked at him carefully. "I can't tell, there's too many of you. Four, maybe five characters in there kinda rubbing up against each other. They all have names that sound kind of alike, but they're all different."

"Oh, for god's sake," Jason mumbled.

Andrew nodded. "I guess," he said. "I don't know what any of that means, but all right."

She laughed. "I don't know what any of this means until I know what it means, you know? I can tell you this, though," she said, flashing that broad, bright smile. "The central one, the real one, is getting stronger, and the others are fading."

"I don't know what that means either, but that's cool. Do you think maybe you'll see anything more?"

"I think so. I think maybe that's one of the reasons you're here."

"Will you tell me when you know something?" he asked. "Even if the news is bad."

"Oh, yes," she said, "as soon as I know. But I don't think the news will be bad."

Cecelia drew a map to get them to the festival entrance by a different route that crossed Happy Avenue and left them just outside the gate in front of the stage.

"There's a stage? Why is there still a stage there?" Jason asked.

"It's not the original, god knows," Cecelia said. "There is a concert next weekend, sort of an anniversary, or close to it. Some of the original acts are going to perform."

"Really?" Andrew said. "Do you know which acts?"

"Um, I know Country Joe will be there, but the fish have all swum upstream or something. I have a brochure somewhere I'll find for you." She went to a kitchen drawer and came out with a flyer titled, "Another Concert in the Garden." It had the familiar picture of the guitar neck with the dove on it, and below it in rainbow colors, "One Full Day of Peace and Music." It listed Country Joe McDonald and Melanie from the original concert, and eight unknown local bands.

"Oh, man," Andrew said. "Oh man, oh man. Cosmic. This must be some kind of a sign."

Jason said, pointing at Cecelia, "You're sounding like her. What are you talking about?"

"Melanie. Melanie's playing. Melanie who sang in the rain the first day I was there and has been flashing me back ever since. For years, man, I come over the hill, and there she is. Melanie, man! Melanie. Blonde, angelic face, voice like, I don't know, God, if God was a beautiful blonde woman."

"Bitchin' babe," Cecelia said, and slapped her leg.

"We gotta get tickets," Andrew said. "It could help us spot that tree. We could get a real good look in the daytime."

"Gee," Jason said. "What a bright and creative idea. I wonder why no one else thought of it. Oh, I know. Most of us are single units, and there's a whole bunch of you."

"Yo, bro. The truce," Andrew said." He looked over at Cecelia and said with a grin, "Melanie."

Six

A couple sat stiffly in a large, richly decorated office on the eighth floor of a building on 6th Street in Washington DC. In the middle of yet another argument, she heard her son yelling and ran to the other room.

"What did you do?" she screamed at the man standing near the entrance. "What did you do to him?" She picked up the little boy who was holding his head and crying.

"I barely touched him."

"You hit him? You hit a four-year-old? What the hell is wrong with you?"

"Look around you," the man said. He was pudgy, pink skinned, dressed in a grey pinstriped suit, a regimental striped tie with a silver tie tack, and a U.S flag pin in his lapel. "This is a place of business," he said, "not a pre-school."

There were toy trucks and toy dinosaurs scattered all over the floor. She kicked one and it shot across the room and hit him in the shin. He did not react.

"Cole!" she called. "Cole, please come out here and see what your favorite mannequin did."

In the inner office, a man stood up wearily and walked slowly to the doorway. "What?" he said to his wife.

"What? Really, all you can say is 'what?' Your faithful retainer here smacked your son, your four-year-old son, on the head, and your response is, 'what'?"

The man casually leaned against the door frame. He was tall, trim, athletic, in shirtsleeves. He had a longish and slightly askew face. "Gary, what happened?"

"You called me, sir. When I came in, I almost tripped on one of these toys. I may have over-reacted."

"May have?" the woman said. "You hit him, you soulless bastard. His doting father here won't have him in the main office, so I left him to play out here. What the hell is wrong with you? Are you some kind of a robot?"

"Jennifer, that's not helping," Cole said. He took his son from her arms and put him on the floor. The boy was just sniffling and rubbing his eyes. "Son, you need to pick all of this up. Please put them back in that box." The boy looked at his mother who just nodded at him. He started to pick up his toys.

"You aren't going to say anything to your mechanical friend here?"

"Jennifer, stop that. Gary is the best research assistant on the East Coast, and I can't get along without him."

She was not surprised by this, but stood motionlessly for a moment, making a decision. "Good," she said. "Then get along without us." She took the box of toys, tossed it at her husband and then walked out. The boy began to cry again before she made it to the elevator.

Cole watched her go without expression. "Gary, call Marty at Stevenson and Partners. Ask him to dig up my pre-nup and give me a call tomorrow."

~ * ~

Two days later, they stood in the great hall of Union Station in Washington, the man with a natural scowl, and a young woman holding the hand of her little boy. "Gary," she said. "Gary, it just had to be you, didn't it? He couldn't leave it to someone less hateful."

"Jennifer, you know I just follow his instructions. This isn't personal." He took an envelope out of his jacket and handed it to her.

She hesitated and then took it with a curtsy. "I wonder if he usually leaves it on the dresser. Do you happen to know?" she said with a smile.

"It's enough to take you anywhere that Amtrak goes. His guess was Baltimore."

"Right. 'The Lady Came from Baltimore.' That will give you some idea how well he knows me. I haven't been in Baltimore since I was a year old, so he can keep guessing."

The little boy holding her hand tugged on it and asked, "Mommy, can I get a snow cone?"

"Yes, Benjamin. We'll both get snow cones as soon as I have the delicious pleasure of seeing the back of this android for the very last time."

Gary smiled and said, "Yes," turned quickly and walked away. Jennifer held back her tears and took her son for a snow cone, with only a vague idea where they would go after that. With a snow cone in one hand, and the other hand wiping her boy's mouth, she figured it out.

That evening, she stepped off the train at Grand Central Station, New York, carrying a sleepy Benjamin and pulling a suitcase behind her. She had two minutes of panic and almost hyperventilation until she spotted her friend, Cheryl, waving and walking toward them from the far end of the concourse.

They hugged and rocked and then hugged again and said at the same time, "It is so good to see you!"

Cheryl bent down to Ben. "It is very nice to see you, too. I met you when you were much younger, and you have grown into a fine young man."

Jennifer said, "You are a life saver for letting us stay. I didn't know who else to call."

"Yes, you did, but that's okay. We'll be a little cramped, but we'll work it out. It will be so good to be with both of you. But I'm so sorry about, you know." Jennifer swallowed and nodded.

Benjamin reached out and touched Cheryl's face. "You have brown skin," he said.

"Yes, Ben, and you have white skin," she said. "What do you think about that?"

"Blue is my favorite color, but brown is good, too."

~ * ~

Jennifer and Ben settled into the small second bedroom, formerly the office, in Cheryl's apartment and worked hard at being invisible and, as often as possible, elsewhere. Cheryl and her fiancé were planning their wedding, a joyful activity, but also somewhat private. Jennifer was usually skilled at keeping Ben occupied at crucial moments or taking him shopping or to the park. Tonight, though, she lapsed. She was focused on writing a letter, a difficult and long overdue letter, and he had wandered out of the room. Jennifer was stressed, and Ben was four.

Jerome, the fiancé who truly did love Cheryl and enjoyed playing with his young nieces and nephews, had just totaled up the cost of the wedding and was not actually reeling, but a little off balance. He was a respiratory therapist at the hospital where Cheryl was a nurse, and he had lost a patient that day. So, Jerome was stressed, Jennifer was stressed, and Ben was four.

Ben erupted across the living room with an airplane and was looking for somewhere to land it. Jerome's lap seemed the perfect spot.

"Babe," he said with an airplane in his lap, "this is becoming..." Jennifer came quickly out of the bedroom and apologized. "It's my fault. I lost track...it won't happen again."

Jerome had just met her, and sympathized with her situation, but the voice in his head shouted, "It's been two weeks!" He had a roommate at his apartment, and private time between him and Cheryl was more than desired; it felt at times like a physical necessity.

"Jerome, it won't happen again."

He breathed hard for a moment and looked over at Ben. "Jen, it's okay. He's a great kid. And I get where you're at. It's just..." he looked over at Cheryl. "I better be going anyway. Too many numbers floating around in my head right now."

Jen said, "Jerome, really..."

"It's okay, Jennifer, really. Hey Ben, I'm gonna take off, buddy. Can you fly me to the door?" He kissed Cheryl, and Ben grabbed his sleeve and "flew" him to the door. Ben flew back into the living room and plopped on the couch, the airplane taxiing from his belly button to his chin.

Jennifer put her forehead on the kitchen table. "Cheryl, I was writing. To my mother. But it's hard, it's so hard."

Cheryl was calm, ER nurse calm, and took Jennifer's hand. "This is reminding me of our first week in the dorm at Strayer, how awkward that was."

Jennifer lifted her head a little. "Yeah, white girl, black girl feeling like we were in enemy territory."

"Yeah, but we figured it out. We're here. Friends."

"It was the cookies that did it. Oh, those oatmeal raisins your mom made. Big ol' things and somehow still soft and warm when they got there."

"Yeah, I hated them, and you scarfed them down. And your mom made those ginger snaps. Oh, Ginger, how they would snap."

"I grew up with them and by college I hated them. Traded them for your mom's oatmeal raisin."

"I used to lend you my clothes so you'd dress like a black chick."

"I loved those outfits except that the ass was always too big."

Cheryl tilted her head a little. "But you grew into it, from what I can see. That was cookies, too, I bet."

"I did, didn't I?" Jennifer laughed. Cheryl laughed. In the other room, Ben made noises like an airplane.

"Honey, you know I love you. Always will, whatever. But, your mom..."

"I know, I know. But you don't understand what a total bitch I was. Slamming doors, literally and figuratively. A total, total..."

"But she's a mom. And a really sweet old babe. You know she wants to see you. And him."

Jennifer stood up and peeked in at Ben. "I tried to write a letter. 'An Unsolicited Letter From a Hateful Daughter To Her Sweet Old Babe Mother.' What can I possibly say?"

"I don't think you have to say a word, honey. Not a damn word."

"You think I should just...How can I just go there? How can I just show up with a four-year-old she hasn't even met?"

"A better question is, how can you not?" Jennifer banged her head softly on the table.

A few days later, Jennifer and Ben waited in line to board the bus. Cheryl and Jerome had taken them to the Port Authority Bus Station. The second to last thing Jennifer did was to put her hand on Jerome's chest and say, "She is my sister, in any way you want to interpret that word. That means you'll soon be my brother. I know you can handle it."

The last thing she did before getting on the bus was to hug Cheryl and whisper, "I do not have a fat ass."

~ * ~

The bus trip was about three hours long. Ben was asleep against his mother within about twenty minutes, and Jennifer, about twenty minutes later.

She dreamed of a jai alai game she had once seen on television. In jai alai, the ball is thrown and slams into the wall (bang!), ricochets off the side wall and is scooped up by another player to fling it off the wall again (whap). All players must wear helmets because the ball, small and hard, can travel at over 150 miles per hour. It is a game, like life, where the players must pay attention.

Eyes closed and sleepy, she thought of home and her family, and the misfortunes that placed her on this train, virtually homeless, with an envelope full of cash passed to her by the toady of a husband she no longer recognized. And her dreams began to swirl together.

Wham! The ball smacks into the wall. They're walking to the train and Benjamin is asking, "Will I see daddy again?"

Splat! A frog-faced lawyer, on orders from her husband, is reading to her from their pre-nuptial agreement.

Bonk! Eight months earlier, she smacks her husband across the face, and only worries that the sound of their argument may wake up Benjamin.

Crack! In the weeks just after Benjamin is born, she makes the decision not to call her mother and tell her.

Boom! Eight years earlier, she slams the front door leaving her home for what she thinks will be the last time, but she holds on to her key.

Crash! She is eighteen and home from college, and her mother and father talk to her in her pink bedroom. They tell her that he is sick, very sick, and may be going away soon. Bang! ...Whack! ... Crack! ... Splat!

The last memory came in slowly, without sound as if the ball had run out of momentum and was rolling across the floor toward her. She is nine years old. She sits on the floor in an empty bedroom, smiling and proud. She is holding a paint roller and they are both splattered with pink paint. Her mother is saying, "Well, honey, I think we really have something special here."

By the time they reached the first rest stop, which both she and Ben slept through, there were no more jai alai dreams, just fragments of memories in a pink bedroom, at an oak table her father had made, and of a pretty woman in lace braiding her hair.

Seven

After full dark, Jason and Andrew drove to Yasgur's farm using Cecelia's directions. The area near the stage had a chain link fence, high and spiked, but about fifty yards down the road it became a ranch fence, three horizontal planks and a post every eight feet. Andrew and Jason climbed over it. They stood silently, waiting for sirens or searchlights or bull horns, but after a silent minute or two, they started walking single file along the fence toward the stage.

The road behind the stage area split, half going southeast and half going northeast. Jason carried his video camera and a flashlight; Andrew carried a lantern and a shovel.

"Are you getting your bearings?" Jason whispered. "Can you spot anything that looks familiar?"

"Okay, so I was pretty close to where I'm standing now, right in front, looking up at the stage when Pete throws it. I dive, win the scrum, grab it and run, I think, I'm pretty sure, to the left."

"Are you tripping now? Is this from a flashback?"

"No, no. It's memory. It's how I thought about it all these years, and I know it's right."

"So…that way. Those woods over there, right? Do you remember how far? Deep in the woods or at the edge?"

"No, not a clue. I was just scrambling away. It was so long ago, man. Well, wait, if I was thinking straight, which is a big 'if,' I probably thought a lot of people were after me, so I would have gone a good ways into the woods. Yeah, I think maybe that's what I would do."

"This is great, really, you're doing great. I'm not just schmoozing you. You got us in the right area, now we just gotta find the tree."

They walk across the meadow, conscious of the quiet and the half-moon peeping in and out from behind the clouds.

"You said it was early morning and the sun was behind you, right? So, maybe we go west for a while, and then focus looking east. That could help."

"Yeah."

They walked until they were just inside the perimeter of the trees. Jason was looking up at the trees for any signs of lights or damage or anything unusual. Andrew was looking along the ground for fallen trees and exposed roots…then…

The area near the stage had a chain link fence, high and spiked, but about fifty yards down the road it became a ranch fence, three horizontal planks and a post every eight feet. Andrew and Jason climbed over it. They stood silently, waiting for sirens or searchlights or bull horns, but after a silent minute or two, they started walking single file along the fence toward the stage.

The road behind the stage area split, half going southeast and half going northeast. Jason carried his video camera and a flashlight; Andrew carried a lantern and a shovel.

"Are you getting your bearings?" Jason whispered. "Can you spot anything that looks familiar?"

"Okay, so I was pretty close to where I'm standing now, right in front, looking up at the stage when Pete throws it. I dive, win the scrum, grab it and run, I think, I'm pretty sure to the left."

"Are you tripping now? Is this from a flashback?"

"No, no. It's memory. It's how I thought about it all these years, and I know it's right."

"So...that way. The woods over there, right? Do you remember how far?"

"No, not a clue. I was just scrambling away. It was so long ago, man. Well, wait, if I was thinking straight, which is a big 'if,' I probably thought a lot of people were after me, so I would have gone a good ways into the woods. Yeah, I think maybe that's what I would do."

"This is great, really, you're doing great. I'm not just schmoozing you. You got us in the right area, now we just gotta find the tree."

They walk across the meadow, conscious of the quiet and the half moon peeping in and out from behind the clouds.

"You said it was early morning and the sun was behind you, right? So, we need to focus looking east. That could help."

"Yeah."

Jason was looking up at the trees for any signs of lights or damage or anything unusual. Andrew was looking along the ground for fallen trees and exposed roots...then...

The area near the stage had a chain link fence high and spiked, but about fifty yards down the road it became a ranch fence. Andrew and Jason climbed over it. They stood silently, waiting for sirens or searchlights or bull horns but after a silent minute or two they started walking single file along the fence toward the stage.

At the stage area the road split, half going southeast and half going northeast. Jason carried his video camera and a flashlight; Andrew carried a lantern and a shovel.

"Are you getting your bearings?" Jason whispered. "Can you spot anything that looks familiar?"

"Okay, so, I was pretty close to where I'm standing now, right in front, looking up at the stage when Pete throws it. I dive, win the scrum, grab it and run, I think, I'm pretty sure, to the left."

"Are you tripping now? Is this from a flashback?

"No, no. It's memory. It's how I thought about it all these years, and I know it's right."

"So...that way. The woods over there, right? Do you remember how far?"

"No, not a clue. I was just scrambling away. It was so long ago, man. Well, wait, if I was thinking straight, which is a big 'if,' I probably thought a lot of people were after me so, I would have gone a good ways into the wood. Yeah, I think maybe that's what I would do."

"This is great, really, you're doing great. I'm not just schmoozing you. You got us in the right area, now we just gotta find the tree."

They walk across the meadow, conscious of the quiet and the half moon peeping in and out from behind the clouds.

"You said it was early morning and the sun was behind you, right? So, maybe we go west for a while, and then focus looking east. That could help."

"Yeah."

Jason was looking up at the trees for any signs of lights or damage or anything unusual. Andrew was looking along the ground for fallen trees and exposed roots...then:

And then...climb the fence, wait for sirens or searchlights or bullhorns. And then...

They would never be aware that it was happening, but eventually, they just petered out. They were winded and their legs ached from walking.

Andrew said, "Man, I am beat. Do you remember getting close to the trees?"

Jason said, "No, but yeah, sorta, but how could that be? I thought we were walking, but we just got here."

Andrew thought for a moment. "Did you schmooze me? Did you say something about schmoozing?"

"No, I don't think so. Wait, yeah, maybe. Schmoozing, yeah."

"Just for the hell of it, let's take a look at the video camera, see if there is something on there."

Jason looked, cursed and said, "No way, not possible. No, no, no." After looking for a few minutes, he showed it to Andrew without comment and they drove back to the hotel.

In the car, Andrew said, "Didn't we walk? I thought we walked. What was that? What happened."

"I don't know. We were just, and then we were..."

"What? What happened?"

Jason just shook his head. Then he stopped for a while, and then shook it again. They were both silent the rest of the way back to the hotel, and both fell into bed without a word.

~ * ~

In the morning, late in the morning, Jason dropped Andrew off at the Pickle, and headed off to find an electronics store, or a video store, or he wasn't sure what.

When Andrew went into the Pickle, there were no customers, and Cecelia was sitting in the back at the kitchen table with scissors and yarn and something that looked like a fishing lure.

"Ah, you caught me," she said. "This is my meditation."

"Um, like knitting?"

"Like it. It's tatting lace. I wear a little bit of lace every day, since I was a kid. My mom taught me how, so it's kind of a thing with me."

"Huh." Which is what he always said when he did not know what else to say.

"I think I can tell by your not-so-smiling face that you didn't find it last night."

"Probably saying 'you didn't find it' is the world's most incomplete sentence."

"I don't know what you mean."

"Yeah, I was trying to be clever. Never a good idea for me."

"Yeah, me neither, but tell me about last night." He watched her tatting away, paying no attention to what she was doing, like last night braiding her hair.

"Hard to explain. Harder to understand. We hopped the fence and walked almost to the woods, and then found ourselves back at the fence. Apparently, we did that several times before we even realized that we were yo-yoing."

The hands stopped moving. She looked up at him. "Yo-yoing? I don't understand. You turned around and came back? Why?"

He turned a chair around backward and sat at the table. "That's the thing. We didn't turn around. We walked, and then just found ourselves back at the fence, like we had just got there."

"Like you had a memory lapse? A hallucination? Both of you at the same time? Doesn't make sense."

"It was a memory lapse of some kind, I guess. Except that the same thing happened over again. And over again. Jason looked at the video and it showed us walking along the fence, turning near the stage, and then we were back at the car. We climbed the fence again, got almost to the woods and then we're back at the car, over and over. I can't explain it."

"Huh," she said, apparently using that word with the same meaning as Andrew. "Far freakin' out."

"We didn't even know it was happening until we got tired, legs got all wobbly, and couldn't figure out why, until we looked at J's video camera. We had gone across that field several times, don't even know how many, but always ended up on the outside of the fence."

Having finished her lace design, she got up and deliberately put everything away in a small tin container. "Huh," she said again. "That is like, beyond freaky, man."

"Yeah, but weird stuff has been happening to us. Well, to you, too, right? With your visions."

"Yeah, I guess. What weird stuff is happening to you?"

"Words and phrases keep popping up, like that Mcguffin thing the other day. J and I have had a couple of those moments. *Déjà vu.*"

"I notice things with the clocks around here. They sometimes stop, and then just start up again. Crazy city, dude. And J, Jason? How is he taking all of this?"

"He is being scientific, as per the usual. He's gone looking for a techie or a video guru to explain what's on the tape. His legs are as sore as mine. I don't think the video is the problem, but he is on a quest for knowledge. The town of Poughkeepsie was mentioned."

"That's out of sight, man. Really far out. You just got, like, zapped."

"Tell me about it. I can't figure it out, but it really throws a block on us trying to find Pete's ax. If we can't get to the trees, well...what?"

"Yeah, like, what?"

"I been thinking about it all morning, and I got flat out nowhere except creeped out. So, I really need to talk about something else," he said.

"Well, you're welcome here, although I haven't had a customer all morning, and that creeps me out."

"I really like the atmosphere in here. The posters, that McCartney cardboard cutout. The smell is wonderful, and the sound of that cuckoo clock ticking reminds me of my grandmother's apartment in Utica."

"Utica. You're a long way from home."

"Yeah, I kind of came around by the long route, too."

"I'm still trying to understand how the two of you got together. You don't match at all. You seem like..."

"Peanut butter and anchovies was our last prize-winning comparison."

"Yeah," she laughed. "That one works. So, how?"

He shook his head. "You've been so nice, but I'm gonna have to keep the secret. Our first encounter was not real flattering for him, not real good for his ego. J and I have this uneasy truce, you may have noticed, and talking out of school would not help."

She met his eyes and nodded. "Good. That's, like, righteous. I think maybe your central guy imposing his will a bit. Making good choices. Oh, hey, what about breakfast? Have you eaten yet?"

He hesitated, fearful of hearing the word "farina," but she offered some whole wheat waffles and orange juice. "Sorry, no syrup," she said, "but I have some fresh strawberries, or maybe some almond butter." He turned down a third waffle and a second glass of juice.

When she opened her refrigerator, although he was really staring at her rear end, he noticed that no light came on. "You might need a new bulb in there," he said.

"No, I changed it. The bulb is okay, it's the little switch in the door that's shot. It's an old fridge."

"I'm good with stuff like that, if you have a screw driver. I'd like to give back at least a little."

"Um, central guy again, maybe?"

"Yeah, could be." Andrew just wondered if central guy might be a little horny.

~ * ~

Jason got back in the late afternoon, by which time Andrew had fixed the light in the refrigerator, tightened a loose hand rail on the stairway, glued a wobbly leg on a tea table and put caulking around the kitchen sink.

"You, sir," she said to him "are a gem. A diamond in the rough. In repayment, you are entitled to two meals a day, and also experienced nutritional guidance."

Jason, just coming in the door, said to Andrew, "You and I need to talk."

"About what happened last night," Cecelia said.

"So, you told her all about it." He glared at Andrew.

"Why would I keep it a secret? We're sitting in her store, she saw the light, she painted that picture. She's part of all this weird crap, too."

Jason sighed. "I know, but it makes things...She's just..."

She walked over to him. "I need to know. I don't mean it would be nice to know...I need it. I need to know what I saw at Woodstock, and I need to know why I couldn't get that picture out of my head. If you think I'm nuts or running some game, then don't listen to me. Just keep your distance. But I'm part of this."

The room went dead quiet except for the ticking of the cuckoo clock.

Andrew asked, "So, what did you find out?"

Still looking at Cecelia, Jason said, "Mostly what I already knew. There is no rational explanation for this!" he shouted. "No astral projection, no transporter technology, not hypnotism, not poltergeists, not alien abduction, none of that new age, third eye psychobabble that people are so enamored of today."

Cecelia just smiled at him. "Good that you're staying calm about this, J. We need your steady hand."

"Do you understand what happened to us last night?"

76

She said, "Yes, and I'm freaked by it as well. And I agree with you, Jason. Most of that new age stuff is just jargon made up to turn a quick buck. Anyone with half a brain and thick glasses can see right through it. And none of it explains what happened to you last night."

Jason sat and calmed himself for a minute and then looked over at Andrew. "The tapes were fine, just like you thought. They weren't skips or duplicates. The tapes were not overused, the recorder was fine. Apparently, you and I walked into the woods, and somehow got bounced outside the fence."

"Could you tell how many times? Not that it matters, I guess."

"Fourteen. Fourteen times. If you figure seven to eight minutes per walk across the meadow, we were yo-yos for close to two hours. Two hours caught in something that cannot, and therefore does not, exist."

"Which begs the question, what do we do now?"

"No, that doesn't beg the question. Begging the question would be 'since I already decided that we're stumped, what do we do now?' I'm not stumped. No question has been begged. This is a temporary setback."

"Temporary meaning the next step is to go to the reunion concert next Saturday, right?" Cecelia said.

"I guess," Jason said.

"Melanie," Andrew said.

"Solid, man, that's gonna be bitchin'," said Cecelia.

Eight

It was a busy day at the Pickle because there was the "Another Concert in the Garden" in a few days, the fall weather was cooperative, and the town was filling with tourists and aging hippie concert goers. Cecelia was struggling to keep her "translating" in check, and not always succeeding.

"This pattern is beautiful, so unusual."

"I know. It's really a groove."

"You tie-dyed these scarves yourself?"

"Yes, that's my bag."

"I want to keep looking, but let me pay for these now."

"Yes, the bread, lay it on me."

"Your store is so unusual."

"It's a trippy scene. You know, heavy."

She grimaced through each of these translations, but half-convinced herself that the customers thought it was all part of the ambiance. Some of them did.

Business slowed down in late afternoon, and she watched Andrew, busy with leveling a knickknack shelf in the display window. In the days since the abortive visit to Yasgur's, he had volunteered himself to be the Pickle's chief of maintenance. He seemed just a little different doing this; more comfortable, more in charge, but she was still a little nervous about him. She liked his company, being naturally social and having lived alone for several years, and it was not all verbal fencing like with Jason. But she sensed a disconnect somewhere in Andrew that kept her at a distance.

"Take a break," she told him. "I'm not paying you that much, or anything, actually. Do you want a drink or something?"

"Thanks, but not if we're talking iced tea. Oh, yeah, I picked up a new lock for your front door this morning. The one on there is older than me."

"No. No new lock. Sorry, it's just another thing with me. No new lock, please."

"Okay, okay. I'll return it. Are you offering iced tea, 'cause..."

"No, I was thinking beer. I picked up a six pack this morning. In your honor."

"A beer would probably save my life right about now."

"Where did you learn to do all this stuff?" she asked when she brought two long necks back to the oak table and they clinked them.

"On the job training. I was a roadie for twenty something years. You learn to do what has to get done."

"A roadie? Wow. That's wild, man."

"It was a great life. Travel, meet people, hear the best music. But musicians, man, they are the laziest. I fixed air conditioners, speakers, mic stands, guitars, drum kits, you name it. But mostly I carried stuff."

"Work for anyone I would recognize?"

"Yeah, probably a couple. I was with Skynyrd for a little while. That was before they got real big."

"I was never stoked on Southern Rock, or really hard rock stuff either. I was acoustic, folkie, Joan Baez, Buffy, Joni Mitchell, like that."

"I did a few weeks with Tim Hardin, if you remember him."

"Yeah, God yeah. He did 'Lady Came from Baltimore,' my husband's favorite song."

"You're married?"

Her face went blank. She hesitated, got up, sat down again and said, "Yes, I am. You're staying for dinner, right?" She stood up again and walked away.

"You're being too nice. You don't have to cook for me, us."

"That works both ways. You're doing a lot for me around here. And I don't want you to bail on this guitar, bright light, cosmic visitor thing. It's caused me a lot of trouble, and I want to know what it is."

He tipped back his beer and said, "I came up with a couple of plans, stupid ones, to get us into the woods, but J shot them all down. He's a schmuck, but I'm lucky to be with him. He really is a bright guy, but don't tell him I said that."

"Any idea what fortress of solitude he's been hanging out in? I haven't seen him in a couple of days. I'm really hoping he doesn't give it up. That yo-yo thing, that is truly freaky."

"I've barely seen him either, and I live with him, and I really do not like the sound of that sentence."

"He drops you off here, right? Don't you talk in the car?"

"No, he hasn't been driving me. He's gone when I get up."

"You walk all the way here? That's a trek," she said.

"Yeah, I figure it's a mile, maybe two. Good for me. For the central me," he smiled.

"I'm glad you're open to that. Surprised, too. Sometimes I say what I'm thinking and people, well..."

Jason came in then, slowly, quietly, almost sheepishly. He was carrying an oblong box under his arm. "I have a plan," he said.

Andrew grinned at him. "Just having a beer, a real beer, here. Sit down and tell us."

Mornings, for much of his life, Jason would brood. In his room at home, at a desk before class, at a large table in a library before he dug into the books, he would brood. Singly or in small groups, all the people and situations of his recent life would parade by and he would silently condemn them, debate them into submission, and move on.

Here in Liberty, it was no different. He would ignore Andrew snoring in bedclothes and drive to the spot where they had first climbed over that fence, and then climbed over it so many times after that. He would turn the engine off and just look.

Early this morning, he sat watching a dark cloud drift slowly over the stand of trees that consumed his thoughts. *Something I don't understand is screwing with me,* he thought. *With all of us. What happened in that pasture does not happen, cannot happen. So, there is another explanation. Of course, cosmic needles that observe and perhaps alter historical reality also don't happen. Unless, of course, they do without our knowledge.*

"Aha," he said out loud. That word was a close relative to the 'huh' used by Andrew and Cecelia. It was the word he used when he did not know what else to say.

"But," he said to his steering wheel, "there is a thread to pull on, at least. That phrase 'they happen without your knowledge.' And of course, that's is what my whole thesis is based on, and why so many stand in opposition to it. Okay, okay so we need knowledge, data, corroboration. Even Rat Bastard realized that. Wait, maybe I should be writing this down. Or, better yet, recording it."

He got the much-cursed video camera from the trunk and spent a few minutes working to prop it up against the dashboard in the front seat. At the lowest setting, it focused so closely on him that he could just about make out his pores. Adjustments only made it worse. "I need to set it so it looks like it's far away," and then he realized what he had said. He tried it once pointed across the field at the stage and saw that it did not have sufficient magnification. He lay it down on the front seat and drove to Modern Times Electronics Boutique in Poughkeepsie with hope in his heart.

~ * ~

"Beer's in the fridge, Jason, and you can see it because the light works," Cecelia said. "Help yourself."

Jason sat, took a gulp of his beer, and it was good. "The key element here," he said, pulling open the box on his lap, "is distance. You agree, Andy, that we seemed to be okay until we got close to those trees."

Cecelia thought, but didn't say, *Andy?*

"Yeah, but then I don't remember even a moment we didn't seem okay."

"Granted, but don't rain on my parade. This could work. At the very least, we may be able to see those trees from a distance, and maybe see something we didn't see before. Maybe learn how close we're able to get. Maybe even another way in. That's something." He pulled out a lens that would fit on the video camera. "This is the longest one they had, good for a hundred meters. I'm hoping that's enough."

"Wow," Cecelia said. "That is a good idea. I was afraid you were just walking in circles, but you came up with a winner."

"Glad you agree, because you are part of the plan. Andrew and I need to walk across again, and we need a cameraman, cameraperson, outside the fence. That would be you. I know you want to stay close to home and hearth, but..."

"Well, okay, but not all night. And it may be a short night, anyway. The forecast is for rain."

"Huh," Andrew said. "I wonder if that was another of those '*déjà vu*' things we keep having. You said, 'don't rain on my parade' before."

"Odd," Jason said.

"Freaky," Cecelia translated.

~ * ~

And, sure enough, as soon as they got out of the car and set up the camera and tripod, a light rain began.

"There's a tarp in the trunk," Jason said. "I think we should try to do as much as we can."

They draped the tarp over the camera, and Jason and Andrew climbed the fence. As before, they stood for a couple minutes waiting for trouble and then moved cautiously toward the stage.

Cecelia trained the camera on their backs, but swung it left to see if she could see anything in the woods. "Uh-oh," she said.

"What, uh-oh," Jason snapped. "The lens is set, just point it and press the red button."

"A different kind of uh-oh. Come here and look."

He climbed back and looked through the viewer. "Damn, double damn, double goddamn."

"What, what?" Andrew said.

"They put up a barrier just in front of the trees. And it seems to go north for a few hundred yards. I'm not sure we can get close enough to even get yo-yo'd."

"That must be for the concert next weekend," Cecelia said, "and I think, not sure, but I think that barrier may go all the way to the pond."

"Can we climb it?" Andrew asked.

Jason looked carefully through the viewfinder again. "Dogs. They picked tonight to get serious about security and bring dogs. They must have brought in equipment they don't want stolen." It began to rain harder. Andrew threw his head back and opened his mouth. Jason walked around the car twice and then put the camera back in the trunk. "Maybe there's something we can discover at that reunion festival," he said, and slammed the trunk.

Andrew said, "Snake bit. We're snake bit."

"No. I'm not getting down about this, Andy. Not getting down. This whole thing was a long shot from the start. The plan is solid, we just need patience. That concert is only for one day, and then the fence and the dogs will be gone. I think."

Driving back, Cecelia said, "I think we need a reset here." Jason and Andrew looked at each other at the word, "reset." I need both of you to stay around a while and fill me in. I'm feeling still outside the loop, mostly about you," she pointed at Jason. "I have a vegan stew in the refrigerator that you," she pointed to Jason again, "will like, and you," she pointed to Andrew, "will have to deal with. And we can rap over dinner."

Jason said, "Oh, a dialogue."

"Don't play, man," she said. "If I'm supposed to be a part of this, then you need to let me in. I need the whole story, from the start.

The three of us are like in a movie script where I haven't read the first fifty pages. Andrew I know was at Woodstock, and saw what I saw, which explains a lot about him, but not all. I don't think he's as freaked about that scene as I am, he just wants that guitar. I don't get how he lost it. I don't get why that guitar is so important to him. I don't get why he waited thirty years to come and look for it."

"Oh please," Jason said. "Do we really need a whole encounter group? Can't we just focus on..."

Andrew put his hands up and interrupted. "I don't know how I lost it and I've been kicking myself in the ass about that ever since. As far as why I want it, I'm not sure I can explain. It's a family thing that took all this time to catch up with me. I don't know if you even have families, so I'm not sure if you would understand."

Cecelia said, "Okay, that's a little helpful, I guess. But where does Jason come in? This is obviously an investment of time and energy for you, but why? You two just met in a bar and started talking about old guitars that light up in trees? Who are you, Jason? I know you think I'm flaky, but I want in, or I won't stay halfway in. I'll give you some stew for the ride home, and we'll shake hands and part friends."

"Fair enough," Andrew said. Jason said nothing.

Over leftover stew and beer, Cecelia looked at Jason and said, "Okay, brother, let's rap."

Andrew grinned and said, "My story here may be the simplest, so I'll start."

He told of his scrambling for Pete Townshend's guitar, thinking it might impress Cecelia.

"I get that part," she said. "But then you lost it? Or traded it for a tab of acid? Or sold it? And then you saw it up in the tree. That's the middle part I don't get."

"That's the part I don't get either, and I guess it's why I'm here. I was high. It was about five in the morning. I buried it, thinking to come back later for it. But when I went back, it was gone. I scrambled around in the woods looking for it, almost cried, but it was gone. And for me, the concert was over."

After the festival he had met up with two of his friends and walked back down 17B to his car, which had been broken into. When he got home to Utica, the reception was not a warm one. "Not gonna tell you about that. Don't ask."

He hung out in a local bar and volunteered his back as a roadie and gained a local, and then a wider, reputation as someone who could do what he was told. He could also tune a guitar, set up a drum kit, and score drugs.

"Life just rolled on from there," he said. He never went back to college, didn't think much about the future, didn't even think much about the guitar. Occasionally he thought about the day they left Woodstock, the frustration and anger of having lost the guitar. But not often. He curled up in buses, drank too much coffee and ate too much snack food, and fully expected to die young.

"About a year and a half ago, an amp fell off a truck and with perfect accuracy, landed on my foot. Three small bones broken, cast, cane, six months of physical therapy, and I'm out of the roadie business. So, like a girlfriend told me once, "Over time I went from Andy to Andrew to Druid when I was skulking around backstage, to my current cover version, Drusome.""

"Your other selves," Cecelia said, softly. Jason rolled his eyes but kept quiet.

"And if I may just add a brief word about our consumer society and its advertising arm," Andrew said, "lightweight amplifier, my ass."

They sat quietly for a minute, realizing that any comment would be a wrong one. Eventually, Jason said, "That's about where I enter the saga, so I guess it's my turn."

"I made a low sugar, whole wheat, carrot cake that might go well with some decaf for dessert." Cecelia stood up, grabbed hold of the chair, wobbled for a moment and said, "Whoa. That one is new."

Andrew stood. "Here, you sit. I'll get the cake and coffee. I think you work too hard."

She sat and stared across the table as he stumbled around the kitchen area looking for things. She called out to him, "Coffee is already made on the back burner, cups and plates in the cabinet, right hand over the sink, forks in the drawer. Whoa…there it is again."

Andrew came back to the table quickly. He said, "What is it? Are you sick?"

"No. That thing I told you was coming is almost here, that's all. Still don't know what, or when, but it's close."

Jason said, "Might not be a bad idea to bring you somewhere, get you checked out."

She took a deep breath and let it out slowly. "Thoughtful, Jason, but really, no. You don't believe me and I don't blame you, but I know what the situation is, and I will be fine. I'm in for a surprise, I think, but I'm fine."

Andrew came back with the cake and coffee.

"Thank you, Andy," she said. "Your mother would be proud."

Andy? thought Jason. *And what the hell did that mean about his mother?*

"I really want to hear about you, but I think I'd better talk next, Jason, if you don't mind. I'll try and keep it short and to the point."

He nodded, relieved. He really did not want to share anything.

"Okay," she started, "I'm from Baltimore. Cecelia is actually my middle name. My father was a bail bondsman who kept us safe and relatively secure, if never rich. He was wonderful, and growing up was wonderful, even after my mom passed away. I came to Woodstock with a boyfriend and two girlfriends, and ended up going home alone." She told quickly of stepping on glass and going to the medical tent and later seeing something high up in the tree.

"It freaked me when I first saw it, but even more so now. There were days when I could not get past it. Could not think of anything else."

She told of hearing Joan Baez singing "I Live One Day at A Time" and, even though stoned when she heard it, thought that was a good idea.

She skipped the part where her girlfriend spent the night in a sleeping bag with her boyfriend.

"I sat in a field of trash and listened to Hendrix play the 'Star Spangled Banner' and never gave a thought to how I was gonna get home. I met someone shortly after," she said, "and we moved here and opened this store. Long story short, deliriously happy for years until he died. Relatively happy since. The fool in the tree, the need to paint, really got into my head when he got sick. And, you know, after."

Andrew hesitated, but interrupted. "You told me today that you were married."

She grew thoughtful, cut more cake, poured more coffee and said, "You asked me if I was married and I said yes. That was not quite accurate. I should have said 'yes and no.'"

"*Sic et non*," said Jason, showing off.

Andrew said, a little too loud, "Huh?"

"*Sic et non* is a medieval book of philosophy. The title means 'yes and no'."

"Was he one of your dead historians?" Andrew said to Jason.

"No, he came later."

Cecelia said, "Please. I need to get through this, let me explain. When I married, I promised myself and my husband that it would be forever. To me, forever means exactly that. For. Ever. Not 'til death do you part, not divorce, not until someone better comes by. Forever. So, when he died, a good, long, wonderful time into our marriage, I thought of myself, and still think of myself, as married to him. And that won't ever change. The church, the State of New York, my friends and family and all the local yahoos looking to get laid don't see me as married, but I am. So, yes and no. He's gone and I am still married to him."

Silence descended, eyes lowered...the ticking of the cuckoo clock captured everyone's fascination.

Andrew said, careful to get the words right, "I think telling us that is about the most you could tell us about yourself. It says..."

The silence was broken, shattered, by a key being turned in the lock at the front door. At the same moment, the pendulum from a small clock fell off, and the ticking stopped.

A woman stepped in, holding the hand of a little boy, and stopped just inside the door. Both were soaking wet, and tears were streaming down her face. She took a few steps in and said, "The old key still opens the door, Mom."

Cecelia said, "Oh!" and got up and walked slowly over to her. She stopped for a long moment and stared at the two of them, her arms out wide. They hugged and cried and said no more words. The little boy stood awkwardly beside his mother, just looking up at them.

"Oh!" Cecelia said again. And again, "Oh!"

She held her daughter and rocked back and forth and was wordless. Finally, she stepped back and held her face in her hands, tears streaming down both of their faces. "Jennifer."

Jennifer managed to sob out, "Yes, Mom, it's me. It's us."

Cecelia looked over at the little boy and sobbed. She knelt down in front of him and said, "Do you know who I am?"

Benjamin said, "Yes, you're the lady who came from Baltimore. My mom used to sing to me about you."

"Oh, yes, I am. I am. And what is your name?"

"I'm Ben. Benjamin."

Cecelia looked from Ben to Jennifer back to Ben and then back to Jennifer."

Jennifer, her hands over her face, could only sob.

Ben took a few tentative steps toward Cecelia and held his arms up. She picked him up and held him tight. "Grandma," he said.

"Ben," she said. "Oh, Ben."

Jason and Andrew had the good grace to circle around and leave quietly.

Interlude

The evening that Jason and Andrew climbed over the fence the first time and entered the festival grounds, all of these things were happening:

The guitar player that Andrew tried to help, weeks before on the hillside, was sitting alone at a table in the lounge at her college, still working on "Let It Be." She had changed the key from C to G, which made the chords a little more familiar, but she was still missing the minor, and it sounded, even to her inexperienced ear, not quite right. G to the D directly to the F chord, just not right. She pulled out her book, *Beatles Made Easy,* and saw that after the G, the guitar lowered to an E minor and then back to the G.

"What the heck is an E minor?" she wondered. She looked it up in the chord list on the back page, fingered it carefully and tried it out.

Yes. Just right. Fits right in. The minor fall, the major fifth.

At the moment Andrew's foot touched the ground inside the fence, the girl thought, *That fat guy on the hill wasn't such a jerk, I guess.*

89

~ * ~

The senior clerk in the NYU History Department was at home with her feet up thinking about her retirement. She was ready financially, she was ready emotionally, and feeling that familiar twinge down her sciatic nerve, she knew she was ready physically. She thought how people had changed, gotten colder and more demanding since she started this job almost thirty years before. And then she remembered a surprising moment when a student had asked her if she wanted a cup of coffee.

"I bought it," he said, "but I really don't want it. I'm too nervous about my meeting with Dr. Braithwaite. You're welcome to it."

"Oh, how kind of you, but no," she said. "I often have a cup of tea in the afternoon as a pick me up, but coffee gives me heartburn." He nodded and left.

At the moment that Jason's foot touched the ground at Yasgur's, she realized, yes, that was the student who was arrested on her front lawn.

~ * ~

R. Hotchkiss, whose first name was really Reagan, a fact he chose to conceal, was filing reports and paused at that of Jason Nelson. He read from his own notes: "A cosmic event, cosmic in the sense of originating somewhere in the universe outside of our knowledge or experience. Mister Nelson believes that these events, at least two of which he has found very limited evidence of, have impacted history at crucial junctures."

That guy could be a chapter, he thought, *if not a whole book on abnormal psychology. Hope he doesn't do any damage out there.*

He felt a small ache between his first and second molars at the same moment that Jason and Andrew found themselves back at the car for the first time.

~ * ~

Gary, who may have had a last name but had little use for it, stood obediently in front of the big desk and said to his boss, "She didn't say where, except that it would probably not be Baltimore."

"Knowing her, that means it probably will be Baltimore. A miserable city, but she just kept singing that annoying little song."

"May I ask, sir, only out of curiosity, what song that is?"

"Something about a woman from Baltimore. I don't really know anything else about it."

Gary, who played stand-up bass for the folk group, Maryland CrabCakes, decided to look it up just at the exact moment that Jason and Andrew found themselves back at the car for the second time.

Part II

King of the Franks, King of the Lombards, conqueror of Saxony, warrior by necessity and statesman by nature.

He and his retinue entered St. Peter's Basilica, with full pomp and ceremony, to attend Christmas Mass celebrated by a grateful pope. But he was uncertain of his role here, an unusual position for someone of his accomplishments. International diplomacy, even before there were true nations, was as fraught with snares and intrigue as it is today.

Charles the Great, Charlemagne, Carolus Magnus, was son and grandson of the two men who had consolidated power and policy over a state encompassing modern day France, Germany, and half of Italy. A fierce and sometimes brutal warrior and defender of the papacy, he had delivered Pope Leo III from a violent confrontation and restored his authority as leader of the western Christian church.

On this Christmas morning in 800 A.D., during the celebration of the Mass, Charles had taken his place on the altar, knelt, and prayed. The pope carried a crown to elevate Charles to the role of Holy Roman Emperor, further stabilizing the relationship between church and state, and granting lasting security for the successors of St. Peter.

In the darkened church, flickering candles splashed dim shadows on the benches and statues of the altar and faded to darkness in the high vaulted ceilings. A soft light appeared above the crown that Pope Leo was solemnly carrying toward Charles. The light pulsed, deepened from silver to gold and back to silver, and descended slowly to the crown, now held just over the head of Charles. Gasps of fear could be heard, but neither the emperor nor the pope paid attention to them.

Once on the head of the new emperor, the light pulsed again from silver to gold and back to silver, and then faded to nothingness.

The onlookers, ministers of Charles and bishops of Leo, had drawn back in fear, and now fell to their knees, believing they had witnessed a manifestation of the divine.

A torch at the entrance to the basilica blew out in the windless cathedral and smoked for a moment. Then the flame re-ignited and flared up. No one noticed.

Nine

The girl with the lace wristlets and waist length, golden brown hair left the medical tent with a fresh gauze bandage wrapped around the arch of her foot and some newspaper shoved in her shoe to staunch the blood. She heard music coming from behind her, at the "Free Stage," another misnomer, because almost anything you could get that weekend was free. She had smoked several joints and been handed pipes and capsules, but just handed them on to someone else. She had never been this high and was totally disoriented. She knew there was a problem with her foot, but it didn't seem important, so she followed the music to a clearing in the woods where someone had built a small crude stage. A young and pregnant woman was alone on the stage singing, and Susan was mesmerized. The voice seemed so pure and clear, like this woman was not from earth. *Alto?* she thought, *or soprano?* As if that made a difference. But the lyrics aimed right at her, too. The song spoke of dreams, but not the meaning. Through her haze, Susan understood that, at eighteen, her life was not ahead of her, nor behind her. It was now, here, today, and living any other way was wasteful and stupid.

And, she thought to herself, *this alone makes the trip worth it.* She limped up onto the stage and shook the woman's hand but couldn't find the words to say anything. The woman, Joan Baez, smiled warmly at her and moved down the stage to greet someone else.

She found herself walking to where she thought her tent was. After about twenty minutes of going in circles and poking her head into the wrong tents, she sat with her back against a tree and cried. A stream of people were walking in single and double file, mostly naked and wet. Some of the women carried towels, and Susan remembered vaguely that there was a pond down that road.

She dried her tears and fell asleep. When she woke, it was full dark and her foot was throbbing. She tried twice to stand, worried about finding her friends, but finally sank back down against the tree and went back to sleep.

Next morning, she was stiff, and logy, and thirsty. She tried to stand and got a sharp, shooting pain in her foot. The rain was a fine mist.

"Damn," she said. She sat again, took off her sneaker and pulled the wadded and blood-soaked newspaper out of it. The part stuck up in the toe was still legible. It was the *New York Times* from a few weeks ago, and the headline read, "Astronauts Coasting Homeward Accelerated by Earth's Gravity." She refolded it so the bloody parts were on the inside, and stuffed it back in. That was a little better. She could walk, not well, but at least she could walk.

Leaning against the tree and humming, she was able to get her bearings better than last night. The main stage, huge and dark beyond the tent city, was her best landmark. She figured her tent was a few degrees to the left of center stage, and maybe fifty yards away. She remembered a rusted out VW bus parked nearby. She was hungry but even more thirsty. A girl in cutoffs and a bikini top came up to her and asked if she had anything to smoke.

Susan fished around in her pockets, came out with a joint and said, "Trade you for some water."

"Cool," the girl said. "We got a big jug." Susan followed her to a tent where six or seven others were stretched out asleep, next to and on top of each other. The girl, who had a rainbow painted on her cheek, tiptoed around them and found the jug and a plastic cup. She poured a little water in, swirled it around to rinse it, and filled it again for Susan. Susan drank thirstily and asked for more. The girl filled it again and said, "You look really strung out."

"Yeah, been toking some pretty wicked stuff," Susan said. "But what a trip this is. I mean all of it, you know? The music is just what got me here. The rest of it is, man, I don't even know, like so, so far out." She drank the rest of the water and gave the cup back to the girl who raised her arms for a hug. They hugged and the girl lit the joint. She offered, but Susan just shook her head and left.

Limping again, looking for her tent, she just realized how muddy and wet everything was. Like last night, she poked her head into a couple of wrong tents, and slipped and fell one time, but her foot didn't hurt her too badly. After about ten minutes, she saw the VW van with the rusted top and her friend's green tent a few feet behind it.

She poked her head in cautiously and saw three sleeping bags, two full and one empty. In the corner she recognized the duffel bag she had picked up at the Army/Navy store just before the trip. Her mom had said, "Are you really taking that, honey? I have an almost new suitcase you can use. That white one you always liked." No, that was the pot talking. She realized through her haze that her mom hadn't actually said that, but that's what she wished her mom was still around to say.

Brenda's curly, dark head was partly out of her sleeping bag, and was using the still packed duffel bag for a pillow. Susan wiggled her way between the two occupied sleeping bags, and on top of the empty one, which she was pretty sure was hers.

She slept, or dozed for a little while, but was awakened by movement on her left side. Brenda, on her right side, said, "Jesus, the whole night long. Will you two give it a rest?"

"Brenda?" Susan said. "I need my duffel bag. Man, I had a crazy night."

"Yeah, we all did. You look all wrung out."

"I'm soaked, and I wanna get changed. And I cut my foot, but man, this is so far out. Joanie Baez did a song at that little stage. I was so stoked, and I shook her hand. She is exquisite, man."

She rooted through her duffel bag, found a water bottle, and drank about half of it. "I had a spot cleared out for me and David to listen to Arlo, but he never came back. I don't know what happened to him. That was after I stepped on the glass. I think it was after. Everybody is handing around doobies, you know? I slept against a tree on the way back here. This whole trip is just so groovy. So totally cosmic."

She heard David, her boyfriend of three months, mumbling something behind her. He was saying in a strangled voice. "It was all, like, two-dimensional, man, everything. Trees, cars, people just, like, tall and wide, but not deep. And colors. You've never seen such colors. I feel a little sorry for you, 'cause you won't ever see those colors."

Amanda, naked to the waist, opened up the sleeping bag. "David, I told you, man, I'm not dropping any of that stuff. I wanna have kids someday, and that shit will mess you up."

Susan turned to see her friend, half naked Amanda, and a fully naked boyfriend, David, in the sleeping bag behind her.

"Susan," David said. Amanda slipped back down into the sleeping bag and covered her head. "What happened to you?"

"Me? What happened to me? You came back here to get sandwiches for us. We were gonna catch Arlo. You stayed here all night?"

"Took me a little while to find the tent, and this guy gave me this stuff, some really good shit, you know. And I know you don't indulge."

"So, you were ballin' her all night?"

From the other side of the tent, Brenda said, "All goddamn night. She's a screamer, and turns out he's a screamer, too."

David's eyes were wide, and his face, in the dim light of the tent, had an unnatural color. "I went looking for you, babe, I did. But everything was just so funky. Just so incredible. Everything was flat, but the colors were like from another planet or something. It was such a groove, man, I got lost in it, dig?"

"So, things were flat and colorful so you came back here and balled Amanda all night?"

"I figured you were all right. This place is so mellow. People giving you stuff. And those colors, you gotta believe me."

"Son of a bitch!" Susan swung her bag at him. "You miserable bastard."

Amanda's muffled voice said, "I don't...I wasn't...it wasn't on purpose...we just sort of..."

"He's a son of a bitch, cheating bastard, and you're just a bitch. Both of you go to hell." She grabbed her duffel, then flipped open the cooler and threw the top at him. She grabbed a bag inside and yelled, "And you ate half the sandwiches, goddamn you!" She left the tent, stopped a few yards away, went back and grabbed the camp stool. She spit at the tent on her way out. Twenty feet away, she heard David call her name, and then scream it, over and over and over.

"Susan! Susan! Don't do this! We can work this out!"

She walked back to him and slapped him across the arm.

"Don't you use my name! Don't even speak my name out of your mouth, you son of a bitch. We were supposed to have peace here. Two days of peace and music, that's what you said. And you trashed it! Don't even speak my name." She turned away, sobbing.

Her foot was throbbing, and probably bleeding again, and she hadn't quite realized that she was alone now. There were vaguely musical sounds coming from the stage, and some mumbling over the PA system. She had decided she was there for the music, so as long as her foot wasn't gushing blood, she was going to get near the stage and listen.

John Sebastian, who she liked but didn't love, and then Canned Heat were supposed to be up. During the Sebastian solo act, a girl came over to her and asked if she had anything.

"Turkey sandwich and some water," Susan said.

The other girl, tall, pretty, with a long face and wearing a poncho, laughed. "No, I meant something to smoke."

"No, not anymore," Susan said. "I pretty much blew my stash yesterday, and now I'm just here for the music."

"What happened to your foot?"

"Like a dope I took off my sneakers. Some cat was nice enough to break a bottle, and I was lucky enough to step on it. It doesn't bleed much when I rest it."

"Cool," the girl said, and sat cross-legged beside her, leaning against her legs. "Where you from?"

"Up from Baltimore. You?"

"Down from Syracuse, me and my old man. He sent me on a mission for some weed."

"I'm kind of on my own now. Found my old man in the sack with my best friend. Not going back there."

"I can dig where you're coming from. That's an ugly scene. Sorry I can't ask you to crash with us. My old man worries about me being with another chick. It only happened one time, when I was really wasted, but he won't let it go." They talked for a few minutes and then the tall girl kissed her on the cheek and said, "Have a great time. The Who is playing sometime tonight. Their drummer is insane, and that guy Roger Daltrey is just, he's just…I mean just his hair, you know?" She blew her a kiss and walked away.

Susan looked around, trying to make up her mind. The medical tent was about a fifteen-minute limp to the northwest; the food stand about as long to the southeast; the Porta Potties about twenty minutes up a hill straight behind her. Amanda said she had used one of the Porta Potties yesterday and even on Friday there was a long line and it was seriously funky. *Good. Hope she catches something*, thought Susan. But she was hoping to avoid a similar sensory experience. She wondered if maybe there was an out-house near the medical tent and decided to give that a try. A nurse and a bathroom within limping distance would be perfect. Before she made it to the path that went into the woods, her foot was bleeding again. The ground had gotten wetter, and especially carrying her duffel and the camp chair, it was turning into a heavy slog. She sat for a few minutes on her camp stool, and after a few minutes a guy came up near her, shirtless and soaking wet, eyes wide and wild, and started dancing in circles. "We're not on earth anymore," he said. "This is nirvana, or paradise, or the Garden of Eden, man. I think I'd like to stay here, please." He handed her a half empty can of something, and danced away. Her tall friend in the poncho had told her about people handing out soft drinks laced with LSD, so she poured it out. "I am here for the fucking music," she said out loud.

She kept walking and made it to the medical tent. She waited patiently, in some pain, listening to Canned Heat behind her. *This must be some bitchin' sound system*, she thought.

The woman taking care of patients—who knew if she was a nurse—was middle aged and had some grey splotches in her Audrey Hepburn pixie cut. She was gentle and thorough and helped Susan get her sneaker back on without too much discomfort.

"This isn't too bad," she said, "but if this is your second visit, you're going to have to find a way to stop walking through mud or it will definitely get infected. Maybe just hang out in your tent for a while? Or maybe there's some space down by the pond where you can stop?"

"Yeah, I'll try to prop it up for a while down by the pond. Do you know if there is an outhouse, or any kind of facilities within limping distance?"

The woman smiled. "Best I can offer you is the 'thoid' tree. Do you know about the 'thoid' tree?"

Susan looked at her with a half smile. "No."

"It's a Brooklyn thing, I think. The thoid tree is the toidy."

It took a minute for Susan to react. "Oh, I get it. A toidy."

The woman smiled wearily. "I'm sorry, honey, bad joke. It has been a long bitch of a day. I'm just saying you'll have to find somewhere in the woods. It's your best bet."

Susan nodded and said, "Thank you, honestly, thank you very much. And thank you for all you are doing here."

"Welcome, please be careful," she said, and then she was looking at her next patient.

~ * ~

The path to the pond wasn't a long walk but was as muddy as everything else, and not as crowded as the rest of the scene. She skirted around until she found a relatively dry patch under a tree not far from the water line and sat. She ate the last of her sandwich and drank most of her water. She tucked the camp stool into the duffel bag and lay down with her sore foot raised a few inches on a fallen branch. It wasn't bleeding much now. She wrapped the duffel shoulder strap around her arm and positioned it so it would be a pillow. She wanted to listen to the distant music, but she was fast asleep within minutes. She woke when a couple were thrashing around in the water near her, but they giggled and moved off, and she stayed awake but unmoving and just listening to the far-off music.

I'm crippled, she thought, *cheated on, alone, filthy, wet and hungry and I'm having just a great time. This is the best ever. It's insane. I hope they do this every year.*

She could hear the thumping bassline and some of the lyrics from Creedence's "Suzie Q" coming from the main stage, and she remembered that after Creedence, Janis was supposed to go on. She wanted to see Janis, but she didn't trust her foot to get her near the front stage. With some struggle, she got her sneaker back on, and the rest and elevation had done it some good. She walked a few steps without too much pain and decided to walk as far as the woods just past the medical tent and find a place to sit and listen. There was a guy on the free stage in a slicker and cowboy hat making a wreck of "If I Was a Carpenter," and the silence from the main stage told her that she would need to wait a while for Janis. It rained a little harder now, and rain sluiced off the cowboy's hat and onto the poor guy's guitar. He paid no attention. She sat with her back against a tree at the edge of the woods where she could see the stage. It would be far away, but it would still be Janis.

She watched the rain and the drip from the trees and listened to the murmur of a million voices all around her. She was offered drinks, which she turned down, and tokes, a few of which she took, and was feeling mellow when she came to realize there was music playing. There was a crowd around her now, but she could see the stage and pick out the woman hanging on the microphone stand at the head of the stage. And she owned the audience. Every one of them were riveted to her every gyration, every change in inflection. *Owned*, thought Susan.

Bought, packaged, and put on a shelf for later use. Susan cried a little at "Piece of My Heart," thinking of David and thought, *that won't happen to me again.* She couldn't even think about Amanda yet.

She stayed there for Sly and the Family Stone, screaming like everyone else when he called out "I wanna take you higher!" And she stood, with pain, when he sang "Stand."

There would be a long wait for the next band, The Who, she knew, so she dug into the duffel bag and found some squashed up crackers and drank her last bit of water. She took the time to scrape the mud off her sneakers, inside and out, and wipe off the bandage as best she could. She put her foot up on the camp stool and waited.

The Who was the group that the term "power band" had been invented for. The girls around Susan in the woods were saying "Roger Daltrey" like it as a mantra, and the boys were saying, "Oh, man, it's the fucking Who!!"

At the end of their performance, the guitar player, Pete Townshend, went all out with his solo, and then bashed his guitar on the stage a few times before tossing it into the crowd. A few of the stoned-out freaks that were still self-aware dove into the mud for it, and for a few minutes she could only see writhing and thrashing around. A small section of the scuffle broke off and it looked like one guy followed by a small stumbling mob, headed toward the pond. She put up a peace sign and said, "Peace and love, fellas."

It was still full dark, but at least not raining. Moonlight peeked out and then faded. Clouds were blowing westward under occasional starlight. She walked back toward the pond, being very careful, searching for a new thoid tree.

When she finished, feeling filthy, she walked back toward the main stage just to have a direction to go in. It was so dark, with just an occasional glimmer of moonlight, until she saw the beginning of sunrise, a thin line of light in front of her. She could see a corner of the stage with people moving around on it, setting up for the next band and kept walking toward it. She tripped on a root, and just sat quietly for a few minutes letting people walk around her. A squeal of laughter from the pond behind her startled her to her feet and she turned to look up through the trees at a bright, bright, light that was blinking slowly, silver, deepening to gold, back to silver and then fading. She squinted in the weak, pre-dawn light and moved around the tree for a better look. Halfway around, she could see the bright outline of a person, she thought a man just because he was large, with one hand extended and holding something high above him. And then it was gone, the vision ended like a movie that just goes instantly to black. *Wow*, she thought. *Am I trippin'?*

She sat again for a few minutes, wondering about what she had seen and waiting for the sun to make her trek a little easier, and then she followed the line of trees away from the main stage and toward what she hoped were the food tents.

The next band, Jefferson Airplane, would not begin for a while, and Susan hated them anyway. As she went, the crowds got progressively thinner and she wondered if people were going home already. Then she realized it was just past dawn, probably around six in the morning, and it hit her how tired she was.

She moved into the woods a few yards, found a clear spot against a tree and collapsed against it. She used the duffel bag for a pillow and propped her foot up on the camp stool. She wanted to stay awake for a while and just think about where she was, but it was so dark and so quiet, she was asleep within a few minutes.

When she awoke—she thought about four hours later—the sun was above her and streaming through the trees. Out in the field she could see people, of course lots of people, moving around, playing guitars, dancing, throwing frisbees. She stood and took a few tentative, painful steps and realized the camp stool was gone. Gone. While she slept, someone had gently lifted her foot, pulled it away and lowered her foot again. She scrambled to her knees and checked through the duffel bag. That all seemed to be all right, but her foot was throbbing again. It hadn't bled very much; the nurse at the medical tent had done a careful job of packing it and wrapping it. She thought it might feel better if she could just keep it raised for a while, so she propped it up on a branch. The duffel bag served again as a pillow, and she just sat quietly, thinking. David and Amanda, the glass in her foot, shaking hands with Joan Baez, Arlo, Sly, The Who, Janis, that lit-up guy in the trees. Jesus, what the hell was that anyway? She had seen helicopters going overhead, but this thing was dead quiet. And the guy in that tree was lit up like he was electric. What the hell was that?

She sat, just marveling, being astounded by where she was and what she had done; with all the people around her, a hundred thousand maybe, at the mud, at the music, at the rain, the drugs, at all of it. She shifted around so the mist was not blowing directly on her. She was dirtier than she had been yesterday, angrier at David, hungrier, thirstier and wetter than yesterday, and at any time in her life, but she knew she was having the time of her life. She sat back and listened to the faraway music. She thought it might be Country Joe doing that "One, Two, Three" thing, but wasn't sure.

The rain slackened, and she ventured out of the woods. She saw a puddle on the fold of a tent and drained the water into her bottle. *I don't see how anybody can spike a tent*, she thought.

She moved up closer to the main stage. Still a huge crowd, but thinned out a little bit. She found an opening near a couple that were making out on a tarp. "Can I squat next to you guys for a while? I'm alone, and I won't hassle you, I swear."

"Yeah, welcome," the girl said, and stretched out the tarp to make room for Susan. She had one of those diamond-shaped faces, wide at the cheekbones and narrow at the chin, and dark, dark eyes with smeared makeup. The guy was tall and skinny and had a three-day growth of course beard.

"I just got some water I can share, if you want," Susan said.

"We're kind of leery about drinking stuff," he said. "Some guy gave me half an orange soda on Friday, and I was trippin' until Saturday afternoon."

"Yeah, I heard about that, but I know this is good. It's rainwater I poured off the top of a tent a little while ago."

"Oh, great idea. Yeah, I'd love a swig of that," the girl said.

"Oh, cool. Give me that bottle, Shug, I'll go look for a wet tent. There's probably only two or three thousand of them around here."

The girl took a long pull on the water bottle. Susan said, "He calls you Shug? Is that like Sugar?"

"Yeah," she said, a little sheepishly. "Brown Sugar. We're gonna be workin' on that soon. He's Ian, and I'm Billie."

"I'm Susan."

"Oh, yeah, hey, we got some granola before from the Hog Farm. They gave us extra; you're welcome to some."

She ate some granola. It was dry and bland, and the best thing she had ever eaten in her life. She flopped back and watched the stars for a while with the distant music of Johnny Winter filtering through the breeze.

"Is this the best place in the world?" Billie said. "Is this just fucking outrageous?"

"It is," Susan said. "I'm really strung out and I want to go home, but I want to stay here forever. I want to build a cabin right in front of the stage."

"Yeah, I know. I hate to do it, but we're gonna split tonight before the big exodus. We're going north. Montreal. There's room in the van if you're going that way."

Until then, Susan had not considered how she was going to get home. She had not thought of home at all and felt a little guilty about that.

"Oh, that's cool, but I'm headed south. Baltimore. I got a couple of girlfriends around here somewhere I can meet up with."

"Well, just be careful, because cats are splitting early."

"I just wanna hear Crosby, Stills and Nash, and Hendrix. I can't miss them. Can't."

"I dig where you're coming from." Ian came back with some water, they went back to making out, among other things, and Susan dozed. When Billie poked her a couple of times, Stephen Stills was saying, "We're scared shitless," and singing his love song to "sweet Judy blue eyes."

Unbelievable, thought Susan. *This whole scene is not to be believed.*

She helped them sing "Helplessly Hoping" and then crashed again. When she woke, Billie and Ian were gone. Her water jug was full, and there was another bowl of granola next to her. It was almost dawn. Her foot hurt like hell, but she scrambled up, got her bearings, and went looking for Brenda and Amanda and their tent. She found the van she recognized, but the whole area around it was clear; full of trash, but no tents, no people. Back toward the rise of the bowl, streams of people were climbing over the hill and heading for the highway. But Hendrix was warming up, so she limped back toward the stage and found a spot to wait.

The rain had stopped, and she overheard one of the people leaving say, "Figures, man. It rains for three days and when we're on the way out, it stops."

Susan listened, rapt, to Hendrix' set, and was blown away by the "Star Spangled Banner." She watched as the band and the roadies and the construction crew started to break everything down, and she didn't move, not wanting it to end. People streamed by her, and she just looked at their shoes and then lay back and looked at the clouds.

Ten

A while later—she didn't know how much later—she woke up to a horn blowing. A man got out of his truck and walked over to her. A few guys jumped out of the truck bed and started stuffing trash into garbage bags.

The guy said, "Sorry, miss, you're gonna have to move. Clean up crew."

"Oh, yeah," she said, "Sorry." She pulled herself up and started limping toward the exit. He came trotting after her.

"Stepped on some glass, I'm guessing."

"Souvenir of the festival," she said without looking at him.

"Are you with anyone? Friends? Got a ride home?"

She looked at him now for the first time, and a few tears rolled down her cheeks. It dawned on her that it was over, and she had to figure out a way to get home.

"We had a bit of a falling out," she said. "Poor timing, but it happens in the best of families." She kept walking.

"Well, wait, wait. The least I can do is get you some kind of a walking stick. Take the pressure off your foot."

She just looked at him, tears still rolling down, her eyebrows raised in a question.

"Tell you what, I think these guys can stuff trash in bags for a few minutes by themselves. It may tax their mental abilities, but I'm optimistic. I'll drive you over to the performers' cabin, and I can find you something from there. It isn't far, just back there," he pointed to a small cabin behind the stage.

"You work for the festival? You can get us in there?"

"Yeah, I'm a carpenter for the festival. I have keys and combinations and stuff. It won't be a problem."

"It's very nice of you."

He helped her into the truck. "You look pretty wrung out. Eaten lately? Had water?"

"I'm fine," she said. "I had plenty of rain water and some of that granola they were passing around."

"Oh, okay. That'll keep you for a little while, I guess. How far is home?"

"Baltimore."

"The lady came from Baltimore," he said.

"Tim Hardin. He didn't do that one here."

"Yeah, I was hoping. It's his best, but not the best known."

At the gate, he jumped out of the truck and fiddled with the combination lock, pushed the wide gate open, and drove through. He got back out, closed and locked the gate, and drove up to the small cabin. She watched him, trying not to stare. He was tall and wide, but not heavy. Big hands, strong looking forearms, tanned. His hair was long, almost to his shoulders, and pulled back; sideburns and a bushy mustache, both of which needed a trim.

He parked near the cabin and helped her up the ramp into the almost empty cabin.

She sat on a table and took both of her shoes off. "Oh," she said, looking at the injured one. "That is not good." It was swollen and blackish and purplish around the edge of where the glass had gone in.

"That nurse warned me about the mud."

"You know that line about 'it's not the heat it's the humidity,' right? Around here, it's not the mud, it's the cow shit." She laughed, and then he did.

"Keep it up higher than your heart. I have a first aid kit in the truck."

"I don't want to be a big problem for you," she said. "You were just gonna get me a stick."

He just nodded and said, "Be right back."

While he was outside, she looked around the room. A sink, a couple of benches, a recliner, a cot. In the corner, there was what looked like a phone line that led into a desk drawer.

He came back in with a small plastic box and a stick about four feet long. "This one is oak, strong enough," he said. "Looks about the right size for you, too."

"Uh, before we get into all that, would there be a phone around here? A phone call home would be, you know, like, a minor miracle."

He looked around, spotted the phone wire and pulled the phone out of the desk drawer. "These egos can't survive more than a few minutes without talking to their agents. It's like oxygen for them."

Monday afternoon, she thought. *He'll probably be at his desk.*

She dialed her father's work number and he picked up on the first ring. "Hughes Bail Bond Agency. This is Alan Moore."

"Dads, it's me."

"Susan, thank God, are you okay? The stuff on the news is just crazy."

"Yeah, I'm fine. I had a crazy weekend, but such a great time. It was wonderful."

"Are you on the way home? Where are you?"

"No, not yet. I had a small accident. Stepped on a piece of glass, and someone is fixing it up for me right now."

"Oh? Serious cut?"

"No, no, not at all. Just being careful with it."

"Amanda is still with you? And Brenda?"

"Well, long story there, Dad, but no. We got separated, and I think they're on the way without me."

"What? You're alone up there? How about, um, David? Where is he?"

"Dad, I'm fine, I'm taking care of all of it and I should see you in a day or two. I'm fine,"

A long silence. "I'm driving up there, just tell me where you're going to be. I can be there in six hours."

"No, in six hours I'll be on a bus halfway home. I'm fine. I will get home by myself, Dad. I love you and I miss you, but I will get home by myself."

She watched the carpenter take a quick glance at her, and then move quickly outside. He sat on the steps whittling the knobs off the stick and smoothing the handle. When he heard it quiet inside, he went over to her and said, "This first aid kit is for nicks and scrapes, carpenter occupational hazards, but it should do it for your foot."

She lay back on the table and stuck her foot in his lap. He looked carefully at it. He got a washcloth, and some warm water, carefully washed all the mud off and dried the cut. He opened a package of antiseptic cream and said, "Deep breath, this is probably gonna sting." She yelped just a little and held her breath while he spread some cream on.

"Gonna just let that sit for a few minutes and then do it again," he said. "Next time might hurt even more, so..."

"He worries about me, my dad."

"Well, that's good. He should."

"You're really going way out of your way for me."

"Yeah, well, hold your applause until the show is over. You're a long way from home."

They were both quiet for a few minutes, he rinsing off the washcloth, she trying to see the bottom of her foot.

"Sorry," he said. "Didn't mean to bum you out. You have options. We'll work something out." He rubbed off the excess cream and dried the area again.

"This may be the tough one," he said, "depending on how much infection spread in there. So, hold on. Call me names if you have to. There's no one around, so scream or grunt or whatever works. Here goes."

He held her ankle tight and put the cream on the cut and she shouted, "Oh, you fat ass, two-faced bitch!"

He laughed. "I was expecting some language out of you, but I wasn't expecting that. Never been called a fat ass, two-faced bitch before."

She sniffled a little. "I was thinking of someone else." He laughed again. And then she did.

He cleaned the wound, covered it with the gauze from the first aid kit, and taped it. "What else do you have for shoes?"

"Moccasins, in my duffel bag."

"Mocs won't be as tight but won't give you any support on the bottom. Walking on the blacktop, even with a good stick, is gonna be a problem."

He looked at his watch. "Look, I don't know how it ended with your dad, but I have to get back to those knuckleheads out there picking up garbage."

She started to get up.

"No, no. That's not what I meant. Let me go roust them a bit, and then we can talk options. You just mellow out here for a bit."

"It's okay if I'm here?"

"Probably not technically, but if anyone does come in, which I doubt, just tell them that you're waiting for Chip."

"You're Chip?"

"No, Chip is the boss, and basically a patron saint around here. Mention his name and you are pretty close to sacred. I'm not sure how long, but I'll be back as soon as I can. Keep that foot elevated."

"Thank you. I, um...thank you."

~ * ~

He was gone for about two hours, and she lay on her back with her foot up. She had a strong desire to walk around and explore, but resisted. After a while, she was aware of a strange feeling that she could not place, like she had been here before...but no, that wasn't it. Why did everything seem so familiar, she wondered? And then she realized that it was her whole shrunken habitat. It was now Monday afternoon and she had been living outdoors surrounded by the voices and movements of thousands of people since Friday. Now it was only her, listening to her own breath in a small, empty room.

"It's me," he said, knocking on the front door before he came in. He brought in her duffel bag. "Looks like I'm gonna need to work tonight. The whole farm is a mess, and it just isn't right to leave it like that."

"You're gonna be doing cleanup? Doesn't sound like carpentry to me."

He smiled. "'Carpenter' around here includes engineer, electrician, plumber, lawn care specialist, engine repair, and sanitation. Good thing there are no windows on this farm, 'cause I don't do windows. Anyway, I have been thinking about your options to get back to hearth and home. What I've been hearing is the roads out of here in all directions are a mess, one big parking lot. Probably will be until tomorrow. You can hit the highway and hang your thumb out, but it won't do you much good."

"I was afraid of that, but you know, Hendrix."

"Yeah, I get that. Hendrix. So, option one is for someone to come up here and get you. Sorry, I overheard your dad suggest that. He'll have a better chance getting in than anyone will getting out, but not very much better."

"Last resort," she said. "Only as a last resort."

"The other option relies on patience and perhaps a little bit of faith. I can get you to the bus depot in Kingston tomorrow morning, but that means you'll need to stay with me tonight. Not what you had in mind, I know, but it is your best bet."

"Stay with you? And how would that work?"

"I have an apartment over my uncle's hardware store in Liberty. That's about thirty minutes from here. I can take you there. I'll have to come back to work here, and you can have the run of the place.

There's a shower, hot water, full size bed probably unmade, might be some leftover chili in the fridge. It's not much, it's not the Plaza, but after three days at Yasgur's farm, it may seem like it."

"Ah, I am really taking advantage of you. You are being much too accommodating."

"I don't mind, really. And I can't imagine leaving you to limp down 17B until your foot turns gangrene. If you're worried about me, you know, a stranger, I think there is a hook and eye on the bedroom door, and the way it looks, I'll be tumbling in exhausted at about three a.m."

"And I have my stick."

"Yes," he laughed, "you have your stick."

"I don't know what to say. You're saving my ass and I can't tell you how much I appreciate it."

"That's a yes, then. Good. Put your moccasins on and use the stick on the opposite leg. It's your left foot, so the stick stays on the right. You'll see."

~ * ~

He drove up a cow path above the main stage area and turned out of the farm onto a rutted path that led to an unpaved back road that twisted and rose and finally led them to a chopped up two-lane road heading away from 17B. It was late afternoon, and after the invasion, the beleaguered town was just about closed. He pulled up in front of Liberty Hardware and helped her out of the truck. She was struggling a little with the newly wrapped foot and the walking stick. The darkened store had an old-fashioned, friendly smell to it, like wood and wool and fertilizer.

They went up a flight of stairs in the back. His apartment was small and self-contained and had that same earthy smell. There was a small living room, kitchenette, bedroom and bathroom.

She stopped halfway in and said to him, "Just confirm something for me. Is that an actual working bathroom?"

He laughed. "Yes, and I can find you some working towels."

"Be still my beating heart." She laughed.

"I don't have time to give you a tour," he said. "You can see it all from here anyway. But let me just do a quick reconnoiter and make the bed and kick the dirty underwear under the dresser."

"This is wonderful. It's the Taj Mahal. The Ritz-Carlton of Liberty, New York. Thank you, thank you. I do keep saying that, don't I."

He looked in the kitchen. "Yes, there is cereal and milk and coffee for the morning, some cold cuts that I just got yesterday, and some leftover chili. Not the hot variety. Help yourself to whatever you find. My Uncle John and Aunt Bette will be downstairs in the morning. They usually open up around eight. I'll leave them a note that you're here. I think that's everything and I gotta go. I'll be the lump on the couch in the morning. Get a good night's sleep," and he was out the door.

Within minutes she was in the bathtub, sore foot hanging over the side, soap dripping into her eyes. She dressed in jeans she hadn't bothered to wear over the weekend, a clean T-shirt, with her favorite lace blouse over it. A lace anklet on her injured foot reminded her of her mother. It took a minute or two to figure out the microwave, and then she warmed up some chili, ate it and cleaned up the dishes.

Sitting at his kitchen table with clean clothes, clean hair and a full stomach, she sighed, "Civilization." Fully dressed except for shoes, she went to bed and didn't even check if there was a hook and eye on the bedroom door. In the brief few minutes before she fell asleep, she thought about the small wrinkle he had at the corner of his mouth that folded in on itself when he smiled. Which, she had noticed, he did a lot.

In the morning, he was a lump on the couch like he said he would be. She tiptoed around making cereal, and feeling a little guilty, drinking some of his orange juice.

He woke up slowly and looked over at her for a minute without seeing her. "Good morning," she said.

"Hello," he said. He got up, grabbed some clean clothes from the bedroom and went into the bathroom for a shower. When he stepped out, dressed but still wet, he said, "Good morning, hope you found everything okay."

"Yes. And I made a promise to myself that I would only say thanks one more time today. It's becoming an obsession. But can I pour you some cereal or juice? Or I can make coffee."

"If you would make coffee, we can switch roles and I can start thanking you obsessively."

She laughed. "Rough night, it looks like."

He thought for a moment. "I had an aunt who used to say 'there are more horses' asses in the world than there are horses.' As a kid I didn't know what she meant, but dealing with that crew of dim bulbs last night, I figured it out."

Sitting at the table with coffee and toast, they heard some noises downstairs. "John and Bette are opening up. If you're ready, now would be the time to get you to Kingston. I don't know when you can get a bus, so you may be hanging around there a while. Just let me finish my coffee. Please, by all that's sacred, let me drink coffee." She saw that little wrinkle next to his lip raise and stretch into a dimple.

Downstairs, she saw an older man and woman busy behind the counter. They looked up at her and smiled. She said, "Thank you very much for your hospitality last night."

The older man nodded and the woman said, "You're welcome, dear. Please travel safely."

They rode to the Trailways station in Kingston, and he went inside with her. "There is one more thing, but you may not like it," he said, and held out an envelope.

"I have money," she said. "I had a stash sewed into my jeans. Dad insisted."

"I figured," he said, "but I want you to have this anyway. You'll probably have to switch at Port Authority, and it's always a good idea to have some extra cash in New York. No telling how often buses run to Baltimore."

"Uh, I don't know...this is too..."

"I tucked a note in there with my address and phone number, and I do expect you to pay me back. And Woodstock Ventures, Inc will owe me a shitload of overtime, so it's not a problem. Please take it, otherwise I will worry that this job is only half done. A pleasant job," he smiled, "but only half done."

She took the envelope and nodded. "As soon as possible," she said.

"And I have to be getting back," he said. "Horses' asses, you know."

"Then, this will be my last thank you," she said.

He took a step back, and she turned to climb on the bus. "Wait," he said. "In all of this, I don't know your name."

"I'm Susan," she said, smiling. "But I go by my middle name, Cecelia."

They shook hands. "I'm Ben."

Eleven

Andy sat with his knees up against his chin trying to hold his head on straight. Some of that brown acid shit he'd swallowed an hour ago was making him think his head was a balloon tied with one tiny little string to his neck. It wasn't a bad feeling, and he wondered what it would be like if he just let his head go, float over the whole scene, look down on the crowds and the rain clouds and the pond and the stage and the whole scene.

But he was afraid if he did that, he would miss The Who. He hadn't come way the hell over here just for The Who, but they were in the middle of the whole plan. Even though the plan sucked.

The plan was to borrow money from his father and let his parents know where he was going, which didn't happen. His father said, "you're not going." Andy said "yes, I am." His father said, "you're not." Andy said, "I am," and slammed the door on his way out.

The plan included borrowing Rich's father's car, which didn't happen either, because Rich was supposed to trim the front hedge last week and didn't. So they had to take Andrew's clunker and hope it could make the round trip.

The plan didn't include a completely bonehead calamity by Carl. The plan did include being stoked on acid for the whole weekend, which also didn't happen, mostly because Carl was the premier moron of the twentieth century.

Carl, who worked as a rate clerk for a freight hauling company, had a contact that could get them acid. They pooled their money, came up with enough of the sugar cubes to keep them soaring through the weekend, and stashed it under the burner of their propane gas stove. There was little thought of using the propane gas stove as a stove—cooking was not part of the plan—but they were thinking that someone at the gate might be looking for drugs. When they got to the top of the bowl and saw the staggering mass of people, they knew that was out the window, too.

They got as close to the stage as possible, which wasn't very, and set up the tent. Rich and Andy tried to walk through the crowd just as Richie Havens was doing "Freedom," but you couldn't walk. They sat near the edge of the mass and just listened, stood up with everyone else and clapped. Carl had stayed behind to finish setting up the tent and smoke a joint.

After Country Joe did the "Fixin' to Die Rag," Rich said, "Hey Andy, I don't care much about the rest of these half-assed bands, let's walk around and see what we can see." They each lit a cigarette, still not quite believing that you could just fire up a doobie.

They tracked around to the woods and down the path toward the pond just blown away by all the people and amazed at how many of them were cute chicks.

They found a seat against a tree and shared a joint, watching girls go by. "Paradise, man," said Andy.

"Paradise with some bitchin' live music, man," Rich said. They were close enough to hear the band on the stage and listen quietly to Melanie and Arlo.

Walking back to the tent site, Andy looked on his schedule and said, "I liked that Melanie chick. Pretty ballsy to play without a backup band, and she has a voice I could fall in love with."

Carl was sitting outside the tent, just listening to the distant music. "Is this unbelievable, or what? Is this just too freakin' awesome for words?"

"There's a pond back there, man. Chicks walking back and forth with bathing suits, some with almost bathing suits. It is incredible."

Rich asked first. "Where's the acid, man? Not for now, but for the morning."

"You got it...I don't have it."

"It's in the stove, dumb ass. I hid it under one of the burners."

"You hid it, what?"

"The burner on the right side, the bigger one. It pulls out and there's room under there."

"Oh, shit," Carl said. "You didn't tell me that. Tell me you're kidding."

They both made a dive inside the tent and took out the stove, pulled out the right side burner. There was some blackened paper and five or six gelatinous blobs that were at one time very special sugar cubes.

"You cooked 'em. You cooked something here? What is wrong with you?"

"I was making sure everything worked, man. This is gonna be a long three days and you never told me it was under there!"

Andy came back from the Porta Potty. They were both sitting on the ground staring between their legs. "Do not try the bathrooms, man. You will melt before you get out of there."

"Andy," Rich said.

"Andy, it's not my fault," Carl said.

"What? What?" They showed him the blackened cubes. They told him what happened, and they spent the next ten minutes screaming at each other. Andy walked to the woods, smacked a couple of trees, and then walked back. "Maybe they're still good," he said.

Rich laughed. "Look at 'em, man, they look like used chewing gum. I'm not swallowing that crap."

They all looked from one to the other. Finally, Andy said, "Okay, I'll try one. But not here. Over by the medical tent in case something goes wrong."

In the woods near the medical tent, he took the blackish lump and washed it down with water. Within minutes he was leaned over a stump, retching.

"That answers that question," Carl said,

"You should probably just shut up," Rich said.

When Andy was able, they walked toward the main stage, single file, and heard the beginnings of Arlo Guthrie's set.

Rich yelled back, "I am so sick of Arlo goddamn Guthrie."

Carl said, "Pete goddamn Seeger, too."

Andy said, "Don't even get me started me on Peter, Paul and Mary."

They weaved through the crowd, looking up occasionally at the threatening sky, and struggling to remember where their tent was. Rich's mother had made them sandwiches, which hadn't lasted long, and they spent the last hours of daylight tossing a frisbee and rolling joints.

"I am wiped out," Andy said, slipping into his sleeping bag. "And tomorrow is gonna be just incredible." He didn't notice that Carl was talking to someone a couple of tents away.

~ * ~

Andy was up first, grabbed a few crackers and some water from the cooler and walked toward the main stage. He knew The Who was scheduled to play sometime that night, he thought around nine or so, and he wanted to get close to the stage. Rich joined him about an hour later, and they took turns watching the spot while the other went into the woods to pee. Around dusk there was an announcement that the brown acid that was circulating was "not good."

"There goes that," Rich said, and tossed his tab onto the ground.

"Where'd you get that?" Andy asked.

"Guy stuck it in my hand on my last trip back from the woods."

"Huh," Andy said, and picked the tab up off the ground.

Not all the bands on Saturday were A list, so they got to ignore or snore through some and groove to Santana and Canned Heat and The Grateful Dead, Janis Joplin and Sly and the Family Stone. But it was really The Who they were waiting for. There was a long, long wait between acts, but others got bored waiting, so Rich and Andy were able to move up pretty close to the stage. It rained off and on, sometimes just a drizzle, sometimes a steady rain. Andy and Rich held a tarp over their heads for a while, but it leaked and splattered all over them, and pretty soon it wasn't worth the effort.

"Rain must be really screwing the schedule up," Rich said.

"Indeed," Andy said. "I'm just so terribly damp and inconvenienced. Personally, I'm considering writing a strongly worded letter to Mister Yazgur. In other circumstances, I would seriously take the time to ponder if this trip was all worth it if I wasn't having such an incredible fucking time. Seriously, man, Santana? Janis? Sly? For eighteen bucks? And then The Who on top of that? Go ahead and rain buckets, rain frogs, rain cow shit. I ain't moving."

Rich kept looking around. "Carl is never gonna be able to get up here, even if he can find us."

"Yeah, where is our chef?"

"Last I saw of him, he was trying to make it with this chick a couple of tents away."

"Oh, yeah? What was she like?"

"Actually, better than his usual."

~ * ~

It was full dark when all of those bands had played, and almost dawn when The Who finally went on. Andy dozed for a while, then swallowed his tab of acid and waited to see what would happen. Within half an hour, he was giggling and trying to keep his head from flying off. When they started their set, Townshend in his white jumpsuit and Roger Daltrey swinging his microphone around, Andy let go of the string attached to his head. It floated up above the trees, but then he grabbed the string and pulled hard on it. It settled slowly onto his neck and stuck. He saw and heard Pete's solo at the end of the show and watched with awe as he carried the guitar to the edge of the stage and tossed it underhand into the crowd.

Andy leapt for it, grabbed a piece of the headstock and landed on top of it. Bodies slammed into him, but he squirmed around until his full weight was on it, and just absorbed the blows. The strings and tone knobs were cutting into him, but he barely felt them. His head was in the mud and he had to turn it to breathe. He heard someone shout, "Get off him!" That was Rich maybe, and a little of the weight came off. He was able to pull his knees under him, and still twist and wriggle to keep other hands off the guitar.

"Come on, man, you're gonna kill him," someone shouted. "You gotta let him breathe."

After a few minutes, a couple of the bodies shifted and got off, and Andy was strong enough to clamber up to a crouch and then run through the crowd. His head was down, and the guitar was still clutched to his body, and he ran like a fullback just knocking into anything that got in his way. He heard shrieks and curses and paid them no attention. He moved along the stage area and toward the woods. A few people followed him, but by the time he was near the free stage, he thought he was alone and safe. He ran into the woods, collapsed against a tree, and watched and listened, trying to keep his breath as quiet as possible.

He was alone. He knew he could never get the guitar past those other assholes and all the way back to his tent, so it had to be buried or hidden somehow. Despite the rain, the ground was too hard to dig with his hands. He looked around for a tree to climb, but the branches were all too high. He walked closer to the pond and saw a tree that had toppled part way over, exposing deep roots and a hole almost big enough. He clawed the hole a little deeper with his fingers and shoved the guitar in as far as it would go. He stepped back for a better look and then took it out again. He took off his shirt, wrapped the guitar in it and shoved it back between the roots. He covered it as best he could with loose dirt.

Not good, he thought. *Too easy in the daylight, but it might be okay for a little while, and I can come back for it tomorrow.* The eastern sky was just starting to lighten up with the sunrise.

He sat for a few minutes, trying to think of a better plan, and then walked out to the pond, stripped down to his skivvies and walked in. It was dark, the water was cold, but he felt a need to get clean, and maybe a little more sober. He dunked himself a couple of times, and, while underwater, decided to go back and guard the guitar. He sat on the shore for a few minutes to dry off a little. *I'll lay in that hole and sleep with it,* he thought, *and sneak it back somehow tomorrow.*

He went back to the woods where he thought he had turned off before, and walked in, but he could not find the toppled-over tree. Rain and mud made walking treacherous. He tried to remember how far he was from the lake, but couldn't. He tried to recall any kind of landmark, but all he remembered was the uprooted tree. So, he walked in a straight line for a few minutes, and then in a circle for a few minutes, and then in smaller circles until he saw the tree. He knelt and dug under the roots, but found only his shirt and one of the guitar tuning pegs. He put his shirt on, and put the shiny metal peg in his shirt pocket.

"Can't be, man. Can't be. This is the place...this is the tree." He sat back on his heels and tried to cry when he heard Jefferson Airplane start their set and Grace Slick mumbling something about "morning mania." She was trying to arouse a little enthusiasm from that enormous crowd that had been up all night, stoned all night, and celebrating all night.

Without thinking, he stood and started toward the music. He tripped once and fell flat on his face in the mud but scrambled up and kept walking. He got to the road, just past the medical tent, and saw a girl on the ground looking up at something, and a weird kind of light. It wasn't the light from the sunrise, it was brighter and more focused and was pulsing slowly from silver to gold and back to silver. In the middle of the light was the figure of a person, ten or twelve feet up in the crotch of a tree, holding one arm up. The pulsing light was coming from him.

The light blazed one more time, stayed lit for what seemed like a full minute, and then was gone. And so was the figure.

Andy walked around the tree, fell twice, walked a few yards in each direction looking for tracks or something, anything. He sat in the mud, spent. Several people over on the path looked at him as they passed, and then moved on. The girl on the ground pulled herself up and limped away.

He sat, still trying to cry because he was sure that what the figure was holding up was his guitar. His guitar. But it was gone now. Gone. He plodded back to the pond and dunked himself again to get the mud off, and then went back to the fallen tree. He pawed at the ground for a while, pointlessly, until his fingers hurt, and then took that long walk back to the tent. The crowd had thinned, and Jefferson Airplane was just getting into "Somebody to Love," but he hardly heard it. He found their tent without too much trouble. A lump at one end was probably Rich, and there was no sign of Carl.

Before he fell asleep, almost crying again, he thought of his father.

~ * ~

It was grey and overcast again when they awoke on Sunday morning. Rich wanted to stay and see Crosby, Stills and Nash, but Andy argued that they probably wouldn't play until very late tonight, and he was anxious to start home. He looked a couple of times toward the tree where he had seen the light and beyond it to the pond but was too discouraged and too tired to walk back there and look. He barked at Carl, who was taking his time saying goodbye to the girl he'd met. It was a long ride home, he had lost his prize, and he just wanted to go.

Carl was looking pale and shaky, but said he was fine. "I met a girl last night," he said, and that's all he would say.

They packed up, and by the time they were back walking along Route 17B, the clouds opened up and soaked them and everything they carried. Andy was too gloomy, and the others were too tired, too full of music and adventure, to care.

They found Andy's car, a seven year old Plymouth, parked on a bare spot off the highway. The front right and rear right lights were smashed, the vent window on the passenger side was broken. The tape deck and all of the eight tracks were gone.

"Oh, man," Andy yelled. "The music's all gone, too."

The real exodus traffic jam hadn't begun yet, and they only hit a few bad spots. Andy drove, found his way back to the Northway, then to the New York State Thruway, and west to Utica. Rich snored. Carl, still looking bewildered, sat in the back and stared out the window.

In Utica, Rich and Carl got out on the same block, and Andy said, "A lot of shit went wrong, but that was the best weekend I ever had. The absolute best in-fuckin'-credible weekend."

Rich slapped him five, and Carl just closed the car door and walked into his house. "He's pissed because we yelled at him," Rich said.

Andy pulled up in front of his house; his sister's car was in the driveway. Before he got across the lawn, his older sister opened the door and just looked at him. Her eyes were red.

"What?" he said. "I know I'm in the doghouse. Don't make it worse."

"Dad," she said.

"What?"

"He had another one."

"Heart attack?"

She could only nod.

Inside the house, his mother and other sister were at the table in the dining room and neither said anything to him. They each looked, made eye contact, and then looked away.

"I'm sorry," he said. "I shouldn't have..." No one said a word.

He sat next to his mother. "Ma..."

"We didn't even know where you were," she said. "We couldn't even tell you."

His sister said, "So, where did you go? You stink."

"It was a music festival downstate. We camped."

"That one on the news, Woods Gate?"

"Woodstock, yeah. He seemed fine when I left."

His mother got up and went into the kitchen, a tissue against her eyes.

After a few more quiet minutes, he followed her in there. "Ma," he started.

"A nice Saturday afternoon," she said. "We don't know where the hell you are, but we're getting used to that. Your sisters are out there somewhere and he's watering the lawn. I look out the window and he's down on the ground, I don't know for how long. They're not here, you're not here, I call the ambulance. Them, I can track down. Who knows where you are, or what you're doing? That's his third one, did you know that? He's had two before."

"Yeah, I know that."

She reached for him, hugged him and cried on his shoulder. "Andy, oh, Andy." And then she slapped him.

He showered and shaved and stayed around the house trying to be invisible, and next day drove to the hospital to visit his father. He pulled the curtain around his father's bed for a little privacy and all he was able to say was, "Dad." His father reached for his hand, squeezed it weakly, and closed his eyes. Andy sat a few minutes, but it was pretty clear his father had fallen back asleep, so he went out to the desk and asked about his condition.

"Are you a member of the immediate family?" the desk nurse asked.

"Yes," he said. "I'm his son." He thought, *the prodigal son. The unforgiven, son of a bitch, prodigal son.*

"I can't tell you much," she said. "You'll need to talk to his doctor, but he is stable and resting comfortably."

"Sleeping a lot?"

"Oh, yes. Rest is the best thing for him."

"So, no prognosis, then."

"I'm sorry. You'll have to speak to a doctor."

"Of course, thank you."

On the way home, he pulled up in front of his usual hangout, the Kingsman Tavern, and debated with himself for ten minutes before he decided to drive away. He went the long way home and circled the block twice before going in.

He went back the next evening with one of his sisters, and his dad was a little more alert. He smiled at them and called them both by name. When he said, "Drew," Andy almost wept. But his dad faded quickly again, and they didn't stay long.

His sister, the younger one, Adele, in the driver's seat, cried a few minutes before she started the car. Andy had been home for three days, and no one had said more than a sentence to him.

He said, "Everyone is really pissed at me, I guess."

She pointed at him, "Don't. Don't even." And they drove home in silence. The thought that played through his head was, *He called me Drew. What the hell? Dad never calls me Drew. No one ever calls me Drew.*

Early the next morning, his father had another attack and died.

The wake was miserable, packed with cousins and aunts and uncles he hadn't seen in years. One aunt, his mother's half-sister who looked like Almira Gulch after Toto bit her, looked at him accusingly and said, "She really didn't even know where you were?"

Rich came one night, and he was able to sneak out and share a joint with him, but Carl never showed. Mostly, he sat alone on those uncomfortable chairs and looked at the coffin. Or tried not to look at the coffin. Or thought about the good times with his father, fishing mostly, and camping. But he wouldn't cry, would not allow himself to do that. Relatives sat with him briefly, patted him on the back, promised to call, promised to visit. He nodded and smiled and let it all pass through him like wind through the roots of a knocked down tree.

The funeral was almost as dismal, but mercifully brief. Afterwards, his mother and sisters walked away, weeping, and he was left standing at the gravesite. No Rich, no Carl, no guitar. Judas, Benedict Arnold, the prodigal son. He sat in his car with the broken lights and the missing tape deck and was finally able to cry. He stopped and had a couple of beers on the way home. And then a couple more.

Andy lived for the next three months with his mother and his younger sister, but when she got married, they sold the house and his mother moved in with the older sister. Andy found a small apartment near his job with a wholesale beverage distributor. There was not much discussion about where the mother would live, and the little there was did not include him.

He saw Rich now and again, and they laughed about the acid hidden in the camping stove. Carl had quit his job and moved away. No one knew where, or why, but it didn't seem important. His family was always weird and distant. His mom had been divorced twice, and Carl had always been shuttled between parent and step-parents.

A few years later, he rented the Woodstock movie and bought the album, and slowly the concert and the guitar grew in myth and consequence until they conflated with his father's death, his home and the scattering of his family. In time, he came to believe the guitar was the reason he had gone to the Woodstock Festival. It had been his plan all along to get it, and losing it somehow became an offense to his father's memory.

~ * ~

While he was still living in Utica, his girlfriend brought him to a roadhouse called The Old Log about twenty miles out Route 8 where the beer was cheap and the music was not good, but free. Andy volunteered his services as setup man, and soon equipment repair man, and eventually the guy that scored the weed. He would perform a little, too. Tuesdays were open mic night, and he would club through a couple of songs with his three chord repertoire and wandering baritone. Wednesdays and Saturdays belonged to an act called Cherie, Willie and Cherry. Willie did acoustic covers, and Cherie and Cherry stood smiling nearby wearing hot pants and fedoras. Willie, whose real name was Stewart, scored a one-week gig at a hotel bar in Buffalo, and he asked Andy to come with him to help with the equipment. Willie/ Stewart was related by marriage to an assistant manager at the hotel and thought it would look professional if he traveled with a roadie. A warm smile from Cherry, or maybe it was Cherie, and a deal was struck.

He lasted the week, but just barely. Cherie, Willie and Cherry were to be the warm-up for a local hard rock band, The Dilemma, who had more equipment than talent. The last night, an hour before they went on, their manager approached Andy with a crisis. Two of the microphones were dead. Dead. Could C, W and C possibly lend them a couple?

Andy looked briefly at the microphones and asked, "Changed the batteries lately?" The manager, the bass player and the lead singer said, in almost perfect three-part harmony, "Batteries?" The manager was appreciative and found him a place on the bus.

He traveled with Dilemma for a few months on a tour through the Midwest, and when they broke up, got a job doing setup for a folkie club in Rockford, Illinois.

He got fired from that job and drifted south to New Orleans where he picked up work with a couple of blues bands. New Orleans, exactly eleven years to the day that he had found and lost the guitar, at sunrise, is where the flashbacks began. By that time, his drug of choice was grass, moistened on occasion with Jack Daniels.

Some of the early flashbacks were benign, most were no worse than a fifties sci-fi movie, and most seemed to be built around that weekend at Yasgur's. But they varied. The mud sometimes sucked him down and at other times lifted him up so he could see the crowd. The roots of the trees were sometimes snarling dogs, but most of the time were colored rectangles like on a kid's xylophone that played "Für Elise" or "Twinkle, Twinkle."

The gentle ones, Melanie singing "Peace Will Come," and walking down 17B and seeing the mass of people, came much later.

When drunk or stoned, he often wanted to brag that he was the one that got Pete Townshend's guitar at Woodstock, but he was too ashamed he had also lost it.

Gradually, probably without even a dim awareness, Andy had already expanded into Andrew, and skipped past the positive qualities of Drew into his alter ego, Druid. Druid, the roadie, with hard work and application, mastered the art and science of being a useful minion. He established a reputation as someone who was reliable, who had some connections, and who could keep his mouth shut. Time went by, a diet of Jack Daniels and coffee took its toll, equipment got more unwieldy, and so did he. Backaches competed with headaches in the morning, and by the time the amp fell off the truck onto his foot, the transformation to 'Drusome' was complete.

Twelve

Mid-week in October, just before leaf peeping season took hold, was traditionally very quiet at the Penultimate Pickle. After a busy summer, and the arrival of her daughter and grandson, Cecelia was happy to have the time to slip into a relaxed routine.

Jason had gone home for a few days, so Andrew spent the time looking around in Liberty for a less expensive place to stay. He figured he had enough in his savings account for about three more weeks, and he did not want to rely on Jason. He avoided the Pickle, realizing that Cecelia and Jennifer, and also Ben, needed time to themselves. This was the middle guy doing the thinking.

And he walked. He took long exercise walks, twice a day, breaking a sweat and pushing himself a little further each time. He couldn't keep himself completely away from the television, but mostly he avoided the soap operas and sitcom reruns and waited for the news shows. He tried reading the paper, but that skill remained, at best, a work in progress.

After four days, Jason was due back the next day. The Woodstock anniversary concert was Saturday, and Andy felt it was time to peek into the Pickle.

The wind chimes over the door jangled as he came in, and he saw Jennifer at the far end of the room, looking over one of the displays. She was a younger version of her mother, a little thinner and with shorter hair, but with the same blue eyes and same quick, inviting smile.

"Please come in," she said. "We're open for business."

"Hi. I'm Andrew, a friend of your mom. I just came in to say hi."

"Oh, you're the handyman guy. The helper. I saw you the other night."

"Yeah, that's me. Kind of a volunteer fix-it guy. Your mom seems to appreciate it."

She walked over with her arm extended, and they shook hands. She was working at being non-judgmental, and he was trying not to be intimidated.

"Mom is upstairs with Ben, my son. She should be down in a minute or two. Coffee?"

"I have never in my life refused coffee," he said.

They sat, she with juice and he with coffee. She said slowly, "It really is not my business, or barely, but I'm not sure what you and your friend are around here for. Mom talked a little about it, but it wasn't real clear."

"No, it wouldn't be. It's nothing illegal, or dangerous for your mom, just a real complicated situation, and I'm not the best one to untangle it. Cecelia could do it, or maybe Jason."

"Jason is your friend, smaller guy with glasses, so you are Alan, right?"

"Andrew," he said. She nodded.

"Your friend is coming, too?"

"He went home for a few days. We both live downstate, I'm in Brooklyn, temporarily, and he's from, I think, White Plains."

They were quiet for a few moments, sipping, stirring. She said, "Please help me out here. We're hoping to stay for a while, but I'm completely at sea. Maybe we can trade. Some info from you, some info from me."

"Well, yeah, I guess. I'm not the best one to tell it, but I can at least give you the basics."

She took a deep breath and looked quickly toward the stairway. "I'll even go first. It may have been obvious the other night that my mother and I were, I guess the word is 'estranged.' Had been since before Ben was born. Since right after my father died and I was a selfish little shit. Whoo! That's more than I meant to say."

He drank some coffee and thought about what to say, and what not to say. "My turn, I guess. Um, I was at Woodstock, the first one, and um, something happened there that, um, we both, your mom and I, saw."

It took her a minute to process this. "The Woodstock Festival? In the sixties? You met my mom at Woodstock all those years ago and you come up to visit now?"

"No. Not quite like that. I didn't meet her. We never met until last week, but we both saw, um, we saw...wait, let me show you." He went to the display window and got the picture. "I saw this. Not a picture, but this in real life. And she saw it, too. It has been in and out of my head for years, and I came up here to look for it and try and figure out what it was. I saw this painting in the window, she and I talked, and..."

Jennifer looked at the painting like it was a Russian tank coming down Main Street. "It's been in and out of her head, too. For years." She heard footsteps coming slowly down the stairs.

Ben jumped the last step and burst into the kitchen. "Mommy, look, I helped grandma tie her shoes! I did the over and under and she did the loops." Cecelia was looking at the painting, and from Andrew to Jennifer and back at the painting.

"Oh, honey, that's great!" Jennifer said to Ben. "Doing the over and under is a hard part."

Ben looked over at Andrew and moved closer to his mother. "Hi," he said.

Andrew waved and said, "Hi. Your mom's right, the over and under is a hard part. Takes a lot of practice."

Cecelia was looking at him strangely. "We were actually discussing you, upstairs, Ben and I. He was wondering if you are able to fix that little cuckoo clock over there. The one with the broken pendulum."

Andrew brought it over to the table, and he and Ben studied the inside carefully.

Andrew said, "Hmmm."

And then Ben said, "Hmmm."

"I think I see the problem," Andrew said, "and I think I know how you can fix it."

Ben's eyes lit up. "How?"

"You see this piece that's crooked? It has to hook up to that little piece up there. That's the thing that makes the tick-tock sound. If someone strong enough were to bend the top piece into a little hook, we could attach it in the right place and hear it go tick-tock again."

"I'm strong," Ben said.

"Well, yeah, sure, but you gotta grip it just right, so I think we need a tool, and I know what tool to use. I don't think we have one here, but I can get one right next door."

"Can I come?"

"Yeah, if it's okay with your mom."

Jennifer looked at Andrew and was not encouraged by his Darth Vader T-shirt and faded jeans. She glanced over at Cecelia. Cecelia nodded, but Jennifer shrugged.

Andrew said, "How about this, Mom. It's just next door. You can watch us from the front door and we won't be five minutes. What we need," he said to Ben, "is a nosey pliers. Special for bending things."

"That works," she said and opened the door for them. She stood just outside the door and watched them go into the hardware store next door. She called over to Cecelia, "Is it still Gundersen's over there?"

"No, Gundersen sold out, but they're pretty nice. He'll be fine."

Ben came out a few minutes later holding a small pair of needle nose pliers and ran over to his mother. "Mom, these are nosey noses. They bend stuff."

Jennifer said to Andrew, "I don't think you'll ever get them back, so please let me pay for them."

Andrew laughed. "Oh, please, no. That look on his face was worth way more than four bucks."

Inside, Andrew set up everything at the kitchen table, showed Ben where to grip the metal rod and which way to twist it. Ben, with his tongue between his teeth, grunted and got a slight little hook at the top of the rod, just enough to catch on the mechanism and swing the pendulum. Andrew placed it carefully inside the mechanism, wound it up in back, and it worked.

"Tick-tock," said Andrew.

"Tick-tock," said Ben. "Mom, I fixed it."

"You did, Ben," said his mother. "You're a mister fixit."

~ * ~

Jennifer and Ben went upstairs to make his bed and straighten his room. Cecelia poured Andrew more coffee and sat down with a bowl of cereal. She looked at him with a funny head tilt.

"What?" he said.

"Different," she said. "Shaved. Your hair is shorter. Different. Thinner?"

"Workin' on it, you know. Been walking a lot, too. Cut my own hair yesterday, and, believe it or not, not for the first time."

"Where's Jason?"

"Went home for a visit. Due back tomorrow. The anniversary concert is Saturday, right?"

She spooned some cereal; he sipped his coffee.

"Have you eaten anything today?"

"I'm good with just coffee."

She looked at him blankly.

"I know, but it isn't fair to keep relying on you. You've been very good, but I don't like doing that."

"What you just did for my grandson, oh God, I called him my grandson..." she stopped herself for a moment. "What you did gets you at least a couple of scrambled eggs."

"We're on the barter system now?"

"We ought to be, for all the little things you've done around here."

From the kitchen, with her back to him, she said, "I was a little worried when I saw you with that picture, you know, showing it to Jen. I didn't know how to broach the subject of you being here, so I'm grateful that you did. The last time she and I talked about that picture, it didn't go well."

"I hope I didn't start anything up, but she was asking. I figured she had a right to know. If there are other, you know, family land mines, let me know and I will tread lightly."

"Yeah, no. Yeah. But she does have a right to know. She really is part of this, and so is her son, my grandson. My grandson, wow. I really like saying that. I'd like to get it all out in the light, pun intended, for their sake and for mine. How about you and Jason have dinner here tomorrow night? We'll put my grandson, ha, to bed early, and we'll, um, talk."

"Yeah." He laughed. "Four people who really don't know each other having a conversation about a decades old event with mystical science fiction overtones. What could go wrong?"

"Yeah, dig it, sounds like a hootenanny. Damn, there I go again."

Later, at Cecelia's suggestion, Andrew was rearranging the display window on both sides, and washing the windows.

Jennifer came over and said, "I want to thank you for what you did this morning with Ben. That clock, he was so thrilled, still is."

"Oh, I'm glad. It was kind of fun. He's a fun kid."

"He hasn't had a lot of male influence in his life. Not enough."

"Huh."

"So, just a warning, he may pester you for a while."

"Yeah, I can deal with that. I think I'd actually like it. I grew up with two sisters, and my dad was not a big talker. I used to just follow him around all the time. But eventually, he taught me about tools and fishing and like that."

"Yeah, I had a dad like that."

Something about the way she said that, and how Cecelia had talked about her marriage, warned him not to ask any questions.

~ * ~

Jason came back to the Pickle late on Friday afternoon. Cecelia and Jennifer were in the kitchen cooking, and Andrew was reading a book to Ben. Cecelia introduced him formally to Jennifer and to Ben, and Jason said stiffly, "Hello."

"A nice visit?" Cecelia asked.

"Well, you know, family. No one bit anyone, so I count that as a win. And mostly I needed to check in with Rat...uh, Hotchkiss. Andrew, do you want to clear out of here and give these folks some space?"

Cecelia said, "I was hoping we could all have dinner later and finish our conversation. And fill in Jennifer on what all this is about."

"Aha," Jason said. Which seemed to say it all.

~ * ~

They had dinner late, after Ben was asleep on the love seat near the kitchen so his mother could watch him and his grandmother could be continuously nourished by his existence.

"Hamburgers for Jason and Andrew," Cecelia said. "Real hamburgers just to grease the wheels here, so to speak."

"And beer, because it's beer," said Jennifer.

"Wow," Andrew said. "Ground up meat and beer. Two old friends I haven't partied with in a while."

Halfway through a quiet dinner, Jennifer started the ball rolling. "I've been looking forward to this conversation because I'm the new kid on the block, sort of, and have only a hazy idea what's going on. I heard a little from Andrew—Andy—about that painting and a little from Mom about something weird at Yasgur's farm. But it really is still murky. That picture you painted, sorry Mom, holds some very unpleasant associations for me. It caused some serious friction between us. She was, sorry again, Mom, obsessed by it but couldn't tell me why. I never understood the appeal for her, and now I'm baffled by why it's important to you. I am planning to live here, hoping to live here, and I don't get what's going on."

Jason said, "It really is not simple. Not straightforward."

"I understand that," Jennifer said. "But, still, I need to know how weird this is for my mother, and for my son. We have plenty of beer and we have more coffee and we have time." This was followed by a penetrating silence, with all eyes looking down at the table.

"Okay, well then, we can start about me. Obviously, I'm Cecelia's daughter, Ben's mom. I've lived in DC for the past six years with my husband from whom I hope to be divorced as soon as possible. And just between us, I hope to mourn his untimely death soon, as well.

"Mom and I have been estranged—God, I hate that word—and incommunicado—I hate that one, too—for all that time. Actually longer, since my dad died. That picture, or whatever craziness it represents, contributed quite a lot to the estrangement. At eighteen, I had just lost my father, and I thought my mother was losing her mind."

Andrew looked over at Cecelia for some kind of helpful signal, but she was focused on her daughter. He shook his head and held tight to his beer glass.

Jason sipped his beer, uncomfortable with emotion. For him, this was all off the track, all beside the point. Cecelia was usually off the track, but she was a witness. Jennifer and Ben, whatever their personal drama, were not involved, not connected to the quest, and so not helpful. He went to the display window, got the picture and brought it over to Andrew. "We should try to keep to the point here," he said. "The light, the tree, the guitar."

Cecelia looked at him angrily. "For me, that picture *is* the point. Why else would I let you in? Decades after Woodstock, I was haunted by what I saw. I was painting it, probably a dozen copies of it, usually at three in the morning. I had just lost my husband, and I was too obsessed with that fool in the tree to comfort my daughter. Doesn't that seem like the point to you?"

A few tears rolled down her cheek, and Jennifer sniffled, reached over, and held her hand.

Andrew turned the picture over and tucked it behind his chair. He glared at Jason for a moment and then said to Jennifer, "I'm sorry this is bringing up so much pain. For both of you. The guitar means a lot to me, but I didn't know it had, you know, hooks into other people.

Maybe we should postpone this little conference, but I don't want to bag it altogether. Maybe Jason and I can..."

"No, no," said Jennifer, "that's not what I..."

"No, please," Cecelia said. "I need to know."

They listened for what seemed to be a full minute to the tick-tock of the cuckoo clock in the corner, syncopated with the ticking of Ben's little clock. It was the only sound.

"Please," said Cecelia.

Jason stared ahead. "I'm not giving up anything. Not postponing anything. I can use your help, the knowledge and experience you had with this, um, thing, but if either or both of you decide it's not worth it, I'm still sticking."

Andrew stood and said, "Okay, I guess that's settled. I can talk a little about what's in this picture." He looked at Jennifer. "One of the bands, The Who, tossed this guitar off the stage at Woodstock, and I got it. I hid it, but I lost it, and later I saw this light up in a tree, or this guy, or this guy holding my guitar all lit up."

Jennifer said, "The Who? Keith Moon, Roger Daltrey, with a reputation for trashing hotel rooms. Them?"

Andrew looked over at Jason, "You see, man. Rock lives!" Everyone else laughed, the tension broken, and Jason even smiled.

Andrew pulled the picture from behind his chair. "That thing in the tree messed with my head for years." Andrew went on, "Decades I guess, and lately I have come to realize that it, the guitar, connects me to a lot things in my past, and I want it." He looked over at Cecelia. "I don't want to hurt you, but I really want it."

Cecelia pointed to the picture and spoke mostly to Jennifer. "I saw the same thing, from a slightly different angle. I must have been standing near Andrew, I think maybe off to his side. That freakish light was just suddenly there, out of nowhere, stayed a few minutes, and was gone. So was the guy. Just gone. The memory of it used to come back, it would just flood my brain and stop my life for a little while, and all I could do was paint it. And they all came out the same, like mass produced."

Jennifer said, very softly, "That was around the time Dad got sick, I think."

"Yes, right then. Perfect timing. I started painting as sort of therapy, but pretty soon, painting the picture was more of a purge."

"A purge? What do you mean purge?"

"Okay. To be crude, it was like puking. I would see this thing in my head, the guy in the tree, and it would just get bigger and more and more clear, until it was all I could see. Sorry to be crude, but it was like eating something bad, and gradually needing to get rid of it. Painting it was like throwing up. The weird speech and the need to paint came about the same time, yes, right around when your dad first got sick. He didn't understand it, either, but you know him, he held his water. He just let it go."

After another long silence. Jennifer looked at Jason. "You weren't there, at Woodstock. You're too young. How do you figure in this?"

Still hesitant to share his story, Jason poured some more beer and started slowly. "I'm a historian, a Ph.D. candidate, and in searching for a novel thesis topic, I found several references to this phenomenon, this light, one around the time of Socrates, and another around the time of Charlemagne."

"Oh, wow," Cecelia said. "I didn't know about that."

"Well, my thesis was not accepted. In fact, it was ridiculed mercilessly." He looked like he had more to say but took another bite of hamburger.

"Really, Jason? Socrates? And Charlemagne?" He just nodded with a full mouth.

Jennifer looked steadily at Jason. "I see what you mean by not straightforward. But I still don't quite see how you two came together. Are you related or something?"

"Oh, no," they both said, quickly. "No relation. None."

"We met on the road," Andrew said.

"On the road." Cecelia said. "This is the part I don't know either."

"Well, it's a hard part for me," Jason said. "Not complicated, and I guess straightforward, just difficult to talk about."

Andrew volunteered, "Cecelia, why don't I bring over the coffee cups and um, make sure the coffee is hot." He got up and moved quickly toward the kitchen.

"Yeah," said Jason. "So, I mentioned that my research was laughed at. Two full years I worked on that thesis, and it was treated like a joke. I didn't take that well, not with my usual stoic demeanor. I mounted a campaign: letters, phone calls and finally threats. I am not in the slightest degree a violent person, but I said much that I regret. I was arrested and forced to undergo an extended psychological evaluation. Andrew was the security employee assigned to escort me to a facility in Saratoga. On the trip, we got to talking and made the connection about the guitar and the light, and we made arrangements to come up here and, well, here we are."

They were all silent as Andrew put out cups and poured coffee.

Jason's cheeks were red. "You're all thinking that I'm a little, um, that I have some kind of..."

Cecelia said, "The word that popped into my head was 'perseverance.' I don't know much about thesis reports, but I know they're make or break. You believed in something that I know is real, so, yeah, perseverance."

Jason, grateful, nodded and said nothing.

Andrew poured carefully. They drank coffee quietly for a few minutes until he said to Jennifer, "We're hoping to get a closer look tomorrow at the anniversary concert. We're all still a little shaky about the actual geography."

"Mom," said Jennifer, "what about Dad's map downstairs? Is that still there?" She had made the decision to get involved, if only marginally.

"There's a map?" said Jason.

Cecelia's eyes widened. "Oh, I forgot all about it. I don't go down there much. Let me go get it."

They heard a grunt and a snort from the love seat and Jennifer moved over quickly to check on Ben. She pulled the blanket up around him and put her hand gently on his chest until he was quiet again.

Cecelia came back upstairs with a framed map of the original Woodstock Festival, complete with stage, entrance, fencing, Porta Potties, pond, woods, medical tent, free stage, information booth, food kiosks. There was a directional compass, a scale in yards, an explanation of symbols, all set neatly inside a grid.

"This is really something," Jason said. "Your husband drew this? Was he some kind of a draftsman?"

"An engineer who was working for the festival as a carpenter. He was working on the main stage and on the speaker towers."

"This is going to really help. Can I take this out of the frame and bring it tomorrow?"

Cecelia looked over at Jennifer, who didn't look back. "No, sorry. You can copy whatever you need, but I don't want it out of the frame."

Over more coffee, Jason copied the map with as much detail as possible. "Wow, this is, um, wow."

Andrew said, "Good, we know where we're going, but I'm still pretty nervous about whether we can actually get there."

"Yeah," Cecelia said. "There's one piece of this that I think we all buried. The loop."

"If you thought this was nuts so far... "Andrew said to Jennifer.

"The, uh, loop? What is that?" Jennifer asked.

They all looked at Jason. "I cannot tell you how much it pains me to tell you this. It goes against everything, everything..."

"So, come on...what?" Jennifer asked.

"As best I can figure it, or describe it, it was some manner or version of a time loop."

"Time loop? That's nuts. That's not real."

"I know. But yes, a time loop."

"Like *Star Trek*, a time loop."

"Yes. Like in *Star Trek*, *Twilight Zone*, a thousand bad movies, on and on, *ad infinitum*."

Andrew could see that Jennifer was getting a little frustrated, so he jumped in. "We, J and I, went one night last week to Yasgur's to scope it out. Reconnoiter. We climbed the fence and walked for maybe ten minutes and then were back where we parked the car, clueless.

So, we climbed the fence and walked about ten minutes and were back where we parked the car. No recollection of coming back, not the smallest clue that something wasn't right, just back at the car and starting all over again. And again."

"Fourteen times, according to my video camera. A full eighty-minute yo-yo session," Jason said.

"Wait," Jennifer said. "You just were back? You didn't *go* back, you were just all of a sudden there?"

"Yep. Just back," Jason said. "Nope, didn't go back, just all of a sudden...back."

"No. No, no," Jennifer said.

"Sorry, but yes."

"I'm not a scientist, but that is not..."

"No, it isn't. And yet..."

"Mom, not you. You weren't there. You weren't there, please."

"No, Jen. I was here. I had nothing to do with it. I was fine."

"And you seriously want to go there tomorrow? And you want me to go there with Ben?"

"I understand, Jen, but I'm going to go."

"No, Mom. Please don't. I don't know if I believe any of this, but don't take the chance. I can't...Mom, I just got back."

This time Cecelia reached out and took her daughter's hand. "I've been to Yasgur's a couple of times, and never had a problem. I'm not sure if I believe any of this either, but Jen, think of the picture. That damn picture. I have to know. I have to help figure this out. For, you know, all of us."

Jennifer looked over at Ben on the love seat. "Not me. And not him."

Thirteen

In the morning, Jennifer again refused to go to the concert. "You're right, Jen," Cecelia said over coffee. "You shouldn't go, but I think I should. This thing has been a roller coaster in my head for too long. These visions or mirages, or whatever they are, affected you and they affected your father. For a while, when he was sick, I was so focused on that fool in the tree that I failed you, and I failed him."

"No, Mom. You never failed either of us. Never."

"I talked like an idiot, or a drunken child or I don't know what. Do you remember the fights we used to have about my speech?"

"I don't remember really fighting."

"No, because I would come out with something classic, like 'It's such a downer, man. Such a total bummer,' and you would just walk out."

"And slam the door, too," Jennifer said. "I got good at that."

"Yeah," Cecelia said, remembering sitting at their oak table and crying.

"So, I want to finish this, Jen. I want to know what happened to me." She reached over and took Jennifer's hand. "But not you, and not my grandson."

~ * ~

Andrew and Jason picked Cecelia up in the Volvo just before noon. Andrew sat in the back seat so he could stretch out his legs. He was stiff from a long walk that morning. "Good morning, team," he greeted and took a quick sip of his coffee.

"I hope that's not breakfast," Cecelia said, "or lunch."

"Well, I ate pretty well last night, you know?"

"That's not how a diet works. That's not how good nutrition works."

"A diet? So, you really are on a diet?" Jason asked.

"Not a real diet like Weight Watchers or any of that. Just trying to lose a pound or two." He said to Cecelia, "How did you know?"

"I don't know, it just made sense. You told me you've been walking, you skipped dessert last night, and you had more vegetables than you did burgers. I just notice these things. And I know you're beginning to merge your different selves."

Jason stifled a laugh. Cecelia said, "Go ahead, say something obnoxious. Get the day off to a good start."

"Merge your different selves? I just love that new-age, third eye kind of jargon. It's just so evocative and specific."

"A lot of people don't dig it. That doesn't mean it's not true. Or helpful."

"I don't see where the word 'true' can be applied. There is no way to prove it or disprove it." Cecelia just turned and grinned at him, then turned and grinned at Andrew.

"It's all very Zen," Jason continued. "The sound of one hand clapping. Very inscrutable. Very cosmic. Andrew, you're not buying any of this balloon juice, are you?"

Andrew held up his cup of coffee and looked at it lovingly. "It's funny about coffee, you know? It can be really bad, but as long as it has those two qualities, hotness and brownness, it is a superior beverage, and it has my approval."

Jason grunted. Cecelia smiled. "How did your visit home go, Jason? You seem to have come back in such a mellow mood." He looked over at her for a long second and then back at the road. That was all the friendly banter in the car on the way to the concert.

They turned onto Route 17B, and saw the crowd walking toward the entrance.

"Oh man," Andrew said, "this sort of looks familiar."

"Yeah, it's a weird vibe for me too, man," Cecelia said, and frowned.

Many of the people walking to the concert looked like they had just awakened from a decades' long coma: rainbows, peace symbols, love beads, bell bottoms, and long hair. Gray, but long. A few carried guitars; a few had children with them.

"So, your daughter is not coming?" Andrew asked.

"No, you heard her last night. She's afraid we're all gonna get that yo-yo treatment again. I can't blame her. He's only four, you know. Who knows what that could do to his head?"

"He's a fun kid, though," Andrew said. "Fun to have around."

It was a dazzling day, the kind they had hoped for at the original Woodstock. A light breeze, white clouds scraping along under blue skies, sunshine not quite warm enough to break a sweat. They parked the Volvo a little way up 17B and walked back to the entrance. Cecelia handed them the tickets. They walked past the kiosks selling T-shirts, maps, hippie wigs, beads, and soft drinks.

"Typical late twentieth century marketing strategy," Jason said. "Put all the junk for sale near the entrance, and the rubes have to pass by twice, once in and once out."

"Kinda like the checkout line at the supermarket," Cecelia said.

This entrance was back a little way from the stage but not too far from the rim of the natural bowl.

Andrew said, "Are we still here? Are we staying here? I really don't want to get bounced back to the car again. One night of that was enough."

"We seem to be firmly rooted in time, space and dimension," said Cecelia. "I think we're okay." Cecelia stopped to talk to someone she recognized near the kiosks. They waited for her, and Andrew whispered to Jason, "Why are you being such a putz? 'Very inscrutable, very cosmic, very balloon juice.' Man, she's feeding us and showing us around. She got the tickets for this, and she even came up with a map. Get off her case, Professor."

"Look, you want to drink her Kool-Aid, that's your business. I prefer to apply a little reality to my surroundings."

"Stuff your surroundings, man."

"Look, Andy, please. The truce, right? We may be finally getting close here. Let's try and hold to that truce."

"Glad to, as long as you get off her case. If you keep pushing and she bails on us, I might go, too."

"And there goes your guitar. Or Pete's guitar, or whatever. You were waffling last night, too. I'm a little worried about you."

"Just get off her case."

When she got back, they walked up a hill and had a view of the field down to the bowl and all the way to the stage. Andrew and Cecelia just stopped and looked.

"Whoa," Andrew said. "*Déjà vu* right in my face. I've been here a few dozen times, but the grass was always purple and the horizon was at an angle. Oh, and the sky was orange. Other than that, exactly the same." He sat and took his sneakers off.

"Yeah," Cecelia laughed. "I get a little jolt every time I come here, but I keep my shoes on."

Jason shook his head. "It's a pasture. Cows come here and eat grass. What's the big deal?"

"I guess you had to be there," said Andrew. Andrew and Cecelia passed a quick glance.

"So, where did you see the light?" Jason asked.

She pointed to the stand of trees to the left of the stage. "The medical tent and the free stage were just past the woods there, and the pond was around the bend of the dirt road."

"I got all muddy and skinny dipped in the pond to clean off. Oh, man, I'm just remembering that was right after I buried the guitar. Walked around in my skivvies for a while, I think."

Cecelia laughed, "Oh, that was you?"

"So, where did you see the light?" Jason asked again.

"Joan Baez played at the free stage, and I got to shake her hand." She pointed straight ahead at the stage. "That's where the original stage was, too, but probably twice as big, and it had a ramp leading back behind it for the performers."

Andrew said, "With the stage right in front of the trees, and the natural bowl shape of the meadow, it was like a concert hall. The music flowed out toward the audience."

"So, yeah, but where did you see the light? Remember the light? The guy in the tree? Can we put the groovy, far out reunion on hold for a little while and try to remember why we're here? Please?"

Andrew pointed. "I was coming out of those back woods, on the dirt path near the medical tent and the free stage," Andrew said.

"And I was coming from the medical tent, I think. There was a stone fence over there, too, but I really doubt it's there anymore, Or the free stage either."

Jason started walking. "Let's go see."

"Oh, man," Andrew said. "Yo-yo time. Wait, wait, don't you want to check out the band first?"

Cecelia laughed. "I think it's okay, Andrew. Melanie won't be on for a while."

They crossed the field and passed a concession stand and a row of telephones. Heading diagonally, northwest, they came to a chain link fence that ran all the way up and across to the stage. It was the temporary fence they had seen through the long-distance lens. They could see some of where Cecelia had pointed, but there was no medical tent, no free stage, no stone fence.

She said to Jason, "It would have been back there, in the woods to the left of the dirt path. And if Andrew saw what I saw, he must have been near there."

"How far up the road, and which side again?"

"I'm not good at judging distance, but from that corner where the fence makes a right turn, it was probably fifty yards, maybe seventy-five. Left side. Yeah, on the left."

Jason pulled the binoculars from his backpack and focused them. "Lots of trees along that perimeter. Damn, we're gonna have to get in there and look closely at them all."

They heard applause from the stage area and Andrew said, nervously, "Could that be her? Could that be Melanie?"

"Way too early, Andrew," said Cecelia. "She isn't scheduled for at least another hour, and you remember how they stuck to the schedule last time."

Jason was staring at the wooded area along the road and mumbling. "Probably not more than two or three trees in from the road, figure maybe fifty yards. We're looking at maybe four or five hundred square feet of trees, maybe a hundred trees or so. Maybe Sonny and Cher back there can think of some other landmarks that can help narrow down where to look."

"See?" Said Andrew. "He's a bulldog. He'll figure it out."

"Yeah, yeah, I'm a bulldog and a loaf of bread. What about your fallen tree? How far was that?"

"A little beyond," Andrew said. "Closer to the pond, maybe another seventy-five yards down. And then off to the right of the path."

Jason nodded and walked along the fence away from them.

"I think we've been dismissed. Let's go check out the bands."

They walked slowly down the hill toward the stage, a couple of aging hippies strolling happily through their shrine. Andrew felt totally disoriented. He was walking with a beautiful woman that he felt comfortable with, and he also felt stretched across the decades to when he was here last. Rain and mud and crowds of young bodies flashed across his mind. He checked more than once to be sure the grass wasn't purple and the sky orange.

He said, "This whole thing...this thing is like..." She patted his beefy upper arm, sending a shock wave through him.

"I know, it blows your mind. First time I came back here," she said, "it was such a rush, a flood of memories. Most people don't get to have a memory this rich, this strong. We were there, man, you and me were at Woodstock."

"Yeah," Andrew said. "I've buried a lot of that feeling over the years. For a lot of reasons."

There it is, thought Cecelia. *There's that disconnect. He's holding it together, but he's feeling like he's missing something.*

"The years can wear you down," she said. "Even the good years. But look where you are. Just go with the moment and don't get hung up. Just relax and take it all in." She said the exact thing he needed to hear.

They walked past toddlers, graybeards and a painfully skinny teen with a patch on the rear end of his jeans that informed the world that he was a "Hippy."

Andrew said, "You've been back here a few times, then. You're from this area originally?"

"No, I grew up in Baltimore."

"Oh, yeah. Ben called you 'lady from Baltimore.'"

"Yeah, my husband, my old man, used to sing that to me all the time. Sang it to Jennifer, too, and I guess she sings it to Ben."

"Yeah, Tim Hardin. There was a verse I loved. Give me a minute, I'll get it. Oh yeah, he was a thief but married her because he was her true belief. Something like that."

She moved away from him suddenly and began to sing a little, and then sob.

She covered her face with her hands and just sat. He went over and knelt next to her. "I'm sorry. Stupid of me. I didn't mean to do that, I just got caught up in the moment."

"No, not you. Just me overwhelmed again. So much lately. You two showing up, the damn painting, Jennifer, Ben, being back here again. That song. That song I love so much. Just give me a minute. I'll be okay."

He walked away, looked at the stage with his back to her for a few moments, feeling like there should be something he could do to make her feel better. He turned half toward her and called, "The music should start soon."

She was getting up and wiping the tears out of her eyes. "Yes. Country Joe is first, I think."

"I'm sorry, Cecelia," he said. "I didn't mean to...I didn't think."

"No, really not your fault. I'm totally cool now. It's just this place. He worked on the original stage, and the original speaker towers. And he helped me get home when my foot got bad."

"Oh. Sounds like a real good guy."

"Yeah, for sure. A solid dude. He died about, oh, a life and a half ago. Being here kinda hits me hard, but mostly good vibes. And that song brings so much back, you know? He made me so happy. Beyond happy, you dig?"

He thought immediately of his father. "I've never been able to deal with death, someone close dying."

She stared off for a little while and then said, "We were lucky, in a way, the three of us. We knew what he had was incurable, so we just lived. We had a couple of months to celebrate."

"Celebrate? Really?"

"Yeah. Celebrate. Me, Ben and Jennifer celebrated our life. It's all just life, man. It's all just life."

He looked closely at her. The sniffles were gone, the red eyes were gone, and she had her familiar smile. "You're a real surprise sometimes, Cecelia."

"Freaky chick," she said, and made a face. "Damn, did it again."

At the bottom of the hill, not too far from the stage, they spread out a blanket and squatted for Country Joe McDonald without a single fish. Joe was shorter than either of them remembered, and of course grayer and thicker, but still had a certain swagger, and did not neglect to do his signature "Give me an F" cheer. The audience, dutifully if not enthusiastically, spelled out the word, and pronounced it correctly all three times, satisfying their brief craving for nostalgic hedonism, and Joe could go on with his show. The cheer had become just another clichè, worn down to meaninglessness by overuse at frat parties and cheerleader reunions.

At the end of his set, Joe redeemed himself by talking sincerely about the war, the Vietnam War, and reading the names of the nine Sullivan County soldiers who had died there and descriptions of how each had been killed. The crowd was quiet, but restless. The older, fatter, grayer ones paid attention, including Andrew and Cecelia, reaching back in memory to that war, that goddamn war that seemed so right and necessary for so many, and so wrong and so senseless to all the rest. And some of the younger ones with cell phones and leased SUVs wondered for a moment what all the fuss was about.

Cecelia said, "I've seen Joe a couple of times over the years, and he always does the same show, but I love it every time."

"Wonder what happened to the Fish," Andrew said.

She looked around at all the kids and teenagers and said, "Probably spawned."

Andrew looked around him and beamed, almost laughed out loud, just realizing that he was in this place, in reality, in the here and now. He was happy just being part of the crowd listening to a couple of local bands.

"This one," he told Cecelia, "has got some chops. The lead singer has a voice and the right look, but they need a better mixer. Half the time the bass is booming over everything else, and half the time it's the opposite. I'm not George Martin, but I could help these folks."

"I'll bet you were good at it," she said.

He smiled. "Yeah, I was. Goddamn lightweight speakers."

"Ever think of moving into management? You know some people, I bet. You know talent and equipment. You probably know how the game is played."

He waited a long time before answering. "The problem is that I do know the game. It's ugly. I've seen too many people chewed up, even the smart ones. I don't want to be a chewer or a chewee. I used to think about it, almost made the leap once, but I'd rather be a poor schmuck than a rich son of a bitch."

Cecelia smiled. "My old man used to say, 'poverty is its own reward.'"

The band finished their set to a smattering of applause, and the band members came to the front of the stage, held hands, and bowed together.

"Kind of hokey," Andrew said. "This ain't Broadway."

"On the other hand," she said, "no musical instruments were harmed during the making of this concert."

~ * ~

"Your queen is the next up," Cecelia said. "But the way they're moving, it looks like another half an hour or so." He took a deep breath and let it out very slowly.

Jason had come back and was sitting behind them. "Is he still hyperventilating about that Melody chick?" He was spitting on his hands and trying to rub out a green stain from his pants.

"Melanie," Andrew snapped, "her name is Melanie. And what have you been doing, man? You're a mess."

"I've been doing what I thought we were all here to do. Remember? What you and I decided on before we came up here and met Glinda the Good Witch."

"I told you, man, get off her case."

"I've been looking for your guitar, or the tree, or some sign there ever was one. I've been leaning over things and crawling under things trying to do that. What have you been doing?"

"What do you want me to do? I told you everything I remember..."

"Which is pretty much nothing."

"...and every time, you just blow me off."

Cecelia said quietly, "Didn't I hear something about a truce?"

"Right," Jason said. "Truce, until we find the guitar or evidence of the light, or something. And you're just sitting on your fat, wrinkled ass watching an oldies concert. How is that helping? If you want to do something, do it. Walk around and see if anything triggers a memory or puts something in perspective or spins something differently. Do something. Help. Function."

Andrew glared at him and then looked toward the stage for a long moment. Finally, he just walked away. "This must be what it's like to have children," he said to Cecelia. "I'll be back in time for her set. Keep an eye on my sneakers, will you?"

Cecelia nodded and pushed the misshapen and grungy Reeboks to the corner of the blanket. "I think they'll be safe."

She sat quietly for a few moments, each very aware of the other. "That was smooth," she said.

"Got the job done."

"I'm gonna go out on a limb and say your expert reconnaissance was not productive."

"Unless one of you star witnesses recalls something useful, we may need to look over about fifty trees in an area that is posted against trespassing."

"I've been waiting years to figure this out. A little while longer won't kill me. I imagine Andrew feels the same way."

"That's very groovy of you, very mellow, but I don't have forever. I would like to get this done and finish my research."

"Oh, so you want the world and you want it now, right?"

"Was that a dig, or were you 'translating' the all-encompassing earth mother Gaia again?"

"It was a joke, Jason. Do you ever lighten up?"

"I have plans, goals, outside of this one-horse, East Podunk, splatter on the map. I'm twenty-six, and you two are like what, forty something? Fifty something?"

"Not seeing your point."

"You two had your run in the sun, and you blew it. You smoked it or you hootenanyed it, or you danced it away, and it's gone. I got things to do, people to see. Time to step aside for someone younger."

"I didn't realize that I blew anything. I have a pretty good life. I like it, anyway."

He snorted. "Well, he doesn't. He's a burnout, and you know it."

Cecelia had seen positive changes in Andrew, the sneakers aside, but didn't want to argue. Jason was even more irascible than usual. She wondered what a visit home would be like for Jason.

"I'm sorry you dislike me so much. I get along with most people."

"I get irritated when people pretend to be something they are not. When they put on airs and condescend to us common mouth-breathers."

"What? What am I pretending to be?"

"Oh, please, you know damn well. Some free-floating, new-age mystical earth mother. 'You're a loaf of bread, but you're not finished yet,' crap. 'I always knew you were coming but I didn't think there would be two of you.' And that weird hippie argot you slip into sometimes. Like you're floating between two time periods. That kind of pretending."

She was quiet for a few moments, just people watching and noticing the breeze making the slightest ripple through the branches of the trees around them. Wistfully, she had a memory of being in a park with Ben when Jennifer was a girl, and Ben was explaining to his rapt and adoring daughter the scientific reason for wind through the trees.

The sun warms the air, especially in a valley or in a hollow like this one where air can get trapped a little bit, he was telling her. *The warm air rises, and pushes the cool air down, and that is enough motion to force air to move and make a breeze.*

She remembered Jennifer, probably ten years old, just saying, *Wow, Dad.*

Some movement on stage brought her back to the present. "Okay, you make some good points. Drama. I'm, you know…a lot of drama. I'll try to dial it down when you're around."

He said nothing, just focused on the map he had drawn from Ben's model.

"This map is good. Surprisingly good for a yokel. I'm gonna go out on a limb and guess that your husband was not a stoned-out freak with rainbows all over his hash pipe."

"Hey!" she yelled, and he jumped. "Hey!" Even louder. "Don't you dare! Don't you goddamn dare! You do NOT say another word about him, do you understand? Not one goddamn word, are we clear, do you understand what I'm saying to you? Is that clear? Don't answer! Don't even speak! Nod your head if you understand. Don't even say a word."

She was glaring at him, eyes wide, cheeks red, nostrils flared, hands fisted.

"I'm…" he started to say.

"Shut up! Not a word! Just nod if you understand what I said!"

He nodded, stunned. She sat back, still glaring at him and then stood and walked away. She moved into a clear spot about fifty feet away and stood with her back to him, breathing hard.

He stayed on the blanket, thinking he should go over and say something but knowing he shouldn't.

Eventually, tears still flowing, she walked away toward where she thought Andrew might be.

~ * ~

Andrew had trudged up the hill, and noticed how many people were walking around, too. Only about half of the crowd was seated and watching the stage, and the rest were moving around for better seats or to the concession stands.

At the top of the rise, he stopped and looked carefully around. His legs were starting to hurt, and he was out of breath already, and he knew it was not that much of a hill. He walked along the fence line, looking up, humming, "San Francisco (Be Sure to Wear Some Flowers in Your Hair)," and trying to remember some of the words. He was thinking he would like to work out the chords on a guitar, and then remembered he didn't have a guitar anymore. Some mook with a mullet landed on it during a bar fight on Long Island. Was that Long Island? How long ago was that?

He walked along the fence line until he came to where the fence made a ninety-degree right turn and headed back toward the stage. He could just see the dirt path that led to the pond and where the medical tent and free stage had been.

"Trees, man. What do I know about trees? They all look alike to me. Kinda dark brown, spread out at the top, roots kinda spread out at the bottom. One looks like another, like beer bottles coming through on an assembly line."

At the post where the fence turned, he stopped and leaned on the top rail to stare at the trees. Most of them, he noticed, went straight up and then split off in a couple of directions, and then the splits split off. But one or two of them split lower down.

"Sorry, sir, you can't lean on the fence."

"I'm sorry, what?" He looked over at a guard standing a few yards away. Brown pants, brown shirt, a name tag that identified him as Thomas.

"You can't lean on the fence that way. The fence is only temporary and isn't made to take a lot of weight."

"Man, are you really telling me that I can't lean on a fence? Is that seriously what you're trying to tell me?" In a second he had changed keys from nostalgic, peaceful concert goer into angry protest mode.

"It's a festival policy, sir," Thomas said calmly. "No one is permitted to lean on or push on the fences."

"Not permitted? Oh, it's a permission thing. They're usually my favorite. They usually paint a clear picture of the lockstep, big brother, bullshit corporate holding cell they think we all live in. Screw your permission, brother."

Thomas looked confused. "Sorry, sir, I don't really know what you mean. It's just one of the rules for safety they asked us to be conscious of."

"Right. Rules of safety. Look, Thomas, sometimes in life..." He looked into Thomas' broad, innocent face, one that had never yet needed a razor blade, and shrank. A fiery rant on protests and passive resistance and a well-placed "Hell, no, we won't go," just weren't gonna make any difference here. He grunted and walked away.

As he walked, he noticed someone well behind Thomas looking over at him. He was older, wore a suit without a tie, penny-loafers, and a Cleveland Indians' cap. There was something familiar about him, something around his eyes, and in the way he stood. He noticed Andrew looking over at him, turned sharply and walked away.

Andrew walked back to where Thomas was standing. "Apologies, Thomas, I kind of got lost in the moment there. You know, sixties, protests, all that stuff. Just got carried away. I'm sorry."

"It's okay, sir, I understand. It's a great day for a concert."

"Can I ask you something? That guy with the brown suit over there. He looks familiar to me, but I can't place him. Do you know who he is?"

Thomas turned around and looked but shook his head. "I'm sorry, I don't. I'm not from around here, but I do know a lot of the Sullivan County government officials came here to observe and make sure everything was, you know, up to code. I think that's why there are so many of us security guards around."

"Yeah, thanks, man. That makes sense. I'll stay off the fence, promise."

He went back to where the fence made that sharp turn and, standing a few feet away and not leaning on the fence, thought about trees. He craned his neck, side-stepped a few feet, tugged hard at his memories, looked at one particular tree in the middle of the wood, and smiled broadly. "I think maybe I just earned my daily bread."

He was still smiling when Cecelia came up behind him. She had traces of tears down her cheeks, and a look on her face like she had just swallowed a bug.

"Oh," he said. "Whatever it was, whatever he said, it was crap and we both know it. I am one snotty remark from bailing on this venture, and I told him that already. I want that guitar, but dealing with his shit is becoming just not worth it."

She reached out and squeezed his hand for a moment. "Thank you, Andrew, you are a friend. I dealt with it, and I'm pretty sure it won't happen again. But I'm where you are. I'm one insult from walking away from this. I want to know what it's all about, but it's getting to the point..." She hesitated a moment and then sang, "...where I'm no fun anymore."

"Oh, Crosby, Stills and Nash! Cool!" Andrew said.

"I was asleep over there," she pointed behind them, "and someone woke me up just as Stephen Stills was saying how he was scared shitless."

He laughed, reached, took her hand in both of his without a word, and just nodded. They stood silently, looking over each other's shoulders for a long moment, until he dropped her hand. "Don't bail on this yet. I think I may have found a little something that will file off Jason's edges for a little while. Look at that stand of trees over there."

"You spotted something?"

"Actually, yeah, believe it or not. Something, maybe. Your painting is pretty much from the knees up, but in my head our light, or light guy, whatever, was kind of standing in the crotch of a tree, I think not too far up. There aren't too many of those around near the path. In fact, I don't see any. But look at that one over there." He pointed and she followed his arm to a pine tree about fifteen feet past the fence, and a little more from the road that curled around toward the pond and near where the medical tent would have been.

"So, I would have been standing roughly there," she said, pointing to an area on the far side of the path and a little past the tree.

"Sounds right. And I think maybe I was behind you, so you were just a little bit forward on the road. I think I was down near the pond, and that's where I buried Pete's ax."

"Yeah, because I walked around the tree a little bit to get a better look at whatever, and then backed off."

"Yeah, yeah, this is good."

"It's great! That could be the exact tree. This is big, eagle eye!"

A guitar chord sounded from the stage that sounded like it was something more than just warming up. A voice over the PA said, "Ladies and gentlemen..."

"That's her, that's gotta be her," Andrew said.

"Go. Go, I'll catch up. Get as close as you can, and I promise I'll find you. Go."

His first thought was, *please let this be real. Please don't let this be another flashback. Please...'*

"Please welcome, Melanie Safka!" Andrew ran, weaving between the blankets as fast as he could manage barefoot. When he was close enough to the stage to clearly see the faces, he looked for her. There were musicians and backup singers on the stage, but none of them was the twenty-year-old blonde of his memory. The backup singers off stage right were too young, and the acoustic guitar player center stage was too heavy and not blond enough. But she started to sing. The overweight brunette with gray streaks opened her mouth and started to sing "Candles in the Rain." He found an empty spot to sit and listen, thinking all the time that this was some kind of a setup, that Melanie would come strolling out any second.

Cecelia came up and sat next to him. "Who is that singing?" He said to her. "That's not Melanie."

Cecelia said, "Close your eyes for a minute, Andrew. Don't look. Just sit and listen for a minute. Close your eyes and listen to her voice."

He concentrated on just the sound, and in a minute, he knew it was true. This was really her, here and now. The thin, twenty-year old, long-haired angel was gone, but the woman with the voice was here. "Yes," he said. "Yes, that's Melanie."

He opened his eyes and looked at her, and then looked around slowly. The grass was not purple, the sky was not orange, the horizon held steady at a hundred and eighty degrees. He accepted that this was not a flashback...this was her.

He grabbed Cecelia's arm. "She's so different, but she's the same. Listen to that voice."

He sat, mesmerized, unmoving, through her set, with Cecelia next to him humming along and bobbing her head. Melanie did "The Bicycle Song," and "Beautiful People" and a version of "Purple Haze" and a couple of songs that neither of them knew. Her voice was as strong and mellow and distinctive as ever. For half an hour, the voice enveloped him in a time loop from thirty years ago. She spoke for a few minutes about being so young and inexperienced and being asked to sing in the rain before a crowd of a few hundred thousand people. A few giggles, a little applause. Andrew called out, "Do 'Peace Will Come." But she didn't. He couldn't understand it, but she didn't. *Maybe,* he thought, *she didn't believe it anymore.* Maybe he didn't either.

After she left the stage, they walked back to where Jason sat. Cecelia hugged Andrew and said, "I'm going to take off. I'll call Jen for a ride, and maybe take Ben out for ice cream or something. You can show him what you found, what we think. I'll see you tomorrow. I had a great day, hope you did, too." She leaned in and kissed Andrew on the cheek. Jason didn't look up.

Andrew sat and put his sneakers on, folded up the blanket and said, "C'mon, I got something to show you."

Jason stood up, stiffly, "I don't even know what I said that pissed her off."

Andrew said, "Shut up," and walked away.

Fourteen

Jason, although excited about what Andrew had seen among the trees, realized it would be wise to wait a few days before going back to the Pickle, or even talking about their quest. This was personal growth for him; unrecognized, but genuine.

He stayed in the motel, walked some with Andrew, drove by Yasgur's, read every newspaper he could find and most of the magazines he thought he could agree with.

On the third day, late in the afternoon, he walked into the Pickle.

Cecelia was in the far corner of the shop, wiping down some figurines. She did not turn around.

"Hi," he said. She turned and looked at him but said nothing.

"I was hoping we could talk."

She walked to the kitchen table and sat, pushed a chair in his direction. "Be very careful," she said in a low voice.

He sat and was very quiet for a full minute. He said, "Cecelia, I am not only sorry for what I said, I am ashamed. I am ashamed that I hurt you as badly as it seems I did. I am often sarcastic, it's a flaw, but the sarcasm usually only cuts so deep. What I said to you cut a lot deeper than I meant it to. Which is not an excuse, I know. I have no excuse. But if you can forgive my callous stupidity, maybe we can start over. That's my hope. If not, just say so, or even say nothing, and I will just leave. No whining, no argument. I'll just leave, do what I can do here without the two of you, and share with you anything I learn."

She thought he was finished, but he took a deep breath and added, "It will not happen again."

She was very still, not looking at him. He was just about to leave when she stood up and walked over to him. She put both hands on his shoulders and kissed him on the forehead. "Okay, it's over. We're good. Let's just move on, Jason."

"Good, good," he said.

She sat again and looked carefully at him. "Did Andrew tell you about what he saw in the trees?"

"Yes, yes. That's great news. And good thinking by him. There may be more trees with that split in it, but maybe not nearby. That narrows the field considerably. Great news."

"It still remains to get near it."

"Yes. And that 'tis a puzzlement'."

"Ah, 'tis a puzzlement'. *The King and I*. Always loved that movie."

"Yeah, me too. Yul Brynner."

"I liked the Rex Harrison version."

Another few minutes of awkward silence and Jason asked, "So is Andrew around somewhere?"

"He went shopping with Jennifer and Ben. Ben insisted."

"Andrew talks about Ben a lot, you know, back in the hotel room. Doesn't say much about Jennifer, though."

"Huh." Cecelia had noticed that Andrew seemed a little distracted when Jennifer was around. And that Jennifer never mentioned him but seemed to look at him for just a second or so too long.

She stood and went back to wiping down the figurines. He sat, unsure of what to do next. After a few minutes she said, "I could use your help with something."

"Uhm, sure. Vacuuming? The dishes? Not my specialty, but I can manage."

"No," she laughed. "Nothing like that. I need your, I guess it's your ears. I need to talk to someone about something, and you are the most likely candidate."

"I am? Well, I will if you think so, but you know I'm not the most understanding guy in town. Would you be better off with Jennifer? Or even Andrew?"

"No, I couldn't get through it with Jen, and she knows most of it anyway. Just not the punch line. And not Andrew either...he's too sympathetic, if that makes sense. I need neutral, I need distant, and that's you. And it's related to the meltdown I had the other day. You should understand what was fueling all of that."

He nodded, wide-eyed. "To be honest, you're scaring me a little. But, yeah, I'm glad to listen or do whatever helps."

"But we can't do it here. Not in the Pickle. Too many ghosts."

"Ghosts."

She laughed again. "Oh, don't worry, I don't mean ghost ghosts. Not Stephen King, poltergeist kind of ghosts. Just memories. Strong, sometimes wonderful memories."

"Oh, well, I have an idea. Shoot it down if you hate it, but why don't I take you to dinner? Just you and me. I wanted to do that anyway. I'll find a place that's ghost free, and we can dress up and go soup to nuts."

"Huh," she said. "That's...huh."

He shrugged. "How 'bout it?"

"Fuckin' A," she said, and slapped her leg.

~ * ~

He picked her up in the Volvo the next night about five. Jennifer and Andrew were helping Ben with a puzzle when Cecelia came down wearing heels, white slacks, a red blouse with a lace jacket over it, and pearls. Jason had on a tie and a blue blazer.

Ben said, "Grandma, you smell really fancy."

Jennifer said, "Mom, wow, it's been a long time..."

Andrew said, "Cecelia, um..."

Cecelia said, "Yeah, thanks. We won't be late. Make sure you lock the door, turn the lights off."

It was a long drive from Liberty to Kingston, both realized how unexpected and uncomfortable this could be, but neither felt like they needed to create conversation. The anger in Cecelia was gone, and the remorse in Jason had been replaced by uncertainty. He was really not sure what to expect this evening.

Traveling east and southeast, the setting sun was behind them, and the rolling farmland was soft and orange and sleepy. About halfway to Kingston, Cecelia said, "I hope you don't feel like you had to do this, but even if you do, I'm really enjoying it."

"Just such a beautiful evening," Jason said. "I guess you have to get away from the town to really appreciate it."

Mildred's Restaurant was candlelit, spacious, high ceilinged and quiet. They sat at a table for four and spread themselves out. She had the crab cakes, he had the flounder, and they ordered a carafe of wine. She was a little on edge, and Jason still had no idea what to expect.

"It's a story in two parts," she began. "The first part is easy to talk about, the second part, the one I need to talk about, is not. But that is the part I need to say out loud because I have been silent about it for too long. So, history. Background.

"By the end of the Woodstock festival, I was a total mess. Alone, limping badly, and not really sure how to get home. He drove up in his truck, and just, um, took me over. Cleaned up my foot, gave me a place to eat and sleep, gave me bus fare and drove me to the station here in Kingston. He was Indiana Jones, but maybe a little better looking."

She dug through her wallet and found a picture; he was a big, rangy man with a crew cut over a strong, tanned face, smiling and gap toothed, a mustache drooping over his upper lip. On the back of the photo it said, "Ben in his prime, '75."

"Men don't ever appreciate pictures of other men, I know, but, from a female perspective, he was just something to see.

"But once he put me on that bus for Baltimore, I thought that was it. It's like a six-hour drive from Liberty to Baltimore, but a few weeks later, my God, there he was at my door. He just came, didn't tell me he was coming. We started going out. For a couple of months, he made that trip every weekend. My dad liked him, my friends couldn't figure him out, and I was just bowled over in love. He didn't even kiss me until the third date. We got married that February and moved to Liberty. We lived in his apartment over his uncle's hardware store, the one next to where the Pickle is now. I worked a double shift, he worked all the jobs he could, and with help from his parents and my dad, we bought the Pickle. Up until then, it had been the Liberty Wine and Spirits Shoppe, and I remember sitting in the middle of the floor crying because it was so empty. One great big room, whitewashed walls, and so empty it echoed. He painted murals on the walls. He built all the shelves and display cases, converted the upstairs into a two-bedroom suite. All the stuff you see there now, we bought almost nothing…he built everything. And somehow found time and energy to get me pregnant."

The waitress brought a carafe of wine, and Cecelia drank down half a glass. Jason had a sip.

She said, "I'm not saying any of this to make you feel bad, to punish you. Not even a little. This is for me. This is therapy, I guess. All of this has been rattling around in my head for a couple of years and, you know, overloading my warp engines. This is the first time in years I've done a, um…not sure what to call it."

"A data dump."

She laughed. "Yeah, data dump. That's perfect. I knew you would know."

They both ate quietly for a few minutes, and then her eyes lost focus on the present. She drank more wine, poured more, and began again.

"I've heard other mothers say kids can be tough on a marriage, but not Jennifer. It wasn't even an addition, more like a multiplication. Everything among the three of us seemed deeper, you know, realer. Is 'realer' even a word?"

"Not generally, but I think in this case it is, yeah."

She focused on her meal again, baked potato, string beans, salad. "Would you pour me a little more wine, please?"

"Sure, but are you keeping track at all? As far as I've seen, you don't usually drink, and this is already a lot for someone not used to it."

"I know, I know," she said. "But I have a lot of shit to get through. I really have a lot of shit to get through. I'll try to slow down, though.

"Okay, where was I...yeah, the connection between Ben and Jennifer was, from the start, something special. I know you scoff at this stuff, but they had this, like, joined at the hip, finish each other's sentences kind of relationship. She knew when he finished a job and would be home early, she would set a place at dinner for him. He knew when she aced a test at school and was ready with a hug or a ribbon or something. That kind of stuff. I loved them both so much, but at times I was actually jealous. Some mother, huh?"

More wine and a few bites while she struggled to hold in the tears. She stopped and looked over his shoulder for a moment. "I'm gonna visit the ladies' room. The hard part is coming up next. Don't let them take my plate, I want to finish this. And can you ask for some more, what is it, Chablis? Maybe just another glass."

A waitress came by and asked if the lady was all right. "She's just had a couple of rough days, but she'll be fine, I'm sure. She did ask that you leave her plate because she wants to finish it, and can we have another glass of Chablis and more water, please?

She was gone for about fifteen minutes and Jason was just about to send a waitress into the ladies' room to look for her when she returned.

"Sorry," she said.

"It's fine. We have all night; the restaurant doesn't need the table. We can walk or sit in the car and talk, whatever you need. It's fine."

"Thanks. This is harder than I thought. No, actually it's just as hard as I thought. But here we are rounding third and heading for home. Or on the final straightaway or coming down to the wire. And dodging it for all I'm worth." She said the word as "doshing."

He shook his head. "I understand you need to do this, but you have options. You can wait and finish tomorrow, or next week...or you can write it down and mail it to me, or someone, or bury it. I just hate to see you beat yourself up like this."

She thought about it for a minute, picking at her crab cakes, and then pushed her plate away. "No. Now, Jason. And can we do coffee? Decaf, please?" She drank some more of the wine.

He gestured, and the waitress brought coffee. Cecelia looked at her and said, "Sank you."

"At the end of Jen's first semester of college, Ben began feeling sick and was diagnosed with a variation of Wilson's Disease. That was the first diagnosis and there were two or three others. I don't think they ever really knew, but we just called it the Green Ripper. You'd think it would have a fancier name, or something in Latin or Greek, but that's what it was. They told us he had about six months, and it turned out to be only about four." She drank more of the last glass of wine and started rearranging things on the table: spoons, the coffee cups, the creamer, the napkins.

"Jen finished her semester but never went back. She came home and helped me with Ben. We nursed him as much and for as long as we could, as well as we could, at home. Changed him, washed him, shaved him, repositioned him in his bed, fed him, read to him, pretended with him that everything was going to be okay. Jen was so good, so, so good. I would break down and she would pick me up. She would break down and I would pick her up. We never let him see. We got through almost four months of that.

"It was around then that I began painting the image of the fool in the tree. I guess it was stress that brought it on, but that's when I started seeing that image, over and over. And also when I started talking, you know, that way. That really got under Jen's skin, like it does you.

"Toward the end, he asked me to let him go, and I could not. I could not do that. But his pain could barely be managed anymore, and he kept asking me. 'It's ruining all three of us,' he would whisper, because a whisper was about all he could manage. We spoke to the doctor, Jennifer and I together. She was angry that we would even consider ending his life. For weeks, I could not do it. Jen and I told each other that things would change, that he was strong and would rally. I didn't have the strength. He had always, always, always done what I needed, since he treated my foot that afternoon at Yasgur's, but I failed him for weeks. And I watched a strong, energetic man shrink, until I finally made the decision. I don't know what changed my mind, what flipped the switch, but I finally made the right choice. And Jennifer... Jennifer...

"We took him off all medicine, all monitors, all those tubes and hoses, and in six days, he was gone. I sat with him for those six days, just talking about our life, singing to him, showing him family pictures. Jennifer tried to stay, but she couldn't. Six days. He was gone in six days.

"She was wild, irrational, and she blamed me. We screamed at each other for weeks, and then she was gone. A note on the kitchen table. 'Mom, I can't. I just can't.' Six days, and then six words. Never another word from her. Never a postcard or a picture of her son, until the other night."

Jason reached for her hand, and she pulled it away. She poured out the last of the wine and drank it quickly, and then sat quietly, looking at her glass. "That was six years ago. Six ungodly years."

She sat so quietly he was sure she was finished. He got the check, and they left. She said, "I'm going to hold on to your arm on the way out."

Neither spoke on the drive back. She looked out the window at things he could not see. He helped her out of the car and took the key from her to open the front door at the Pickle.

She said, "That was a very good dinner, Jason, thank you." Without thinking, he reached out and hugged her close to him, expecting her to pull away. But she didn't. She held him tightly, arms around his shoulders, face to his shoulder, breath on his neck.

After a full minute, she pulled away and went up the stairs to the bedroom suite.

He double checked that the door was locked when he left.

~ * ~

The next morning, Jason was up early at the small desk in his hotel room, writing on a legal pad. The words were not coming easily. They started off, "Mrs. Koch, I know I am the very last person on earth you want to hear from, but please, if you will just read the next few lines, I think you will be gratified to read the rest."

Andrew woke, always an extended process, and took a shower. Rubbing a towel on his head, he asked, "Anything on the agenda for today? I know we're kinda stumped by that yo-yo thing, but any ideas?"

"I'm off on a tangent today, Andy. I need to go up to Saratoga and see Hotchkiss the shrink."

"Thought your next meeting with him wasn't for a few weeks."

"Yeah, this is kind of impromptu. Unscheduled. Mostly for my peace of mind."

"I guess she did a number on you last night at dinner."

"A number? I guess, in a way."

"We figured she read you the complete text of the riot act with full orchestration."

"Yeah, well, in a way, yeah. Do you want a ride to the Pickle?"

"Yeah, thanks. Look, I got something. An idea, but it is the longest of long shots. I need to get something from home that might help, but I'm talking long shot." Jason just nodded.

He dropped Andrew off in front of the Pickle and had already decided not to go in.

A long drive on country roads on a cloudy day was just ideal for planning what he would say to Hotchkiss. It was easy, though. No embellishment, no rhetoric, no chess strategy. Just lay it all out.

Route 52 bends northeast onto NY 28 and then to the Northway at Kingston. Coffee and a sugar-coated donut at a rest stop, and then a straight run past Albany into Saratoga and a deep breath in the parking lot of Halcyon.

"No, I don't have an appointment," he told the guard, "but I'm a patient of Dr. Hotchkiss, or Mister Hotchkiss, and I'm hoping I can just talk to him for five minutes." He wondered if a tip would help or get him thrown out.

He found a bench, and Hotchkiss poked his head out the door about a half hour later. "This is unusual, Jason. People aren't usually in a hurry to see me."

In the office, Jason handed him the two letters he had written that morning, one addressed to Mrs. Koch, and one addressed to Doctor Braithwaite. Hotchkiss read them both carefully, twice. "This is the kind of honesty and candor you and I were fencing about a few weeks ago."

"Yes," Jason said.

"I assume there is a back story to why you wrote this, and why now."

"Yes. A window into how the other half lives. I don't want to tell you the whole story, but while staring at someone's unfinished crab cakes, I realized I haven't experienced as much of life as some others. I don't know very much. I have so much to learn."

"Crab cakes often have that effect on people." Hotchkiss smiled. There was nothing stuck in his teeth.

"Can you get those letters to Mrs. Koch and Dr. Braithwaite? I know I can't. Sorry they are handwritten on a legal pad. I don't have access to a printer right now."

"I will explain the situation to the university attorney, and, yes, I can see that they get them."

"Thanks for seeing me on short notice."

"We have a scheduled appointment," he checked his calendar, "on Tuesday the eighteenth. I think in light of these letters, we may be able to make that our final meeting."

~ * ~

In the Pickle, early that same afternoon, Ben was coloring at the kitchen table, working hard at staying inside the lines and having moderate success. Jennifer was reading the paper, and Andrew was removing an air conditioner.

Cecelia came downstairs, a little shaky, a little pale, brushing out her braid.

"Hi, Grandma," Ben called, without looking up.

"Good morning, honey."

Jennifer said nothing, Andrew said nothing. Cecelia poured herself coffee and sat at the table. "You're not interested in my dinner last night?" she said.

"Well, yes, but we don't want to be nosy."

She laughed. "Sure you do, and I'm willing to share. But I can't tell you the best part." She nodded over at Ben. "Little pitchers have big ears."

Jennifer said, "Hey, Ben bear, would you go upstairs and get my sweater, please? The blue one, I think it's on the bed. Thank you." Ben stood without hesitation and walked upstairs.

"Okay, you should know that last night was not about Jason. It was about me. I had, well, we had settled our differences the day before, but I needed to talk to him."

Andrew said, "You settled your differences, but you still needed to have a talk with him?"

"Yes, not so much with him, as talk at him. I have been holding some things in for good while, and I needed to vent." She looked over at Jennifer and Jennifer avoided her gaze. "Jason was very much the neutral audience I needed, and he was a good sport about it."

Andrew asked, "But you straightened his ass out?"

"As much as his ass could be straightened, I did that back at Yasgur's. But the real breaking news from last night is that I got drunk. Hammered. Knocked off a whole carafe of wine and needed help to get out of the restaurant. It was not a fun night, but that part of the evening was just glorious, and I have a glorious headache to prove it."

Ben came back downstairs with his mother's sweater, and Cecelia beamed at him. A few customers came in. Leaf peepers were plentiful this time of year, so fall colors and anything with the name "pumpkin" in it was popular.

Jennifer took Ben upstairs for his nap and came back down to help with the customers.

An older woman came in with another woman and a little girl. She said to Cecelia, "We were here several weeks ago, and you were kind enough to give my granddaughter a stuffed animal. She still loves it."

"Oh, I remember. How nice," Cecelia said. "Thank you for coming back."

"You keep that wonderful ambiance in here. It's really nice."

Jennifer was waiting for a "groovy" comment or, "far out," but Cecelia just said, "Yes, we're really proud of it."

"Last time it was okay to let my granddaughter walk around in here. You said it was 'cool'."

Both Jennifer and Andrew cocked an ear waiting for an "I'm hip" or "you can just hang loose," but she just said, "Sure. We have a four-year-old living here, so we're very careful."

When they were leaving, the woman said, "Peace and love, sister. I thought that was so funny."

Cecelia responded quickly with the peace sign and said, "Power to the people."

When she turned around, both Andrew and Jennifer were looking at her. "I said that on purpose," she laughed. "I think there may be another benefit from venting." Cecelia smiled. "Or maybe from drinking a full bottle of wine. Jen, say something. Say, 'this is good.'"

Jennifer said, "This is good."

Cecelia nodded and said, "Yes, it really is. It's kind of wonderful. Now Andrew, you say, 'Do you know what I mean?' Say that."

Andrew looked confused, but he said, "Do you know what I mean?"

"Yes, Andrew, I understand the full import of your comment."

"What? What are we doing here?" Jennifer asked.

Cecelia smiled, and teared up a little. "When you said 'good,' I didn't say 'groovy.' When you said, "know what I mean," I didn't say, 'I dig it.'"

"You didn't. You didn't! That's great! What happened?"

"It's just gone. Just gone, since last night. I've been struggling with it since I painted those damn pictures, and now it's gone. Just gone."

"I will confess," Jennifer said, "I used to think you talked that way just to honk me off, embarrass me in front of my friends. But you're sure it's really gone? What the hell was it?"

"I tried so hard not to embarrass you, but I was embarrassed, too, about the speech. I think I finally figured out it wasn't translating in any real sense; it was more like channeling someone else's speech."

"Channeling? Really? Like a medium, like a spirit thing? Someone talking through you? That kind of channeling?" Cecelia stood and walked slowly around the room. Jennifer just watched, a little afraid.

She sat again, and grasped her daughter's arm, looked her in the eye. "Forgive me, honey, I really don't want to throw any more crazy crap at you. I think I was channeling myself from thirty years ago."

"That's... that's..."

"I know, Jen, I know. It's nuts."

"Yeah, it is that, but it kinda makes sense, as much as any of this yo-yo stuff makes sense. It's also kinda like *déjà vu*. It's like that time loop thing they've been experiencing."

Andrew said, "Channeling herself from the sixties? A thirty-year *déjà vu* time loop thing? Is that even possible?"

"No," Jennifer said. "None of this stuff is possible, but it keeps happening."

"Wow. That is really far out," Cecelia said.

"Mom..."

"Oh, it's okay. I said that on purpose. Because it really is. It's crazy far out."

Andrew, perhaps under the influence of his central guy, figured out that they could use some time together. "I'm gonna go buy a paper, or some gum or something," he said, and left them alone.

Jennifer said, "So, Mom, you wanted to vent to Jason? Rather than, maybe, me?"

"Yes. I decided it shouldn't be you. I needed neutral, not family. Not comfort. It has not been an easy couple of days, and last night was a total bummer. I said 'total bummer' on purpose, too. What it's been is just a stone bitch."

"You haven't been yourself, we all noticed."

"Since that festival at Yasgur's, I have been thinking a lot about your dad, my Ben. And about you and your Ben. And it was breaking me down. Jason was an opportunity for a, um, data dump. We, well I, talked a lot about Dad, and some about you. And the wine helped."

Jennifer said, "Mom. Mom, I apologize. I know I'm late getting around to this, I know. I know. We have so much to talk about. I've avoided it like a coward, but I have loved being with you so much and seeing you with Ben. I was afraid. I was afraid to break the spell. But I want to. I want to go face to face with you about everything."

"You don't need to, really. Having you here, Ben here, is, I don't have words. You don't need to do anything for me."

"Well, then for me. And for Dad, maybe. I need to get some things, you know, clear with you. Clear. For my sake and his."

"Gonna take a whole box of tissues."

"At least one. And I also need to tell you about Cole."

"Cole?"

"That's my husband. See, you don't even know that. We really need some time, Mom. And tissues. Maybe some ice cream. Tonight, after Ben is asleep. Pjs, ice cream and tissues. Tonight."

Cecelia could only manage a deep sigh.

~ * ~

They came prepared with tissues, as promised, and as needed. The ice cream would be available later. They met in Cecelia's bedroom, part of the two-bedroom suite Ben had remodeled upstairs years ago at the Pickle. Four-year-old Ben was tucked in safely in the pink bedroom across the hall and breathing peacefully.

Cecelia sat on the edge of the bed, and Jennifer pulled up a chair, leaned across and held her mother's hand. They both had a hard time finding words, and some difficulty swallowing. Before a word was spoken, each had tears in her eyes.

Cecelia was able to speak first. "What's important to know here, I think, is that I feel so blessed, so overwhelmed, to have you back. And your son, my grandson. I can still hardly say those words, Jen."

They were both quiet for a few moments. *This is not what it was all about,* thought Jennifer. *This was not what we need to talk about.*

Jennifer said, through tears, "I know how much I hurt you. What a total, bratty bitch I was. At the worst moment of your life, the absolute low point, I abandoned you. I was weak, I couldn't take it, and I ran."

"Jen, honey." Tears flowed freely now, down both cheeks. Cecelia moved the tissue box between them.

"I don't think that's deniable, Mom. I was miserable, and you must have hated me."

"No, don't ever think that. Not for a minute. Not for, what are those things, a nano-second. Never. I didn't understand at first, but then I did. Your note, the one that said, 'I can't.' I understood when I read that."

"But you could, Mom. You did. I couldn't, but you could."

"He wanted it, Jen. I'm not sure you ever knew that. I never talked to you about that, but he wanted it to end. He couldn't bear to be so weak."

"I know. I knew. No one had to tell me."

"I told him no. I wanted to hold out, but in the end I couldn't. He was right, it had to end."

"I know. I know. I didn't know then, because I didn't want to know, but I figured it out later, after I ran. But by then I was so ashamed."

They had been holding hands, but Cecelia grabbed Jennifer by the forearm, just below the elbow. Jennifer gripped her mother in the same spot, and they were locked, face to face.

"Where did you go? What happened to you?"

"I went to Harrisburg. You may remember Ginny Naismith. I kept in touch with her after high school, and she helped me get a job as a clerk-typist in a law office. That's where I met Cole."

"Cole. I'm embarrassed I didn't even know his name. And you are Mrs. Cole what?"

Jennifer laughed. "Yes, we got married. Mrs. Cole Ainsley, pleased to meet you. And so in love, Mom. So in love for about six months. Stupid, naive Nellie here. I believed all men were like Dad. Kind and honest and, well, loving. And he was all that, for about six months. Oh, give him the benefit of the doubt and say eight. Which is when I got pregnant."

"That was a problem?"

"That, and his ambition. He got a position—I was told to say 'position' and not 'job'—with a lobbying firm in D.C. They were representing the butane industry..."

"Butane, like what they put in those little cigarette lighters?"

"Yeah, apparently a big industry in Pennsy and very competitive. Lots of money involved, but very little time for a wife and child. He wasn't ever mean or abusive, just absent. Even when he was in the same room. Even when he was sitting with Ben. Totally, at like the far edge of the solar system, a void. And he surrounded himself with clones."

"So you left him."

"I would have stayed, would have just endured for the sake of Ben, but there was an incident..."

"Oh, God, with Ben?

"One of the chief clones, a guy named Gary, who is made, I think, entirely of plastic, tripped on some toys Ben had scattered around the waiting room one day while I was arguing with his father. This, um, android swatted Ben on the top of his head. Just a glancing blow, no damage, but, you know, Jesus, he's only four. Four!"

They were both crying now, full blown sobbing, gasping for breath, tears and runny noses. But each held on tightly to the other's arm. Each kept eye contact with the other's face.

"I packed and went to Cheryl's. Cheryl from school, you remember. We stayed there a few weeks, while I tried to decide whether I should come home or not."

"I don't like the sound of that, Jen."

"What? You always liked Cheryl."

"I mean that it took you weeks to decide to come home. But you did. You did come home, so shut up, Cecelia."

"I tried to write to you, more than once, but words never seemed to be enough. Cheryl finally convinced me to just 'prodigal daughter.' Just show up and see what happens. I was so scared, Mom, coming through that door. I was afraid you'd changed the lock, I was afraid maybe you moved, and then there you were, standing there, and I knew. I should have known, but I was so scared."

Jennifer reached around and held her mother tightly for a moment. For that moment, she got the little girl feeling again, safe in her mother arms. But in another moment, or generation of moments, she heard her son make a snorting noise in his sleep, and she was an adult again. The soft noise from the other room told them Ben was awake. Jennifer, worrying about his reaction to waking in a strange room, moved quickly to his bed. Cecelia folder her arms and stared at the carpet.

It took a few minutes for Jennifer to quiet Ben, and then she sat on the edge of his bed, streaming tears, looking through the pink wall at her mother who was sitting on the edge of her bed, streaming tears, looking through the wall at her.

When she was calm and saw that Ben was quiet, she went across the hall, sat across from her mother again, and held her by the forearm as before, right arm to left arm. Someone had told Jennifer, years ago, that this posture came from the Indians, or maybe it was India, and that it guaranteed sincerity, and erased all trace of guilt and remorse. Something about the blood vessels running up the arm and into the heart of each person that assured honesty. Neither Jennifer nor Cecelia remembered that folklore or cared about it. Each was content with the physical connection, the long delayed emotional connection, and the conviction that there was more to come.

"Almost ice cream time, my nearly perfect mother," Jennifer said.

"Good. I think I am dehydrated, my beautiful daughter, mother of my charming grandson. I don't think I can cry anymore."

Jennifer held tight to her arm and looked down at the carpet. "I do have another question, though, Mom. Can we paint that room blue?"

Fifteen

Jason avoided the Pickle the next few days, not certain if he knew any words that he could utter to Cecelia.

Jennifer smiled a lot, and hugged her mother about once per hour, certain that she had tiptoed successfully through the mine field. She began making plans to visit Liberty Elementary School and to find a good pediatrician.

Cecelia spent a lot of her day playing with Ben, coloring with him, doing puzzles with him, reading to him, certain she could make up for lost time.

Andrew called home and made a request, uncertain whether the person he asked had forgiven him enough to do the simple thing he needed. And he thought about faces.

Four days later, a package was delivered to the Pickle addressed to A. Barnett from A. Barnett Colavito, Andrew's younger sister.

"She's the one still talking to me," Andrew said as he lifted the box to the kitchen table. He had a small pen knife on his keychain next to the silver guitar tuning key he had kept for so many years. He sliced the top and pulled open the box. Under the balled up newspaper were four Ilion Eagle yearbooks, from 1965 through 1968 with sky blue covers with a large picture of a swooping eagle. He went to the third book, 1967, and thumbed through the photographs of the students.

Cecelia came downstairs holding Ben's hand at almost the same moment that Jason came in and stood tentatively just inside the door.

He smiled at her and looked quickly away. She smiled at him and looked quickly away.

"Damn," Andrew muttered, paging through the yearbook pictures. "I hung around with that guy for two years, you'd think I could remember his last name." About halfway through, into the Ms, he found the picture he was looking for.

"There he is, Carl, AKA, Charles McAllister." The picture, just a head shot like all the others, showed a sincere looking seventeen-year-old, smiling, looking directly into the camera as if facing his future. His hair was brown and curled just over his ears, thinning just slightly at his hair line. His eyes were dark and unusually deep set and seemed too far apart. His face was rectangular, but with bulging cheeks and a pronounced flare outward toward the bottom, making his jaw wider than his cheekbones.

"We used to call him Elsie, 'cause he kind of looks like a cow. I didn't place him at first, but that's the guy I saw at Yasgur's last week. Fatter, grayer, and more wrinkles, but that was definitely Carl."

Jason walked slowly toward the table and looked over Andrew's shoulder. "I'm trying to be positive here, but so what?"

"I told you, man, it's a long shot, although this picture makes it a shorter shot. Carl is the guy I came to Woodstock with in sixty-nine. Him and Rich. Rich I've seen a couple of times since…the poor schnook was an assistant manager at a supermarket in Utica. Wore an apron and a stupid paper hat and everything."

Cecelia put Ben on his mother's lap. "Yeah, but Carl?"

"Okay, follow my, um, theory, and don't shoot it full of holes until I'm finished, okay?"

They all nodded and grunted. "Okay, Carl, as you can see, is not the best looking guy in the world. Or even Utica. Look at that mug and try to think of Tom Selleck. So we're at Woodstock, camping, smelly, stoned, needing a shave and Carl meets this chick. She's with a couple of girlfriends a few tents away, and she's cute. I mean, cute. I only saw her once, but she's built, you know? She's wearing these jeans that..."

"Got it, Andrew," Jennifer said. "She's a pretty girl. Do I need to take Ben upstairs for the rest of this theory?"

"No, no, sorry. It's rated G. But think now, how is a guy that looks like him gonna make time with a girl that looks like, you know?"

"Is he rich?" Jennifer asked.

"No. But money would not have mattered much at Woodstock."

"Was he smart?" Cecelia asked. "Although I'm pretty sure that's a dumb question."

"No. Not smart. I could tell you stories."

"Please don't," Jason said.

"Ah, I know where you're going with this," Cecelia said. "The popular exchange medium at Woodstock was," she looked over at Ben, "special enhancements that permitted the user to temporarily defy gravity."

"Yes. Exactly. Except we didn't have any enhancements. Ours got fried, thanks to Carl. So, he had to think out of the box." He paused, looking around at all the faces, proud to be the only one with the answer.

"What could he possibly use to impress a pretty girl at a rock concert? The guitar," he said triumphantly. "He heard me talk about getting Pete Townshend's guitar, and if he could get his hands on that, he might be able to get his hands on something else."

"Rated G, pal. Keep it rated G," Jennifer said quickly.

"You think he stole it?" Jason and Cecelia asked at the same time.

"He disappeared from Utica right after we got home, like right after. Just disappeared, man. Gone, left no forwarding address. I think maybe he came back here. I think maybe he stole the ax from me, hid it in the woods somewhere, came back and got it to impress this girl."

Jason said, "Yeah, that is a stretch. And it leaves lots of questions, like why was he, if it was him, up a tree? And what in the world, if it comes from this world, blows us back in time whenever we get anywhere near?"

Jennifer asked, "And if he came back and got it, what's he still doing here? Yeah, a long shot."

"What else have we got?" Cecelia said. "It's pretty obvious we're spinning our wheels here, so we should talk to this guy. Can we find him?"

"All that security guard told me was that he was part of a bunch of government officials from Sullivan County."

"Goobersmoochers," Jennifer said.

Ben laughed. "Mom loves to say that word."

"Yeah, Benny bear, and I used to say it a lot," she laughed.

Jason said, "We know his name, and we know what he looks like, so it's computer time."

"You know, I think I may have voted for Carl," Cecelia said, looking at his picture.

"Hold that thought," Jason said, on his way out the door. He came back in with his laptop, already open and turned on. "When did you vote? What district are you in, or is he in? What was he running for?" They were able to find a Charles L. McAllister on last year's ballot within about twenty minutes. He was running for Sullivan County Supervisor.

"I think he won," Cecelia said.

"Wow. Elsie is a big-time county supervisor?" Andrew said. "He always had a head for numbers, I guess. Just not much else."

~ * ~

The office building that housed the Sullivan County Supervisor's office was in Monticello, about half an hour south of the Pickle. Just before five o'clock, Jason and Andrew parked on North Street with a clear view of the front door. Cecelia, Jennifer and Ben sat in her truck in the parking lot watching the side entrance. They watched as office workers, mostly women, came out in small groups or individually until a large man wearing a gray suit and brown tweed cap, came out laughing with a woman and a couple of men.

"I think that's him," Cecelia said.

"That is a face that almost says 'moo'," Jennifer said.

Cecelia jumped out of the truck and waved and whistled to Jason and Andrew.

Cecelia got in front of him and said, "Mister McAllister, I'm one of your constituents, and I want to ask you about your plans for upgrading the elementary school by next September. I have a grandson that will be attending." She nodded toward Ben.

"Ma'am," the man said, "we have an established protocol for requesting information from the town supervisors. There is e-mail, and specific hours to..."

Behind him someone said, "We hid the stash at the bottom of the camp stove, in case someone searched. Never thought someone would actually turn on the stove and fry it, Carl."

The man turned his head briefly and saw Andrew, then turned quickly back to Cecelia and Jennifer. "Please, ma'am. I have a personal matter to attend to. Please e-mail me, or phone. The contact information is on the website." He sidestepped and started walking toward his car.

Andrew said, "Come on, Carl. The game is up, man. It's me. Don't be a wuss, talk to me."

Carl, actually Sullivan County Supervisor Charles L. McAllister, turned and looked at him for a long minute. Then he took a couple of steps forward and hugged Andrew, who was stunned, but hugged him back.

"Been about a hundred years, Andy," Carl said.

"Feels like more than that." They stood for a minute or two, just looking each other over, nodding, shaking their heads at the impossible notion that so many years had passed.

"We have some stuff to talk about," Andrew said. Carl looked around at the others surrounding him.

"Yes, we surely do. But I was being honest with this lady. I do have something personal I really cannot miss. My youngest is starting behind the plate tonight for the South Fallsburg Cyclones, and I'm coaching first base. Why don't we do it this way?" He wrote his home address on the back of a business card and handed it to Andrew. "I'm not weaseling out here, Andy. This is my home. Come by about nine, I should have the troops fed and settled by then. Bring your friends if you want, and we'll swap lies about old times."

Andrew hesitated a moment, and then stepped forward and gave him another hug. "Okay, Mister Supervisor. We'll talk later."

~ * ~

The house was a raised ranch on a side road in the town of South Fallsburg with a wide, rolling front lawn, a long driveway, and no other houses around it. Andrew could not imagine Carl owning horses or pigs or chickens, but he certainly had enough room.

Jennifer, although nervous, thought they would be safe far from Yasgur's farm, and so she kept Ben up past his bedtime and brought him along. Andrew walked up the brick steps and rang the bell. A boy about fifteen opened the door and called back, "Dad! Your friends are here!"

Carl came around the corner at the end of a short hallway and put his hand on the boy's shoulder. "This is Mark, my oldest. The other meatball is finishing his math homework at the kitchen table. Let's go into the living room. I think there may be a fair amount to talk about."

It was a big living room: a long couch, a love seat and a couple of wingback chairs. "We don't drink here, but Mark will be glad to get you a soft drink if you'd like."

There were no takers, and Mark disappeared while Andrew was making the simplest of introductions. He pointed to each. "Jennifer, her son Ben, Cecelia, who really did vote for you, and Jason. Me you know, and I think you know why we're here."

Carl pulled at his chin. "I've been thinking about the best way to share, um, information with you. You all. And I guess it depends on how much you know already. Some of it goes back a long time, and some of it is really surreal. If we do question and answer, even between Andy and me, who probably know the most, it could take some time. My suggestion is just to let me spew it all out, hope Andy doesn't punch me, and then move on from there."

Andrew said, "Two of us have been wrestling with this for weeks, and one of us for years. I think we have one end of the story and you have the other. To save time here, let me tell you what we have figured out. You tell me if I'm warm."

Carl nodded. "Whatever works, Andy."

Andrew started slowly. "Back at Woodstock, you met a girl and wanted to impress her. You thought maybe Pete's ax, which you knew I was after, was the key to her heart. So you stalked me, you let me get the crap kicked out of me in that scrum. Sorry, Ben, I'll try and keep it G rated."

Ben was fast asleep on his mother's lap. "I don't think it will be a problem, Andrew."

"Right. You saw me do a halfback run right up the middle, followed me into the woods and saw where I buried it. I think I buried it, but I'm a little hazy there, having enjoyed some of the local special enhancements. I was planning to go back for it later, but you had a different idea."

Carl hesitated, blew out a long breath and said, "You didn't exactly bury it. There was a tree near that pond that had almost fallen over, and the roots were exposed. You stashed it under the roots and threw some dirt on it. I was behind you, crouched behind a tree maybe twenty feet away."

"So, you stole it."

It took a full minute and one look back at the room behind him, but Carl finally said the words. "Yeah. I stole it." Andrew, sitting on one of the wingback chairs directly across from Carl, stared but didn't move.

Jason squirmed impatiently on the couch, and Cecelia just patted him on the knee. "Then what?" he said.

"I had the same problem as Andy; what to do with it until I could get it past half a million people and into my tent. Or her tent. Or somewhere I could come back for it. I got this bright idea that turned out not to be so bright about a tree. I thought if I could get it high enough, and behind some branches and leaves, and hang it on a branch, you know. So, I walked around for a while until I found a tree I could climb."

Cecelia smacked Jason's knee and yelled, "That was you in the tree! With the light! That was you!"

Carl was stunned. "You saw that?" he said.

"About a hundred times," Cecelia said. "What was it? The light? What the hell was it?" Ben stirred, snorted a little, and settled back into Jennifer's lap.

"I...I don't know. I really have no idea. I was suddenly infused, if that's the right word, with a light. Not even blinded by it, I could see just fine, but I was all lit up. I thought it was a helicopter spotlight at first, but there was no noise. And it froze me. Not like I was frightened, but I was like paralyzed as long as that light was blinking."

Jason said, "It blinked, right? Colors?"

"Yes, you guys know about that?"

"Yes. We know. Was it silver and then gold?"

"How could you possibly...? Yes. Silver to gold then back to silver. When it stopped blinking, the light went out, I was released, I could move and I fell out of the tree."

"You still had the guitar?"

"Yeah. When that light first came on, I was holding it up, trying to hook it onto a branch, like this." He stood and stretched himself up on his toes with his left arm and hand up in the air.

"Oh, God. Oh God, oh God, oh God," Cecelia moaned.

"I believe I've seen that somewhere before," Jennifer said.

"What?" Carl said.

"Mom," Jennifer pointed to her mother, "has painted that pose about twenty times."

"From memory," said Cecelia. "From nightmares."

Carl sat back in his chair, blank. "What? How? Who are you people?"

"First things first," Jason said. "What happened to the guitar?"

A boy came in from the room behind them, a smaller version of the one who answered the door, and leaned against Carl. "This is my younger knucklehead, and believe it or not, destined to be a math whiz."

The boy handed his father a sheet of paper. "Can you check these, please?"

Carl gave a resigned shrug and looked at Jennifer. "Parenting. The gift that keeps on giving." He got up and went into the other room, the kitchen, with his son.

"Sweet Nefertiti, this is like *coitus interruptus*," Jason said, and then looked over at Jennifer. "Sorry."

"It's okay," she said. "I'm familiar with the concept."

They sat quietly, impatiently, not looking at one another, listening to the muffled voices in the other room. Jennifer shifted Ben to a more comfortable position. He breathed softly and didn't seem to notice. Andrew began cracking his knuckles, and then abruptly stopped. Cecelia and Jason just stared at the entrance to the kitchen, each lost in thought, or the past, or the future.

Carl came back smiling. "Okay, sorry about that. Knucklehead number two is all set up and has been assigned pajamas and toothbrush duty. We were at the point..."

Andrew said, a little too loud, "You just fell out of the tree with Pete's ax in your left hand. What did you do with it?"

"Okay, yeah, okay. I don't think I blanked out or anything, but I was like, stunned. No surprise there, right? I landed in the middle of the woods, and just ran. Left for a while, right for a while, straight for a while, and then I sat and almost cried. No one was following me that I could tell, so I either passed out, or I slept. And when I woke up, I just walked. I thought first of putting the guitar back under those roots, but I figured Andy would come back. So, I walked and walked around the edge of the pond and I found this piece of rope, I think from a boat. I tied one end around the head of the guitar and swung the other end over a branch, high as I could get it. I hoisted the guitar up and tied the rope to a lower branch. The guitar was swinging maybe eight or ten feet up. The ground was thick mud so I figured no one would be coming around there. I made it back to the stage area in time to catch the end of Jefferson Airplane. My shoes were mud up to the ankles, but the guitar was as safe as I could get it."

"And you went back and got it, right, and gave it to that chick? And now it's hanging in her basement?"

Carl let out a long sigh. "That was the plan, but no."

In the same moment, as if watching a conductor bring his wand down, Andrew, Jason and Cecelia said, "What?"

"I went back, but I couldn't get the guitar. Couldn't get near it."

Jason looked over at Andrew. "Yo-yo'd."

Carl looked from one to the other. "What? Yo-yo'd?"

Jason explained. "You started walking toward where you hid it, and you found yourself yanked back to where you started."

"How in hell did you know that? Who are you people?"

"Been there, done that, bought the T-shirt," Andrew said.

"No, seriously, how did the four of you, five of you, get involved in this? How can you possibly know this? I never told a soul about this. Not even Irene."

"Irene being the chick from the festival," Andrew said.

"My wife. The mother of the two knuckleheads."

Jennifer and Cecelia nodded. Jason said, "How Andy and I got involved is a very long and funny story, Carl, but better kept for another occasion. We really need to find out about the guitar."

Carl stood and walked around his chair, and then sat again. "I've done all the talking so far, but I could use a little context, here. If you know something, I need to hear it."

"Carl, old friend," Andrew said, "in spite of just finding out that you stole my guitar, I have not yet strangled you and hid your body in a swamp. What happened to the guitar?"

"Carl," Cecelia said. "It's been a long, strange trip for all of us, obviously including you, but I'm freaking out here. Please."

Carl glared at her, and then at Andrew and Jason in turn. "I'm freakin' out here, too. I've been freaked out by this since 1969. I need answers, too."

Cecelia said, "I promise you'll get answers. Look, I am a local shop owner, The Penultimate Pickle on James Street in Liberty. So, I won't be going anywhere. And I promise I will get you caught up on everything we know, and how we got to know it. Please, tell us what happened."

"Yeah, okay, I guess I owe Andy." He hesitated. "No, wait, no. You folks seem to have some inside info here, and I'm still totally baffled. Tell me what you know, I'll tell you what I know, and we can move on from there."

Andrew scowled at him. "You haven't changed a bit, man. As thick headed as ever."

"Fine. It was great to see you again, Andy. Call me sometime and we can do lunch or have a beer or something."

Andy looked at Jason. "Great. He's got us over a barrel here. Professor, I think this is your gig."

Carl said, "Yeah, you look like the brains of this operation. How do you know all that stuff? What do you know about what happened to me?"

Jason hung his head and shook it slowly. "Here's what I know, or at least think I know. There have been three witnessed incidents of the phenomenon that I can document. They happen, I thought, at important pivotal points in history."

"Here we go, man. Pivotal points in history," Andrew said.

Jason ignored him. "The first was on the day Socrates was executed by drinking hemlock. Sources—granted most are secondary sources—outlined the same description of the events. They occur in the early morning, focused on something small, in that case, Socrates' bowl containing the hemlock. A sudden bright light flashing from silver to gold back to silver, and then disappearing."

Carl made a face and stared at him. "Come on, really? Socrates? Hemlock? Two thousand years ago? You're yanking my chain."

"Two thousand three hundred and ninety-five years ago, and I told you that you wouldn't like it. Nobody does. The second incident was a little easier to research. There were more sources, but they didn't resonate through proceeding decades. I think the Church may have squashed it for their own reasons. It happened in Rome in 800 A.D., at the moment when Pope Leo the Third was crowning Charlemagne as Holy Roman Emperor. Same description: a small object, the crown, was the focus, a sudden bright light, silver to gold back to silver, and disappearing."

Carl looked up at the ceiling and shook his head. "Charlemagne? 800 A.D.? Oh, please."

"The third incident was the one you were involved in, and these two witnessed. Socrates and the crowning of Charlemagne are, obviously, important historical moments on which much future history and culture hinged. I can't imagine why this happened at a rock concert and why it happened to someone as common as you, no offense. My hope has been to find the guitar, or the tree, and do some kind of physical analysis. X-ray, spectrum analysis, radio waves, radiation, whatever I can find."

Andrew said angrily, "You didn't tell me about any of that. I don't want that guitar damaged. Radiation, my ass."

"If we can avoid the yo-yo, you'll get your guitar. Intact. But I came for answers. She is here for answers, he is looking for answers."

"Okay, okay. Just understand, I am going home with that guitar. It is gonna hang on my wall between a poster of The Who and a picture of my old man."

Jason turned back to Carl. "Look, I have researched this for more than two years, and written a thesis of two hundred pages with over thirty references to classical and medieval texts. It's true. It all happened, I just can't prove any of it."

Carl laughed and shook his head. "Come on, seriously. What is this? Who are you people?"

Andrew said, angrily, "It's your turn, Mister Supervisor-first-base-coach. What happened to the guitar?"

"After that blather, I don't owe you folks anything, but, okay fine. Long story as short as I can make it. Back then, Utica was pretty much dead to me, Andy knows why."

"And the rest of us don't care. Please get to the guitar," Jason grumbled.

Carl hesitated long enough to stare at Jason. "A few weeks after we got back from Woodstock, I relocated. I was just bowled over from the first minute by this girl, Irene. I packed my stuff and moved up here. Got a job, got involved in local affairs, dated Irene and just generally turned my life around."

"You went back for the guitar, right? And then...?"

"Yeah, not right away. After you and I drove home, and the concert was over, I figured it was safe, so I just left it for about a month, I don't know, maybe six weeks. I was worried about trespassing, too, but I snuck in one night, and I don't know. Could not get even close. Just like you guys."

"And that's it? You gave up?"

"No, I went back a few weeks later. I was worried about trespassing, too, but I snuck in one night, and I don't know. Could not get even close. Just like you guys."

Jason asked, "So, what did you do?"

Carl had not moved. He was leaned forward in his chair, elbows on his knees. *"I was worried about trespassing, too, but I snuck in one night, and I don't know. Could not get even close. Just like you guys."*

"So, Carl..."

Andrew was the first to notice that something was wrong. "Hey, Carl, are you okay, man?"

"I was worried about trespassing, too, but I snuck in one night, and I don't know. Could not get even close. Just like you guys."

Andrew jumped up and tapped Carl on the leg a couple of times. "Carl! Hey, Carl!"

"I was worried...what? What?"

"You okay?"

"Um, I guess. What happened?"

"I think you just got yo-yo'd, Carl. You said the same thing four times." Jennifer took Ben and retreated into the hallway and looked around the corner.

Jason said, "Anybody else feel that? Anything weird? Everyone okay?"

Carl stood quickly and ran upstairs. They heard him talking to his kids for a few minutes and then he came slowly down the stairs. He collapsed into his chair.

Cecelia asked him, "Carl, are you okay? Do you know where you are?"

He nodded and sat up straight. "Yeah, I'm okay. In my living room, sitting in Irene's grandma's chair. Wow."

"And your kids?"

"The kids are all right," he said.

They were all quiet for a few moments, looking around at each other and especially at Carl.

Jennifer waved to her mother and yelled, "Mom! We need to go, please." Cecelia stood, reluctantly, and walked to where Jennifer was crouched with Ben in the hallway.

Jason saw Jennifer pulling Cecelia down the hallway and said, "Carl, get your kids and come with us. Or maybe get a hotel for the night."

Andrew grabbed Carl by the arm. "Just tell me, man. Tell me you know where the guitar is."

"I told you everything I know, Andy. But I would bet my house that it's still at Yasgur's, hanging on that tree."

Andrew turned to Jason, "Square one, man. We are back to square goddamn one."

~ * ~

Outside, they huddled around the Volvo, Jason and Andrew leaning against it, no one speaking. Carl came as far as the front steps and yelled something back at his kids.

Cecelia laid a hand on Jason's shoulder. "What was it you said about something small? That's wrong. A guitar isn't something small." She stopped and turned back to Carl and whispered to herself, "Something small. Silver, gold to silver. Hey Carl, were you wearing any jewelry? A ring, or a watch, or something?"

"Way back then? I don't really remember, but I doubt it."

She shook her head. "On a couple of the paintings I did there was a bright spot, like a reflection, on the arm holding the guitar. Up at the top, like maybe even on the neck of the guitar."

"I never wore a watch back then. Sure wouldn't wear one camping."

Andrew stopped walking, too. "How about one of those bracelets. The Vietnam vets' bracelets?"

"POW/MIA bracelets," Cecelia said.

"Had one for a while. I don't know what happened to it. I don't remember if I wore it at Woodstock, and anyway, it wouldn't be way up the neck of the guitar.

Andrew said to himself, "Small, silver, metal," he put his hand in his pocket and pulled the keychain and silver tuning key out of his pocket. He held it in his palm, and the tuning key glowed, very faintly, silver to gold and back to silver.

"Oh, shit," Carl said. Andrew and Jason stood up straight, Cecelia took a few steps backward, and Jennifer ran with Ben to the end of the driveway and behind the Volvo.

At that exact moment, the nearest streetlight went dark. In a car parked in the driveway two houses down, the four-way flashers started up and then turned off. No one noticed.

~ * ~

Andrew tossed the keychain into the trunk of the Volvo and hoped it would not explode, or signal to an alien vessel, or yo-yo them all from Carl's house back to the hotel. Or the Pickle. Or Yasgur's.

Andrew's souvenir of that morning thirty years earlier had turned out to be a different kind of key. Somehow, it was still connected to the guitar, and the guitar to whatever the light was and to the yo-yo and to the *déjà vu* that had followed him for weeks.

And now he was pretty sure he knew where the guitar was. He wanted to say "yippee" and then he wanted to say "oh, dear God, what the hell." He said nothing. He was the last one back in the car, and sat, unmoving, staring at his sneakers.

The drive back to the Pickle and then afterwards to Jason and Andrew's hotel was eerily silent. The tuning key had only pulsed for a moment and had gone back to its normal chrome covering before Andrew threw it in the trunk.

In the hotel room, Andrew said, "It's been sitting there on that dresser since we got here, 'cause I knew I didn't need my keys. I don't know why I grabbed it tonight."

Jason said, "I think one of us would have noticed if it had been flashing."

"I guess. Yeah, sure."

"You've had that thing all this time? Since '69?"

"Yeah, had it stashed away with some old pictures and stuff. Hooked it on to my keychain just before you picked me up in Brooklyn."

"And sitting on the dresser for weeks."

"Wait a minute, man, I think this might be just what you're looking to analyze. To nuke, or whatever you got in mind."

"I think maybe even better than the guitar, better than the tree."

"Once I get my guitar, you can have it, brother. Put it in a thick lead box and haul it away."

Sixteen

Activity at the Pickle for the next few days was cheerless and leaden. Conversation was brief, dull and stilted, and tended to trail off mid-sentence. Eye contact was minimal, smiles were brief and artificial, the usual greetings and jokes were absent. Cecelia tatted lace and cleaned, hummed a lot, muttered "it was just a guy" several times, and fawned over the few customers.

Andrew drank coffee and went for long walks. He thought of Carl and Rich and that morning at Woodstock. He tried to call Carl, but he was always out of the office.

Jason brooded in the hotel or drove to Yasgur's and stared at the cow pasture for a while.

Jennifer sat upstairs with Ben and drew pictures or colored or read books to him.

The glowing tuning key seemed like it should answer a lot of questions, but even with the answers, none of the questions made sense. They all felt in danger for a while, but that wore off after no one disappeared or reappeared, and the fear downshifted into a vague, throbbing anxiety.

They also realized, if subconsciously, that their personal quests were coming to a conclusion.

Cecelia was satisfied, thrilled, that her daughter and grandson were home with her, that she finally understood what the painting represented, and that she could talk without embarrassment.

Jason, after writing his letters to Mrs. Koch and Dr. Braithwaite and a brief conversation with R. Hotchkiss, had finally come to understand that the mysteries he was trying to unravel were not to be unraveled. He said to his steering wheel, "It's like trying to understand cave paintings or the multiverse or Stonehenge or those stone heads on Easter Island. Not enough data." He slammed his palm against the steering wheel. "Damn! Braithwaite was right. Just not enough data."

Jennifer was just edgy and distant, and on guard that none of this would impact her mother or her son. She listened intently to what everyone said, fearful of the kind of repetitions she had heard at Carl's house.

Andrew, however, still felt betrayed by Carl, and was still unwilling to give up the guitar. Staring at the ceiling in his hotel room, he thought more and more often about his father.

Ben was getting better all the time at coloring within the lines. His mother and grandmother were telling him about school, and he couldn't wait.

~ * ~

By the afternoon of the third day, Cecelia was sick of tatting, had cooked and frozen a freezer full of meals, and was anxious for a permanent solution to the turmoil of the last few weeks.

The angst and need built up in her until she stood in the middle of the Pickle and shouted, "Pizza! Tomorrow night! Eight o'clock! Everyone comes! I'll call Carl, and Andy will let Jason know. And tell him to bring beer. This craziness is not over yet, but it's going to be. It needs to be."

On Saturday night, Carl found his way to the Penultimate Pickle and walked in tentatively, feeling like a hen among foxes. The others—

Cecelia, Jason, Andrew, and Jennifer—were at the kitchen table. Ben was stretched out on the love seat, restless but dozing. Four pizza boxes were spread across the table, and salivary glands were active.

Carl pulled up a chair and sat a little away from the table and directly across from Andrew.

He reached for a slice of pizza and said, "I know I said I wanted more information from you all, but we've spent a couple of nights in a motel, so I think I have all I need. This is too 'Twilight Zone' for me. I just want to be done with it. I shouldn't have even come. I'll have a slice for the road, wish you all good luck, and then I am clear of this Ray Bradbury story."

Andrew had eaten a salad a little while earlier and was determined to limit himself to only one slice of pizza. He took a small bite and looked hard at Carl. "I don't think so, man. You owe me. I want to finish this."

Dead silence. Andrew and Carl stared at each other. Jennifer, Cecelia, and Jason stared at their pizza. Ben breathed softly.

Carl said, "To tell you the truth, I'm afraid of this thing. I haven't slept in three nights. We don't know what we're doing, or how dangerous this can be." They all nodded at their pizza. "No one's been hurt, but who knows what's next if we keep after that guitar."

"That's true," Jennifer said. "That's my biggest fear, but so far no one has been hurt."

"I want my guitar, man," Andrew said.

"I have two kids," Carl said to him, eyes wide and his jaw thrust out. He looked at Cecelia and Jennifer for support. "I need to be careful."

"I want my guitar, man," Andrew said, just a little louder.

Carl stood up and glared at Andrew. "I don't want to go back in those woods. I almost wet myself last week just being back at Yasgur's. I'm not getting bounced around or lit up or God knows what else. I have no reason to anymore." Carl was thinking of Irene, for whom he wanted the guitar in the first place, so long ago.

Andrew, as always when the guitar was mentioned, was thinking of his father, for whom he had convinced himself that he wanted the guitar, so long ago.

Upstairs in Jennifer's bedroom, an alarm went off. It was 8:15, and she thought she had set it for 8:15 in the morning. "I'll get it," Jennifer said. When she reached the stairway, the alarm stopped.

Silence descended again, and much staring at the pepperoni in the pizza. As before, the only sound was Ben's soft, rhythmic breathing and the syncopated ticking of the two clocks.

Andy said, "I want that guitar. I have sacrificed a lot for it."

Carl said, "What? Sacrificed what?"

"I needed to bring that guitar home in '69. But while I was away, getting stoned and wet and muddy, and scheming for that goddamn guitar, my father had a heart attack. And I wasn't there for him. I wasn't there for my family. He died two days later."

"Your dad, Andy?" Carl said. "I didn't know."

"Yeah."

"I always liked your dad."

"Yeah."

Carl stood up again, although this time not angrily, and walked a few steps toward the door. "I did take it away from you. I own up to that. But I had a reason."

Andy reached for another slice, his second, but pulled his hand back. "Sure, you wanted to make it with some dumb ass groupie chick."

Cecelia put her hand on his arm. "Andrew, don't."

"We've been friends for a long time, Andy, but don't say that again," Carl said.

"Say what? Dumb ass..."

"Drew!" Cecelia yelled. "Stop! You don't understand what you're saying."

Everything stopped. Everyone stared at Cecelia. Jennifer went over to check on Ben who had woken up for a moment and gone back to sleep.

"What did you call me?" Andrew said to Cecelia, very softly.

Carl pointed at Andy. "I came back up here to be with Irene. I built a life and a couple years later she married me and gave me two great kids. It had nothing to do with the guitar, man. She could not care less about that. She liked me. And then she loved me. To hell with you and to hell with your guitar. It can rot under that tree."

Andy stood and walked into the kitchen and took a beer from the refrigerator. Then he put it back and poured a glass of iced tea. "Okay, Carl, okay. I was out of line. I'm sorry, man. I didn't know."

Jennifer, looking over at her mom, asked, "Carl, where is Irene?"

Carl turned away and took a minute to answer. "Irene died two years ago. Two years next Thursday."

Jason looked, astonished, at Cecelia. "You knew? How did you know?"

She shook her head slowly. "I don't know how I knew. I knew. It happens to me sometimes. My dad used to tell me I was born with a veil, whatever that means."

Jennifer, still sitting with Ben, said, "I don't have, what do you call it, a horse in this race. I only care about my son and my mother staying safe and not yo-yo'd or teleported or lit up or whatever. But I do have a suggestion."

Carl turned and said to Andrew, "I don't want to fight with an old friend."

Andrew just shrugged. Jennifer said, "I think maybe we should try something with that silver Mcguffin. It's obviously connected to the thing. The guitar, the light, all of it."

"Mcguffin," Cecelia said. "My old man used to...never mind."

"Mcguffin," Andrew said to Jason. "There's that word again."

Carl said, "Mcguffin. I use that word sometimes with my kids... never mind."

They all looked at each other, and Cecelia stared at each of them slowly. "Whatever we do, I think we need to get past this thing, and quickly. So, what are you thinking, Jen?"

"I'm thinking one more shot, the Hail Mary pass, the walk-off homer and that's it. That's the end. Someone takes the silver Mc... thingy to Yasgur's and tries to get the guitar. The little flasher thing is some kind of a key, right? Maybe it turns something off. Or maybe it's just the last piece of a puzzle. Why don't you take one last shot and see if that silver flashing thing changes anything?"

"Tuning key," Andrew said.

"Whatever. If it works, meaning that no one gets yo-yo'd, we all go back to our lives. If not, I guess we still all go back to our lives."

Cecelia said, "I am so done with bright lights and guitars and yo-yos."

"I think I am, too," Jason said.

Andrew came back to the table and sat. Carl sat across from him. Andrew said, thinking of his father again, "It's still a thing with me. I want it. I don't want to go home this time without the guitar. I'll take the key into Yasgur's, and we'll see what happens. If anything happens."

Jason said, "I'll come with you. We started this; we should finish it together. If it can be finished."

"I would appreciate the company, J, but that tuning key gave you what you need. You don't have to be a hero."

"Yeah, you're right, but then, you know, peanut butter and anchovies."

Carl looked over at Andrew. "I'm sorta the one who started this, so I'll come with you. Just someone stay close by and keep an eye on me in case we get yo-yo'd again."

Cecelia was about to speak, but Andrew interrupted. "Thanks, that's solid of you, Carl, but no. You got kids, man, like you said. And we don't know what this thing can do. If it's a thing. And if it actually does what we think it does."

Carl stared at the ground and nodded a few times. "Not gonna argue with you, Andy. Kids, man. You know?"

Cecelia and Jennifer said, "Yeah, I know."

~ * ~

Carl left a few minutes later, and Andrew's eyes followed him to the door. He turned, looked at his friend Andy and said, "Tell me when. I should at least be nearby."

Jennifer took Ben upstairs to bed and both Jason and Andrew

helped clean up. Andrew said to Cecelia, "What did you call me before? When you yelled?"

She sat and looked at him for a long moment. "I called you Drew. It just jumped out at me." She looked sheepishly over at Jason.

Jason reached across the table for a pizza box and said, "I have nothing to say. I think I understand what you mean, but I don't have anything to say." He moved away and took the garbage out.

Cecelia stared down at the table, fidgeting and trying to collect her thoughts. "I never heard anyone call you Drew before, but Drew was the middle one, the strong one that I told you you were growing into. There used to be others, but they're gone, I think. Only Drew is left."

He swallowed hard. His eyes teared up. "Drew. That is the last word my father ever said to me."

Seventeen

Andrew and Jason waited until the following Tuesday to take one last try at finding the guitar. There was no real reason to wait, and they never actually discussed it, they just decided not to make a decision until they had made a decision.

Andrew, now asking to be called Drew, awoke in the motel after a solid night's sleep and said, "Tonight. Tonight would be good." Jason, reading the local newspaper, just nodded and checked the weather forecast.

After breakfast at the diner, Jason called the Penultimate Pickle and told Cecelia, "Tonight. Tonight would be good."

Drew called Carl at his office and said, "Tonight. Tonight would be good."

Carl said, "The sun goes down about seven. I'll come by your shop about seven-thirty."

Jennifer called Jason and said, "My mom will not be there. Or me, or Ben. We will worry about you, light candles, think good thoughts, maybe even pray. But we will do it here. At the Pickle."

Carl met them at the Pickle and sat in the back as Jason drove them to Yasgur's. He gave them, as nearly as he could recall, the location of the uprooted tree and directions from there to where the guitar was, he hoped, still hanging. They parked on 17B, in the exact spot as when they had first arrived in Bethel, weeks ago.

Drew said, "Back here? Kind of a long walk."

Jason said, "Yeah, I'm not sure why, it just seems, I don't know, you know…"

"That's fine, it's really fine. Not like we're in a hurry tonight."

At the Pickle, Ben asked his mother if she could read him one more book before he went to bed. She said, "That's fine, it's really fine. Not like we're in a hurry tonight."

They sat in the car for a quiet moment and Andrew nervously got his keychain out of the trunk. Jason turned and asked Carl, "Tell me again what it felt like when that light hit you."

He shook his head. "It didn't feel like anything. No pain, no jolt, no shock. Nothing. It just held me still while the pulsing was happening."

They got out of the Volvo, Carl leaned on the front fender, Drew and Jason climbed the fence and waited for the alarms and spotlights which never came. A soft breeze murmured in the trees and lifted the scent of grass and cow dung. The three-quarter moon went in and out behind fast moving clouds. When they got near the edge of the pasture, they could see that the temporary fence, erected for the concert, was gone. It would be a straight, almost leisurely, walk to where the uprooted tree was.

"Like a walk in the park," Jason said.

"Hold that thought," Drew whispered.

Cecelia had been pacing but stopped long enough to polish one of the display tables. "Please don't worry, Mom. I'm sure they'll be fine."

"Hold that thought," Cecelia said.

The two flashlights bounced their meager light on the dirt path that went past where the "free stage" used to be, and past where the medical tent used to be. Drew stopped for a moment, looked around him, pulled off to the right and walked carefully among the trees. Wet leaves and downed branches made the footing awkward. The moon burst through the trees for a few moments, and then left them in darkness again. The whispering of wind through the trees was louder, and they could smell the pond.

"It's dead reckoning from here," Drew said. He fingered the silver tuning key in his pocket and wondered for a moment if he should hold it out in front of him. "The last time I got lost here, I made a big circle and then smaller circles until I..."

Jason grabbed his arm and pointed. They both pointed their flashlights at something dark and twisted, only about fifteen feet away. The moon stayed behind a cloud, leaving them in the dark. "I think that's it," Drew said, and made his way over to it. The end of the almost horizontal trunk was rotted and collapsing, and most of the roots were gone, but there was a dirt-filled depression at the end of the tree trunk.

"Oh, man," Drew said. "Oh, man."

The moon came out from behind a cloud and illuminated the whole scene: muddy ground, rotted tree, and two nervous men.

"Carl's directions from here were pretty clear," Jason said. "Starting at the bottom of the trunk, take a forty-five-degree angle to the right, and walk toward the pond. He thought it was about twenty-five or thirty steps from the tree."

"Wow. I'll never think of him as Elsie again," Drew said.

They walked, each counting steps, shoes sinking deep in the mud. Jason went first with the lantern; Drew pulled out the knife on his keychain to cut the rope. The tuning key was glowing, brighter than at Carl's driveway, silver to gold and back to silver.

"Shit," he said.

"I hope that just means we're getting close," Jason said. They plodded carefully through the mud, the lantern and flashlight held high. "Twenty-two, twenty-three, twenty..." Jason started counting out loud.

"Please don't, man. Please don't," Drew said.

Jason nodded and kept count in his head. At twenty-seven, he held the lantern a little higher and saw something long and dark hanging from a tree. He pointed.

"Yeah, I see it," Drew said. They both stared at it for a long moment and then Drew started toward it. He took one step, stopped and looked all around him.

"Where's that coming from?"

Jason didn't answer. He had stopped, too, and was looking around for something. They stood for minutes like that, stuck in the mud and looking at something seemingly far away, both smiling. There was no sound except the wind through the trees.

Drew was the first one to come out of it.

He walked under the guitar and stretched, grabbed it by the body and pulled. The frayed rope gave immediately and Drew almost lost his balance.

"Oh man," he said again.

"Let's get out of here," Jason said. "Let's just go."

They trudged through the mud and to the woods as quickly as was safe, and faster when they reached the dirt path. At the edge of the grass, they began to trot, and were soon in full stride across the pasture. Jason carried the lantern and flashlight; Drew had the guitar clutched to his body. He was still muttering, "Oh, man. Oh, man."

When Carl saw them running, he popped the trunk and opened the doors. He saw the guitar clutched to Drew's body, and didn't need to ask. Drew and Jason climbed the fence, put the guitar in the trunk and got quickly in the car. Jason drove straight, not even thinking which way he should go.

At a stoplight, Jason looked over at Drew with his eyebrows raised.

Drew nodded and said, "Yeah, I heard it."

After riding silently for a few minutes, Carl asked, "Where are we going, Jason?"

"Away," said Jason, "just away for now." He drove northwest on 17B for another fifteen minutes and then pulled over. "I'm gonna pop the trunk and take a look," he said. "We should at least look. I'm scared, but I want to take a look. I want to be sure it's not glowing or humming, or yo-yoing my spare tire. I just want to look, and then we'll go back to the Pickle. Maybe Carl can tell us a long way around, keeping away from that damn farm." Which Carl was happy to do. Jason popped the trunk, and the three of them sat for a few minutes before getting out. One at a time they walked behind the car and looked in the trunk. It was definitely Pete's ax, the Gibson SG that Drew had fought for, that Carl had stolen, and that had attracted a force perhaps ancient, definitely powerful, but certainly well beyond understanding. Jason and Carl climbed back into the car while Drew stepped back and just stared at it.

"Dad," he said.

~ * ~

Carl directed them north and then east, and then north again, ranging far away from 17B and Yasgur's, and finally into Liberty.

"I think we're okay," Carl said, twice. "I know this road, and we haven't doubled back. I'm pretty sure we're still in the same, um, time frame, or whatever it's called."

Jason checked his watch. "It's twenty-five minutes since we pulled away from Yasgur's."

"Yeah," Drew said. "Yeah."

When they pulled up in front of the Penultimate Pickle, all of the neon signage of the hardware store was flickering. By the time they got out of the car, it had stopped. Carl got out and walked to his car.

"Carl," Drew called. "Come on in for a minute, man. I think it's okay now." Carl hesitated but walked to the door of the Pickle.

Jason opened the trunk. Drew carried the guitar in both arms like a load of firewood, like Pete Townshend had carried it to the end of the stage before tossing it into the crowd.

The door to the Pickle was locked. Jennifer called, "Is it okay? Did anything happen?"

"It was where he said it would be. We just grabbed it and ran," Jason called. "It seems to be just an old, beat up guitar."

"Yeah, but did anything happen?" she asked again, louder. Cecelia opened the door a crack. She said, "Something happened."

Drew and Jason looked at each other. Jason said, "Yes, I think, but not dangerous. In fact, maybe something good."

Inside, he went to lay it on the big oak table and Cecelia said, "No, not there. Put it on the floor."

They stood and looked down on it, Jennifer and Ben from the far corner of the kitchen. The body was cracked and dented from where Townshend had banged in on the stage. Only two rusty strings remained attached, paint on the body was moldy, chipped and faded; a corner of the headstock had rotted, and that one tuning key was still in Drew's pocket.

"Not a thing of beauty," Jason said.

"It's in the eye of the beholder," Drew said.

Jason said, "I have to admit, I still don't understand any of this. I don't know how, and I don't understand why. Any of it."

"What happened?" Jennifer asked. "What is it you don't want to talk about?"

Drew and Jason exchanged another glance. "Music," they both said.

"What?" Carl said. "What?"

"Something stopped me just before the tree. Him, too, I think. And for a while, I don't know how long, I had music in my head. Not some half-assed bar band, but the best, I mean the absolute best music imaginable. Acoustic guitars, standup bass, concert grand piano, even a violin. I couldn't move, but I didn't want to. I could have stood there and listened forever."

"That's what you heard?" Jason said. "Wow. For me, it was like the world's greatest jazz band. Sonny Rollins on tenor sax backed up by Miles Davis and Thelonious Monk. I didn't want to move either."

They all kept looking at the guitar on the floor. It didn't light up or glow.

"Maybe that's part of your answer," Cecelia said. "The why part."

Jason looked at her. "I am beginning to see how ignorant I can be, but I don't know what you mean."

She walked over to the display window. "Well, you're the historian. Wasn't Socrates all about truth? Questioning authority. And Charlemagne, wasn't his thing advancing culture?" She picked up the painting of the fool in the tree. "Truth, culture and music.

Didn't the Woodstock Music and Arts Festival sort of embody those three things?"

Carl just shook his head.

Drew said, "I don't know."

Jason said, "Maybe."

From the corner of the kitchen, Jennifer said. "For what it's worth, Mom finally has her answers, maybe Jason, too. And Andrew, I mean Drew, has his guitar. And it only took thirty years."

"I feel kinda sad, like when you finally put the last piece into a five-hundred-piece puzzle," Cecelia said.

Ben rubbed his eyes and said, "Mommy, when do I get to go to school?"

Coda

In the year 2031, a forty-year-old astronomer named Ben Barnett gave a lecture at his alma mater, Colgate University. Attending, and breathless with pride, were his mother Jennifer, his grandmother Cecelia, his stepfather Andrew, his brother Peter, and two honorary uncles, Jason and Carl.

"I have some facts to share with you, and some questions to ask," he began. "Facts are the building blocks of our knowledge of the world. And questions are the things that guide us as to how those blocks fit together.

"The universe, as currently measured, is about ninety-three billion light years across. A light year being the distance light will travel in a year. An unimaginable distance which leaves room, both intellectually and pragmatically, for an abundance of unexplained phenomena.

"The Big Bang set the stage for sub-atomic particles to combine into atoms, atoms into elements, elements into increasingly sophisticated structures. And what did those structures become?

In time, stars, planets, mountains, plants and animals, people, tools, etcetera, etcetera...it's a very long list.

"But do we know everything on the list?

"The beginning, when those sub-atomic particles began blossoming into the incredibly vibrant and complex world that surrounds us, was about thirteen billion years ago. Earth was formed about four and a half billion years ago. That's roughly nine billion years, billion with a 'B,' in which things were combining and blossoming somewhere other than earth in that enormously fertile laboratory across ninety-three billion light years. Sufficient time, and perhaps sufficient corners of the universe, for those unexplained phenomena to evolve.

"Could we possibly know everything that enormously fertile laboratory may have produced? No. In our arrogance we often think we do, but no.

"The possibilities springboard off science, and dive into the muzzy dominion of science fiction.

"Are there other inhabited planets? Are they more or less advanced than us? Is it possible they are curious about us? Should we fear them? Is it possible they are afraid of us?

"Shakespeare has told us that 'there are more things in heaven and earth, Horatio, than are dreamt of in your philosophy.' In my life and career, I have known people whose philosophy is much more robust than that of Horatio, and they have influenced me to feel the same."

"Oscar Wilde, no scientist, but someone who abhorred any kind of personal limitation, said, "'We are all in the gutter, but some of us are looking at the stars.'"

Ben looked over at his family and smiled at his Uncle Jason. "It has become my vocation to anticipate and to translate some of those unexplained phenomena. To me, to many of us, this is the meaning of progress. Thank you."

Meet Gene Murray

Gene is a a retired special education professional living and writing in upstate New York. He has been published before, but this is his first novel. He's been a dirty face toddler, a reluctant student, a crossing guard, body surfer, and Mickey Mantle wannabe. He has a family, nuclear in more ways than one, that he cares for deeply and worries about in the traditional 'wee small hours' of the morning. They are the star around which his wobbly planet orbits.

Writing has become the activity that keeps him balanced in these unbalanced times.

Letter to Our Readers

Enjoy this book?

You can make a difference.

As an independent publisher, Wings ePress, Inc. does not have the financial clout of the large New York publishers. We can't afford large magazine spreads or subway posters to tell people about our quality books.

But we do have something much more effective and powerful than ads. We have a large base of loyal readers.

Honest reviews help bring the attention of new readers to our books.

If you enjoyed this book, we would appreciate it if you would spend a few minutes posting a review on the site where you purchased this book or on the Wings ePress, Inc. webpages at: https://wingsepress.com/

Thank You